MW00897259

Better than Sisters

a novel

by Catherine Gigante-Brown

Cover and interior design by Vinnie Corbo
Author photo by Katy Clements

Published by Volossal Publishing
www.volossal.com

Copyright © 2019
ISBN 978-0-9996916-5-6

This book may not be reproduced or resold in whole or in part
through print, electronic or any other medium. All rights reserved.

To DRL
and all the best friends of yesterday
who make us better people today.

Table of Contents

INTRO

I wanted to write all of this down so I didn't forget it. Any of it. I'm not sure why. It just seems important. But to who? To the people who were there, mostly, although they probably don't need reminding. Desi. Raffi. Matty. Athena. Umbe. Stefan. And all the rest. Oh, and me, too. Especially me.

They say everybody remembers the same things differently. I guess because we see our lives from the inside out while others are looking at stuff from *their* inside out. Our own insides make us see details and incidents in a personal way: through our own tailor-made pair of rose-colored glasses.

Then there's something else...selective memory, I think it's called. It's a kind of amnesia where the victim remembers only certain parts of their memories, nothing more. It's a protection mechanism. Protecting yourself from yourself. Or from the facts. But who's the victim here? No one, as far as I can tell. Maybe we're all just victims of ourselves.

Will people get pissed off at me when they read this? Who's going to read this? Who's left? We've all lost contact by now, drifted apart. I'm just writing stuff down so I can free myself from it, so I can get it out of my head. The stories keep bouncing around inside my brain with nowhere go. At least putting them down on paper—or onto a hard drive—releases them in some way. It sets them free, if only to sit in a box in a basement, forgotten. Or waiting patiently in a three-ring binder, hoping to be discovered when you're looking for something else.

But I, for one, will never forget.

Look at me…I'm just stalling, wasting time by writing about writing. I guess I should just shut up and do it already. Type the story up on paper, I mean. Maybe it will make sense to someone other than me. Maybe it will help someone. Maybe it will speak to them, change them, touch them in a positive way.

But then again, maybe not.

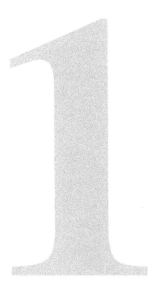

MUSHROOM

We called her "Mushroom" the first time we saw her in the schoolyard. Why? Because she wore a beige knitted hat that looked like a mushroom plopped on top of her head. It was a strange choice for a Puerto Rican kid named Desiree. Desiree Ruiz, to be exact. An old lady hat when most of us were wearing watchman's caps or no hats at all. Freezing our ears off just to look cool.

And that's what me and Desi weren't: cool. Maybe we that's why we immediately bonded—because of our nerd-dom. Desi wore glasses and I wore braces…or "bracelets," like Ralph Martin's baby sister called them. Desi and I were also the shortest girls in the eighth grade and we were runners-up for having the knobbiest knees and the slouchiest socks.

When we met in St. Fiacre's schoolyard, what the rest of us girls didn't know was that Desi liked MushroomHat so much because it was the last thing her father had given her. And her father, who everyone called Big Matty, because he was six-two and built like a four-by-eight, had died in a hunting accident the year before.

Things like that just didn't happen to people in Brooklyn. Gang shootings in Sunset Park and Brownsville once in a while, sure, but not hunting accidents in upstate towns called Cairo. (But pronounced like the corn syrup, Karo, not like the capital of Egypt.) We didn't know a lot of things back then. But we would learn them soon enough.

Desi came to St. Fi's almost three whole weeks after the eighth grade began. There were three Ruiz kids altogether. Besides Desi there was her sister Athena, who was a couple of years younger than Desi, the same age as my bratty sister Laura; and a brother, named Matty, who the nuns insisted on calling by his Christian name, Matthew.

Catholic school kids like us knew that Matthew was not only one of Jesus's main dudes, an Apostle, but that he was also a Gospel-writer. But *this* Matty, Desi and Athena's Matty, was definitely not a Matthew. He was swishy and feminine, even at nine. My Uncle Frankie would say that Matty had a little sugar in his toes or that he was light in the loafers. But Matty was okay. He was funny and he could dance. So, we just dealt with him being girly. It was what he was, period.

And then there was Raffi Ruiz. Real name: Rafaela. She was their mom but she cursed like a dad. Although Raffi looked like she could be another sister. She was short, tiny, in fact. At almost 13, Desi was taller than her mother, and Desi wasn't tall. Raffi was full of fire, like a mini M-80 that blew up in your hand on the 4th of July. Plus, Raffi dressed like a teenager, too, in skirts from Joyce Leslie and jeans fresh from Alvy's Dungaree Outlet. Not in the housedresses and elastic-waisted "mom pants" from Mays Department Store that my mother Tessie wore. Which was another story. For later. Maybe.

I never met people like the Ruiz family before. I guess I never met Puerto Ricans before. Bay Ridge was a mixed neighborhood—Italian, Irish, German, Greek, Polish—but not that kind of mixed. No Latinos. No blacks except for Erik, Derek and Peanuts on Shitty Gelston. Only the Alladice Boys were different because they could play stickball, so the white guys liked them immediately and wanted them on their team. But there were no Hispanics in the Fort Hamilton section of Brooklyn. Not until the Ruiz Family showed up.

Desi's mom Raffi also had these wild-looking eyes, narrow and black as coal, so dark you couldn't even see the pupils. My mother's eyes were big and brown like Bambi's, and you could easily pull the wool over them. But not Raffi. "You can't bullshit a bullshitter," she would snap at Desi when she tried to tell her mom some tall tale. That's another thing, Raffi had no problem cursing. And did. A lot. My own mother still said "the F-word" and "Cripes" instead of swearing. Sometimes I wished Tessie would just haul off and curse a blue streak. It would probably make her feel better, less cooped up and less frustrated. I bet she'd eat less, too. But this isn't about Tessie Piccolo.

Mrs. Ruiz was also quick-moving like a scrappy alley cat. When she was pissed off (which was a lot!) she would spring to action without warning. I once saw Raffi grab Athena by the hair, wrap it in her fist all the way down to the scalp in a second, and yank it with every word she spat into her daughter's face, in Spanish. Although tears of pain streamed down Athena's face, she wasn't crying; she never cried. Not once. Not ever. She was a badass kid, even at 11. Athena had pin-straight black hair (Desi's was short and curly like her dad's, they said) and dark, devil eyes just like her mom.

Ruiz Family folklore said that Athena had been born a twin but that her twin sister had died soon after birth. They were both scrawny and sickly but Athena was the stronger of the two so she survived. Behind their sister's back Desi and Matty joked that Athena had killed her twin in the bassinet, smothered her with a blanket. I always wondered if it were true but was too scared to ask.

Little Matty was rarely the object of Mrs. R's rage. Not because he never did anything wrong but because he was so soft, he would cry at the drop of Desi's mushroom hat. It wasn't worth messing with Matty because there was a fine line between mild torture and tears where Matty was concerned. Plus Mrs. R just kind of accepted the way Matty was. "*Mira*, I got three daughters," she would shrug, taking a sip out of the see-through coffee mug shaped like a globe. The mug had been a freebie from Nescafé or Yuban or one of those Cheap-Charlie coffees. My mom had the same cup but she actually drank coffee from it. Whereas Raffi liked sipping rum from it and didn't care who noticed. "Don Q From PR," she would announce proudly. "Just like me. The best."

Raffi was usually in a good mood when she drank but it could change real quick. She was like an unexpected wind rustling through the Narrows: calm one second then pushing you off course before you knew what hit you. Mrs. R could go from happy drunk to boo-hooing into her Don Q within seconds. Then she would start talking about Big Matty, first wistfully then angrily.

Oh, it would start innocent enough, with her remembering how they met in Ann and Harry's Candy Store when they were both 15. How he asked her to marry him a few months later, slipping a cigar band onto her finger to seal the deal. An *El Producto*, it was. Red and gold and rimmed in white. I know because I heard the story a few times. More than a few. But I loved hearing it. Especially the part about how they got married the second they turned 18. Moved up to the Bronx to make a new start, then began having kids right away, each two years apart.

It would always make Desi uncomfortable when her mom jumped on the Big Matty Pity Train. She would give me the high sign and we'd leave ASAP, saying we had homework or that Sister Priscilla had asked us to run an errand for her. But I knew Desi was making it up, that she just wanted to get out of the house before the waterworks started. The waterworks that soon led to rage. About how Big Matty had abandoned Raffi, left her with three brats. How she'd begged him not to go hunting. How she hated guns. How she was afraid something bad would happen. But when she said all this stuff right before the hunting trip, Big Matty just laughed like he always did when he thought Raffi was being silly. And look at what happened.

Big Matty had taken Little Matty with him on that hunting trip so Raffi would only have two brats to worry about. So that she and her daughters could have some Girl Time. Besides, it was only an overnight trip, he'd told her. Except it wasn't overnight. It was forever.

Big Matty ended up getting shot. In the head. By accident. By his brother, who Raffi said never liked him anyway. And the worst thing was… as if there could be anything worse than getting shot in the head like President Kennedy in Dallas…the worst thing was that Matty, Jr. was there in the deer blind with his dad when he got blasted. Yeah, the kid saw the whole thing and got spattered with his father's brain matter, too. Worse than Jackie Kennedy in her nubby pink suit and pillbox hat.

Athena, who never had a nice thing to say about anybody, said that's what turned her brother gay. As if it happens like that. Not that I know how it happens but I'm pretty sure it's not like that.

Anyway…

THE MAN UPSTAIRS

Like I said, there were no Puerto Ricans in Bay Ridge in 1973 until the Ruiz Family moved in. (This is probably an exaggeration but it's my story and I'm sticking to it.) And then Stefan moved in upstairs. Stefan being Esteban Colon Lazarus. His cousin knew Raffi's cousin in the Bronx, so this made them practically like family.

Stefan was a chef. He worked in the kitchen of the Met—the Metropolitan Museum of Art for those of you who aren't from New York. No, it's not the one with the huge dioramas of elephants, cavemen and the big blue whale suspended from the ceiling. (FYI, that's the Museum of Natural History.)

The Met is art, pure and simple, no filler. Anyhow, cooking at the Met was sort of a big deal but Stefan wasn't one to brag. He also wasn't above making *picadillo* for Raffi's kids and me. *Picadillo* is like Sloppy Joes, but way better, and with a Spanish accent. Stefan told me it had *cumino* (cumin to you whitebreads), peppers, *sazón*, green pimento olives and other goodies, plus raisins. (The last ingredient hardcore Cubans frowned upon, much like they disapproved of "low class Ricans" like Stefan. Hey, everyone knows Cubans are the most sophisticated exports from the Caribbean. Especially

Cubans.) I thought raisins gave *picadillo* a nice sweet-and-salty vibe. But who am I to say?

For an Italian kid like me, *picadillo* was heaven, miles away from meatballs and stuffed peppers and all of that boring stuff. It was exotic, like the Ruizes and Esteban Colon Lazarus. This was before Stefan's friend Umbe came into the picture. That's when everything started to change. Things were lots more peaceful before Umbe arrived from Florida. But I'm getting ahead of myself.

Desi lived in a big apartment building on 92nd Street, around the corner from Gelston Avenue. While I grew up in a four-family brick house filled with family, Desi was in a five-story walk-up with at least 20 units of strangers living in it. Since the super liked Raffi (and who didn't!) whenever an apartment became available, he told her about it, and in turn, Raffi told someone else about it. That's how Stefan got his one-bedroom, directly above Raffi—we could hear him walking on the floorboards because he didn't have any rugs. ("PRs don't do rugs," he explained.)

When a two-bedroom came on the market, Raffi's grandmother, who everyone called "Mami" (sometimes "Big Mami), moved in. Maybe she was big at one time but not anymore. Mami seemed ancient to us kids but she was probably only in her 70s at the time. Small, slightly hunch-shouldered with close-cropped white hair and leathery skin, Mami wore Medicaid-issued glasses several sizes too large for her shrunken face. What Mami said was law, and most of what she said was in Spanish. To her, I was "La Gringa," which I thought meant "Celeste" or "Cici" in *Español*, but it turned out to mean "white girl." Even though I wasn't really white (who is?) but more of a beige. My skin was almost the same shade as Desi's, but not my heritage.

Before you knew it, Desi's Aunt Cassie (real name: Cassandra) came to visit from PR. And never left. With her, Aunt Cassie brought her daughter Jacinta, who was Athena's age. Aunt Cassie, was large, loud and worried. About everything. If it was windy outside, she warned us to be careful of falling street signs. If it was rainy, she told us to watch out for flash floods. (I guess they happened a lot in Ponce.)

Aunt Cassie had once died from an apparent heart attack, and when they pulled the white sheet over her face, she knocked it off, sat straight up and announced, *"No estoy muerto aún!"* ("I'm not dead yet!") Ever since then,

Aunt Cassie supposedly had the sixth sense and could commune with departed spirits. Big Matty seemed to be at the top of her Hit Parade. And Aunt Cassie said that Big Matty was pretty pissed. Now, this was even before things got weird with Stefan and Umbe.

Aunt Cassie swore Big Matty was mad. But not at Raffi or the kids; he was mad he had been plucked from the Earth before he was ready. Hell, before he was even 40! Plus, he didn't like the way he left—too dramatic and violent. "Stop with your crazy ESP *mierda!*" Raffi yelled when Aunt Cassie said this, because Little Matty was starting to whimper. If Cassie didn't let up, the kid would have a full-blown meltdown.

Raffi threw a balled-up ten at Desi and told her to take us all downstairs to Vito's. Desi didn't have to be told twice. The bilingual yelling started between Aunt Cassie and Raffi before the heavy steel tenement door even slammed shut behind us.

Vito's Pizzeria was smooshed between Desi's apartment building and Mary's Dress Shop, where Raffi worked part-time. Social Security for the three kids gave Raffi a halfway decent income but Big Matty hadn't worked long enough as a construction worker to have a pension. There was just a measly death benefit as Raffi told it, barely enough to bury him. So, to make ends meet, Raffi worked a few hours here and there for cash under the table at Mary's. It was the kind of place my mother never shopped; they didn't carry clothes big enough to fit Tessie's size 18 body.

With ten bucks, the five of us could feast at Vito's. I think it might have been the first time Jacinta had Brooklyn pizza. Desi ordered a small pie and small Cokes for each of us, no sharing. "Do you believe it?" Matty worried.

"Believe what?" Desi asked, even though she knew what he was talking about.

"What Aunt Cassie said. About Dad." He shuddered when he said the words and closed his eyes. I could swear that Matty was wearing eye makeup. Not that there was anything wrong with boys wearing makeup. But at nine, he was too young for Maybelline. Hell, I wasn't even allowed to wear eye shadow. But me and Desi had a secret stash in her underwear drawer and tried not to look like Lily Munster when we put it on. I wondered if Matty had found our palette of frosted coppers.

"Sometimes I feel like he's still here," Desi admitted. "You?"

Matty took a bite of his slice, chewed and nodded. "Yeah. I feel like he's watching us. But in a good way. Not a creepy way."

Jacinta was trying to follow the conversation. Her command of the English language wasn't very good, even though she was learning it in school before she left PR a month or so earlier. Brooklyn English was something they didn't teach anywhere on the planet. It was fast, furious, sloppy and hard to follow, especially if you weren't born there. Jacinta's eyes went from Matty to Desi, back and forth like a tennis match, avoiding Athena's eyes because her ebony gaze was starting to smolder. It was scary.

Matty continued, unaware of his sister's seething anger. "It's like Daddy wants to make sure we're okay," he explained.

"And what would he do if we weren't?" Athena barked. "Huh?" Nobody answered. We just silently sipped our Cokes and stared into the depths of our waxed paper cups. "Huh? Answer me!" Athena demanded. "So, shut up, just shut up, just shut the fuck up!" she added.

Desi and I knew her sister was hurting, just like Raffi was hurting, so we let Athena rage. Her long, fine, black hair seemed electric. Her hand shook as she picked up her slice and took a bite like she was chomping off someone's ear. We knew not to say anything or even look at her. Everyone knew except Matty, who could be pretty dense sometimes. He was too young and too dumb to know. In a small voice, he said, "I'm telling Mom. You just said 'fuck.' I'm telling."

We braced ourselves for the Wrath of Athena but it didn't come. "You just said 'fuck' too, so we're even," she said. Then she started laughing, laughing until tears wet her face. We all joined in, me and Desi guardedly, because after a flash flood, a storm could come. But this time it didn't. However, when Athena asked if she could have the last slice, we let her. You never knew what was going to set her off and we didn't want to take any chances.

Not that me and Desi were strangers to the supernatural. Even though it scared the crap out of us, we were drawn to it. Part of the *yin* and *yang* of being "good" Catholic school girls, I suppose. We had gone to see *The Exorcist* together the December weekend it came out. We held hands in horror, cringing when Regan puked pea soup, letting go only to cover our eyes when Regan screeched, "Karras! Karras!" and again, when she muttered, "Dimi, why you do this to me?" sounding more like Big Mami than a Greek immigrant.

When Desi and I walked the block and a half home from the Harbor Theater, we were still clutching each other. It was almost dinnertime during our Christmas break, so it was already dark, which made it even creepier. Demons could be lurking in the White Castle parking lot—for sure there were junkies in the bathrooms; they often OD'd in there. They liked to use those teeny, tiny plastic coffee-stirring spoons to snort. Or so we'd heard. (That's when White Castle switched to plain wooden stirrers.) There were evil spirits wafting out of the greasy smoke that billowed from Kentucky Fried Chicken's exhaust fan. Monstrous possibilities were everywhere.

Desi and I reluctantly said good-bye to each other at the corner of Gelston and 92nd Street, she rushing down to 555 92nd Street, which had the potential of ghosts at every landing. I could picture her running up each set of stairs, breathless and sweaty, until she reached her apartment on the third floor. As for me, I just had just one staircase to conquer but my grandmother cheaped out on the lightbulbs, so the hallway was dimly lit, even in the daytime. I always half-expected a beefy, hairy arm to grab me around the neck, and drag me to the boiler room in the cobwebby basement, never to be heard from again.

The next day, Desi and I vowed never to watch another scary movie again, but that afternoon, when *Queen of Outer Space* was on the *Million Dollar Movie*, we watched it anyway. And were totally creeped out by Zsa Zsa Gabor's face in the last frame, looking like a slab of overcooked bacon. "I kept seeing it whenever I closed my eyes to go to sleep," Desi confessed the following day.

"Me, too," I sighed.

But did that teach us? No. A few days later, when Frances Paladino whipped out a Ouija board, we went along with it. I swore Dino was moving the beige plastic triangle but she swore she wasn't. Then the Ouija board spelled out that Desi would have two daughters, and that the youngest would be raped and murdered when she was five. We finally stopped playing after that. But we were so terrified that instead of going home, we went straight to St. Fiacre's rectory and asked for Father Parsons.

Lucky for us, he was in. Mrs. Barris, who answered the door, didn't even grill us about why we were there, that's how scared we probably looked.

Father P was such a cool priest that he listened patiently to our tearful babbling. He told us not to worry about playing with the Ouija board, which wasn't a venial sin but not condoned by the Catholic church. He made us promise never to do it again. We didn't.

"You don't want to upset the Man Upstairs," Father Parsons added, kindly. We didn't want to do that either.

I slept over Desi's house that night, me and her squeezed into her twin bed with the ballerina bedspread which matched Athena's except Desi's was pink and Athena's was blue. "Do you think the Devil will come for us?" Desi whispered, her breath hot and prickly against my neck.

"He might," I worried. "He came for Regan, right? And she was nicer than us."

"But that's only a movie."

"But still…"

Except for Athena snoring like an old dog in the bed across from ours, the room was quiet. Matty had his own bedroom next to the girls' room, a small one, which had probably been a walk-in closet at one time. He had been running around in his Underoos until a few minutes earlier, when he fell into a deep, immediate sleep like someone had hit him over the head with a brick. Like the Roadrunner did to Wile E. Coyote. Or Ignatz did to Krazy Kat. That's the way Matty fell asleep.

Raffi was in the living room, sipping rum from the globe cup, probably scowling by now. Neither Desi or I could sleep. Neither one of us wanted to get up to turn out the nightlight, which was the same one from when she and Athena were kids. It had painted wooden figures of Mary and her little lamb on its base.

Me and Desi were gently arguing about who was going to turn off the nightlight when it suddenly went off by itself. I gasped.

"Don't worry," Desi told me. "It's only him." But I worried anyway. I didn't have to ask who "him" was.

"Tell me about your dad," I said.

Desi shrugged, curled up in front of me like a human question mark. "There's so much to tell."

"Tell me what you remember most."

Desi's voice was strong and it didn't shake. "I still remember the way he smelled. Like Old Spice and cement. Nice. Even when he worked all day."

Unlike Big Matty, my dad always smelled like Manhattans, Chesterfields and sweat, even after he just showered. With a dash of Jade East thrown in if he'd just shaved. "What else?" I prodded.

"The stories he told. I remember those."

"Name one."

"There are so many."

I nudged her. "Pick your favorite."

I felt Desi smile. Heard it in her voice. "The day I was born, my dad was working on the Bridge." I knew "the Bridge" meant the Verrazano; everyone in this neighborhood did. The Verrazano-Narrows Bridge watched over the streets of Bay Ridge and Fort Hamilton like a sentinel. You could see it from almost anywhere, the longest suspension bridge in the world at the time. Desi's father had worked on its construction. He was a cement man, helping to build the huge stone pedestals that held it up. The Bridge was as long as 14 football fields, and 12,000 men worked on it, including Big Matty Ruiz. Although I'd never met him, I'd heard the story of Desi's father and the Bridge so many times, I felt like I knew him. And I never got tired of hearing it.

"You're not listening," she said.

"I am," I told her. I hadn't been, but I could probably recite what Desi was about to say word for word. "Go ahead…the day you were born…"

Desi elbowed me in the hip. "The day I was born, they had just poured the cement. My dad was way up on the catwalk and there was no way to reach him until the end of his shift. But the next day, when Big Matty went back to work, the cement was still damp. He wrote my name in the cement with his finger. Desiree Rebecca Ruiz. And the day I was born: 10/4/60."

"On which side?" I wondered, though I knew the answer.

"The Brooklyn side, of course," she told me.

"So, your name is on the Bridge somewhere. You'll always be part of it, even when you're old and gray. Even when you're dead and buried."

"Shush," Desi said. "I'm tired."

"Me, too."

"Let's try and sleep."

"Okay," I said.

All of a sudden, I was filled with a kind of peace. I felt relaxed, like someone was stroking my hair, my back, and lulling me into Dreamland. A big, strong hand, with rough skin but a soft touch. The kind of hand that might have cement under its fingernails.

Before I drifted off, I swore I smelled men's cologne. An old-timey scent, not Paco Raban like my cousin Gino wore, but aftershave like my grandfather wore. Old Spice. The kind Desi said Big Matty wore.

Then I fell asleep.

ST. FI'S

Saint Fiacre's Catholic School was the bane of our existence. Let me ask you, what Puerto Rican and Italian kids in their right minds would want to go to a school named St. Fiacre's? I mean, who the hell ever heard of St. Fiacre. He was an Irish monk turned holy man, kind of a poor man's St. Patrick. At school, they told us that he was the patron saint of gardeners and taxi cabs. But dig a little deeper and you found out the filthy truth. Yes, St. Fiacre was the patron saint of hemorrhoids. I mean, do hemorrhoids even need a patron saint?

Oh, yeah, and St. Fi is also the patron saint of venereal disease. And box makers, hosiers (what's a hosier?) and tile makers. Was there ever a more boring, gross patron saint? Born in Ireland, he made his way to France. His fame for miracle-making was legendary. He supposedly cured "all manner of diseases by laying on his hands." Yuck…hopefully not on hemorrhoids.

It was Michael Pollock who came up with the perfect nickname for St. Fiacre—St. Fire-Ass. We said it as much as possible when the nuns and priests weren't paying attention. There's even a stained-glass window dedicated to St. Fire-Ass in Paris's Notre Dame Cathedral. Sure enough, his eyes are rolled up to heaven and he has a pained expression on his face like his ass is on fire.

Because St. Fiacre's feast day was during the summer, August 11, to be exact, we couldn't celebrate it then because school wasn't in session. But the powers at be at St. Fi thought it would be a great idea to celebrate his works on St. Patrick's Day, lumping all of the Irish saints into one holy bucket (St. Brigid, too). This was actually a terrible idea.

The worst day of the school year, of course, was St. Patrick's Day, when all of us, no matter our racial background, were subjected to the torture of sitting through an assembly dedicated to how great the Irish were when darkies like us knew this wasn't the case. I mean, what did the Irish give us besides boiled-to-death meals and dry-as-the-Gobi bread with a few raisins thrown in for good measure? Nothing as sublime as *manicotti*, *mofongo*, Michelangelo and Roberto Clemente.

But still, the non-Irish kids had to endure these March 17th pageants year after year. And I'd been going to St. Fi's since kindergarten. Blame it on school bussing because that's why my parents sent me to Catholic school. In an attempt to better integrate the education system, New York City was bussing shy, stuttering four-year-olds like me across town when I literally lived next door to a public school, PS 104. My parents were all for integration, but not like that. So, reluctantly, my go-to-mass-on-Sunday mom and lapsed-Catholic dad put me and my sister Laura into St. Fi's.

Desi's mom put her kids in Catholic school because she thought it was safer (remember, they'd just moved here from the Bronx, which was a shithole back then) and that the education in private school was better. Both were debatable but one thing was for sure: Catholic school was scarier. The nuns were meaner than any bully you might encounter in public school. Plus, the nuns got away with everything short of murder. There were no repercussions. If you told your folks that Sister Mary Hewer smacked you with the steel end of a ruler, you got smacked again for doing something to make a nun hit you in the first place. You just couldn't win.

Because of this, short, 13-year-olds like Desi and me who looked 10 were practically too scared to breathe at St. Fi's. We bit back the waterworks when Sister Paschal Marie pulled the fine hairs of the boys' sideburns, a sensation so intense it made tears roll down their cheeks. The girls studied their fuzzy black Buster Brown shoes (no patent leathers in Catholic school, which supposedly reflected up so the entire universe could see your flowered bloomers reflected in them) when Sister Mary (who we called "Sister Moron" behind her back) ripped out the hem of Beatrice Garvey's skirt because it came above her shapely knees. I sat there, silent and cringing, afraid to say a word when Maura Fernando stabbed me in the base of my spine with a dissecting needle—three times!—and even drew blood which stained my baggy, white, Peter-Pan-collared blouse.

If it weren't for Desi, I don't know how I would have survived. These injustices *and* assembly. How many chunky-legged girls could you watch doing the Irish jig? How many more years could you listen to Paulie Petitto sing "When Irish Eyes are Smiling" with a pained expression on his face because he didn't believe a word of it? Desi and I passed notes, shared secrets, and during recess, tapped our fingertips in those paper "fortune tellers" we folded, colored and numbered so carefully. (You might know the game as "tipi tipi tap" or "chatterbox.")

Desi and I "officially" met when Miss Coughley introduced the timid girl in the mushroom hat to her 28 classmates, I immediately felt sorry for her, the shrimpy kid from the schoolyard who now stood nervously in front of the classroom. The name "Desiree" seemed to stick in Miss Coughley's throat with a rough, Scottish burr—too close to the word "desire" for the ruddy-faced prude's liking.

In homeroom, we were arranged in alphabetical order, regardless of size or need or anything else. Desi slipped into the scarred, blonde, wooden desk behind me, Ruiz behind Piccolo in the letter lineup. She didn't say much until lunchtime, when we discovered that we lived a half-block from each other.

At St. Fi's, we all went home for lunch, except the kids who lived more than a few streets away. They were forced to eat in the school cafeteria, which was divided into two sides—the hot lunch kids and the cold lunch kids. The smell of rancid tomato soup wafting up from the cafeteria ruined tomato soup for me forever. The complaints about tinny meat ravioli straight from the can could make an Italian kid retch. Ditto for the stench of the messy green gunk that was pea soup.

Lunch at home was always a big rush. Walking the four blocks to and from school took up most of the time. There was only a handful of minutes left for a quick PB&J or a tepid bowl of Chickarina Soup, then we were out the door again.

It so happened that me and Laura were booking down 5ᵗʰ Avenue the same time and pace as Desi, Athena and Matty. Even though I was kind of bashful in those days, I said 'hi.' Desi said 'hi' back and that was that. Maybe we saw something in each other's eyes or in each other's unfortunate haircuts, both done by Aldis, the beautician with the unkempt shop on 92ⁿᵈ Street. Our too-short, slightly lopsided bangs were a dead giveaway and Aldis's trademark.

Matty was in his own head, skipping along, singing the Jackson 5's "ABC" in a loud whisper. Laura and Athena, two mini shrews, got along like gangbusters, laughing and shoving each other as they walked. Me and Desi connected too but in a quiet, calm way, her confessing a crush on Michael Jackson, me admitting that I preferred his older brother Marlon, bringing each other up on the latest issue of *Tiger Beat*, the one with Donny Osmond (who neither of us liked) on the cover. We also agreed that Danny Bonaduce from *The Partridge Family* was funny but not our type. We were both relieved that David Cassidy liked girls with short hair because we both had short hair.

Desi, Athena and Matty were waiting for us at the corner of 92ⁿᵈ and Gelston, just like they said they would so we could walk back to St. Fi's together after lunch. Even though I didn't think it was cold enough, Desi still wore her funny mushroom hat. (It wasn't even October yet.) She seemed attached to it. I didn't say anything about it, though. I didn't want to make her feel uncomfortable.

What cemented us closer together: our birthdays were only five days apart. We'd turn 13 in less than two weeks. "That almost makes us birthday twins," Desi smiled.

"Close enough," I told her.

"Libras rule," she admitted.

To which our siblings said, "Ha!"

"You're just jealous," Desi said. Everyone knew Libra was the coolest sign of the zodiac. So balanced, even-tempered and nice.

"Yeah," I chimed in.

Laura tried to punch me in the arm but I caught her fist and pinched the skin between her thumb and pointer finger. Hard. She squealed even though it didn't leave a mark. "I'm telling!" Laura said in the sing-song voice I hated.

"See if I care," I shrugged. I cared but I didn't want Laura to know.

I wasn't afraid of my mother but of my father. My mom was all bluster, a big windup but her smacks felt like taps. Laura always made the mistake of telling Mom, "That didn't hurt," which is when Tessie would pick up the wooden spoon. It was kind of humiliating to get whacked with the same wooden spoon you made in shop class during summer day camp. Not that Laura didn't deserve it.

But my dad... Although my dad didn't hit us, his yell was terrifying. The threat of violence in his voice was enough to make me sob. Even if I wasn't the object of his rage. It was usually Laura, who was a pain in the butt, even on a good day. My dad devised this punishment where he would make her stand at attention until he told her not to. Once he forgot and Laura was standing there for over an hour. Later, she admitted that she would take breaks when no one was looking.

I wished the walk to school was longer, that's how much Desi and I connected. Four blocks didn't seem nearly long enough to share the secrets of our souls. After that first day, we started going to each other's houses straight from school and on weekends. Since we both shared our rooms with our annoying little sisters, we couldn't talk as freely as we wanted to without comments from the peanut gallery.

My mom liked Desi well enough. She said Desi seemed like "a good egg." Grandma Lou said Desi and me came from the same place—that she was the pot and I was the cover. That we went together like onions and garlic. I got what she meant and it was nice.

But Tessie, Tessie had loads of questions about Desi's family, about her mother especially. My mom went to church once a week and was a good egg herself, but still, the rumors flew about Raffi: how did she get by? Did she date? (Already? So soon after being widowed?) Was she loose? Tessie wasn't one to gossip but the rest of the neighbors were. Didn't they have enough to talk about with Mr. Dursi down the street embezzling from the Teamster's Union, Mr. McNair's drinking and Marnie Otto running off with that Merchant Marine, leaving her two kids to languish with her heartbroken husband? Apparently not.

But I think the other moms were just jealous of Raffi because she wasn't anything like them. She was short, curvy, petite and could pass for a teenager. Unlike them, Raffi didn't wear cobbler aprons, cotton nightgowns or sensible shoes. She did wear mascara, high heels and tweezed her eyebrows pencil thin like Cher. The dads were all smiles when Raffi was around. They walked taller, puffed out their chests and pulled in their potbellies. But was this Raffi's fault? She couldn't help the fact that she was cute.

I think being Raffi was all cheerful and pretty on the outside, but on the inside, it was sad and lonely. One time when me and Desi were doing math homework in her room, I heard a strange sound…like a cat meowing or a baby crying. "What's that?" I asked Desi. She cringed, shrugged, and turned WPLJ louder on the transistor radio. But even over "Delta Dawn," I could still hear it. "It" being Raffi sobbing.

One Friday night after winter break, Laura had a sleepover at Carolyn Russopietro's. Carolyn was an oddball kid, a change-of-life baby with an older sister named Linda who ironed her hair and was old enough to be Carolyn's mother. Carolyn could fart through her coochie at will and her underarms smelled like Campbell's Chicken Noodle Soup, but for some reason Laura liked hanging out with her. I begged my mom to let Desi sleep over. I hugged and kissed Tessie when she said 'yes.' She laughed, pushed me off, then made me go out to pick up a large pie from Pizza Wagon. It was a Friday night and Friday was always pizza night at Casa Piccolo. Back in 1974, you still couldn't eat meat on Fridays and my dad hated all things fish, so pizza it was.

Printed in bright red letters on Pizza Wagon's boxes it said: "You tried the rest, now try the best." And it was true. Pizza Wagon was the best in Bay Ridge, which had a sea of pizzerias. There was one every couple of blocks; bars and churches too. Pizza Wagon was further away than Vito's (which was just around the corner) but it was far superior. Before I left on my pizza pilgrimage, I gave Desi a quick call and she said she'd come over at 7:30 because *Sanford and Son* started at eight.

By 7:40, Desi and me were on my bed, on top of our sleeping bags. My bed was comfy and roomy, a size they called three-quarter, while Laura, who was "a surprise" (I still wasn't sure what that meant), had to make do with a narrow Castro convertible. While it was cool that we lived in a four-family house with aunts, uncles, cousins and grandparents, our apartment itself was small. I'll never forget the time a St. Fi's classmate who lived in a spacious Oliver Street house (with a driveway!) came by after school. LoriAnn Mancuso was amazed that four people lived in such a weensy (her word) place. "It's so adorable!" LoriAnn had exclaimed, trying to cover her blurt and spare my feelings. "Really..." she added for good measure. The "really" wasn't really necessary because I knew what my home was: it was tiny.

But none of this mattered to Desi. The place she lived in wasn't much bigger than mine and she had another person squeezed into it plus the spirit of Big Matty to accommodate. An endless stream of *primos* and *tias* (cousins and aunts) were always visiting from Puerto Rico who ended up staying indefinitely, shuffling from one relative to another like cards in a deck. Desi didn't judge; she liked me for who I was. Whoever that happened to be. I was still trying to figure that out. But it was good to be liked, loved even, for who you were inside, not how you looked on the outside. And loved by someone who wasn't related to you or felt obligated to love you. But by a friend who wanted to love you, in spite of you.

My mom made us a pan of Rice Krispies Treats. That's how Tessie said "I love you:" with food. To my mom, food = love. Maybe that's why she was tipping the scales at almost 200 pounds (my estimate), she was so full of love. Sometimes it embarrassed me, having a mother who was so...large. I hated the way her chub spilled onto my seat when we sat side by side on the B63 bus. Or the way her belly jiggled when she laughed. But at least she laughed, I tried to tell myself, at least she's happy.

And my dad still seemed to like her, big as she was. I only prayed I wouldn't hear the flick of the Zippo lighter in the middle of the night—the sound meant that they were done having sex. And if I heard it, I hoped Desi wouldn't notice. Or if she did, I hoped she didn't know what the sound meant.

Desi didn't seem to mind the size of my mom. Even though her own mom was super adorable. Desi thought Tessie, who she called "Mrs. P," was "nice" and "thoughtful." Tessie thought Desi was "polite," especially when she thanked my mom for the Rice Krispies Treats. Okay, it was nice of Tessie to make them. And if I knew my mom, she saved a couple for Laura for when she got back from Carolyn's the next day.

Sanford and Son morphed into *Good Times* and then *Room 222* began. (We loved all three.) Desi and I hurried up and finished our Religion homework before the Friday night fall lineup started—an essay about the name we would be picking for our Confirmation and why. Yeah, I know most kids make their

Confirmation in the seventh grade but we didn't because Father Mulvaney, who was going to confirm us, died in a motorcycle accident the week before Confirmation last year. (Yep, a priest who rode a Harley, go figure.) St. Fi's had a tough time finding a replacement to do the ceremony at such short notice, and also, they thought it didn't look right to have a joyous sacrament so soon after such a grizzly death. They postponed our Confirmation until next year. Which was this year.

As luck would have it, Desi hadn't been confirmed either. Raffi had yanked the kids out of St. Francis-Assisi in the wake of Big Matty's death—she said she couldn't afford it. At the time, Raffi was so messed up that Confirmation and religious instruction classes sort of slipped her mind while the kids languished in public school up in the Bronx. Big Matty's mom miraculously came up with the cash for St. Fi's when Raffi decided to uproot her already-traumatized kids and move them to Brooklyn. (Desi thought Raffi wanted to get as far away from her mother-in-law, who lived upstate, as possible. And PS, Raffi also thought that Grandma Raquel had taken out life insurance on her son Matty because he had such a dangerous job—how else could the *bruja* (witch) be so flush with cash all of a sudden?

Desi and I tried to rush our Religion homework because we didn't want to miss one second of Lamont (who we thought was cute) or Aunt Esther, not to mention limpy, old Fred Sanford. In my essay, I wrote that I picked the name Margaret for my Confirmation name because it was my great-grandmother's name and also, because I'd heard about St. Margaret of Cortona, who was a "soiled dove." I left out the part about how she ran off with a handsome dude, had his kid, was shamed after said dude was murdered and became a nun when her father and his new wife turned her away. Maggie eventually took care of the sick and needy, then was canonized. "It's a cool story," I told Desi when she asked about the name. "If there's hope for St. Margaret, there's hope for me."

Desi laughed out loud. "You don't look like a Margaret," she admitted. "Besides, you're not nearly as bad as that. Yet."

I snuck a look at Desi's essay, neatly written, no cross-outs, no erases, on the blue-lined paper. "They'll never go for it," I told her.

"Why not?"

"You know why not."

"It's a saint's name," she pointed out. "And he wrote part of the Bible."

"But Matthew's a guy's name."

"So?" Desi said stubbornly, jutting out her lower lip. "It was my dad's name. I want to honor him."

"I know. But a boy's name…they aren't real progressive at St. Fi's, in case you haven't noticed."

"That's not being old-fashioned. It's being sexist."

I lay on my back and walked my feet up the wall. Right next to me, Desi did the same. "The whole Catholic religion is sexist," I told her. "Girls can't be altar boys. Or priests. And nuns are so boring."

Desi knocked her feet into mine. "You would make a terrible nun," she said. "You're too boy-crazy." It turned into a full-blown feetie-fight with us curled up on my bed laughing until we were gasping for breath. "But still, Matthew has a nice ring to it," she added when we stopped giggling.

"It does," I admitted.

"I'm going to hand in the essay."

"Sister Bernadette might fail you," I warned.

"She might. But then again, she might not."

There was a knock on my door and I heard the jazzy junkyard theme music of *Sanford and Son* past the closed door. At half-hour intervals, Phil flipped from NBC to CBS to ABC. Neither of us was crazy about *Adam's Rib* but Phil had a thing for Blythe Danner so we watched it. *Love, American Style* came on at 10 and my folks let us stay up late. (It was a Friday night, big whoop!) But only if we brushed our teeth on the last commercial and promised to go to sleep right after.

That night, *Love, American Style* had an embarrassing segment called "Love and the Sexpert" with Dick Gautier, who had played "Hymie the Robot" on *Get Smart*. It was an especially humiliating episode for a 13-year-old to watch with her parents. Me and Desi sat between Phil and Tessie, who kept shooting each other these meaningful glances that almost made me barf.

When Desi and I came back from brushing our teeth, I swear my folks were smooching but they broke away and moved back to their sides of the sofa before I could tell what was really happening. My mom kept saying how handsome Dick Gautier was and my dad would light a cigarette anytime someone said "sexpert" in the show. I couldn't *wait* to go to bed.

In the dark of my room, Desi and I each crawled into our sleeping bags. I could see the outline of her face in the streetlight's glow that snuck in through my patchwork quilt bedroom curtains. "I miss him," Desi said suddenly.

I didn't have to ask who "him" was. "I think you'll always miss him," I whispered.

"But it's been more than a year," she told me.

"That's not a long time at all."

"It feels like forever." Then after a beat, she added, "You're lucky. Your dad…"

I poked Desi in the side. "…is grumpy as anything?"

She poked me back. "He's not so bad. But at least he's…not gone."

"Phil smokes too much and drinks too many Manhattans sometimes. But you're right, he's okay, I guess." I thought of how my father took the time to read my short stories and poems, stopped whatever he was doing, no matter what, to look at them. I thought of how he used to take me and Laura to the rides at Nellie Bly when we were younger. How he would take us sleigh-riding at the golf links when it snowed. When we got cold and cranky on the walk home, he'd tell us about Tessie's Trading Post, where there'd be hot chocolate and Oreo cookies waiting for us. (That always made us stop whining.) How he'd tell me to think about Cinderella's beautiful dress when I woke up with nightmares as a little kid. How he'd run so hard when we went kite-flying down Shore Parkway that his car keys once jumped out of his shirt pocket. "Yeah," I told Desi. "Phil's all right."

I heard her sniffling and figured Desi was crying. She wiped her nose on her granny gown's sleeve. I took her hand, not saying anything, and gave it a squeeze. Desi squeezed back. Suddenly, my musical jewelry box started playing. I flicked on the light, and there the tiny ballerina was, spinning in her white tutu to the tune of "Swan Lake." "That's weird," I said. "I know the lid was closed when we shut the light."

"It was him," Desi told me. "Things like that happen all the time."

I shivered. "That's creepy. Very *Last House on the Left*."

"Really? I don't think so. It makes me feel like he's kind of watching over me. Like my little brother says."

"Watching over me too?" I shut the light again and got back into bed.

"Sure. You're my best friend."

"You're mine, too," I told her. This time, it was Desi who took my hand. I could feel her smiling against the pillow as the ballerina girl wound down and quieted.

I kept my eyes open wide, seeing stars and sparkles of color in the darkness. Before long, I fell asleep.

On Monday, we both handed in our Religion homework. Instead of getting in trouble, Sister Bernadette took Desi to the rectory when school was over. They were going to talk to Father Parsons about Desiree Rebecca Ruiz taking the name "Matthew" as her Confirmation name in May.

I waited for Desi at the other side of the black wrought iron fence, alone, our sisters and her brother, already having left together. I kicked a pile of gray snow with my boot tip. Nervously pulling the dead leaves off the bushes that pressed against the railing, I looked up the second I heard the heavy rectory door pull open. Desi was smiling wide. After he read her essay and talked to her for a few minutes, to her amazement, Father Parsons agreed to let Desi take "Matthew" as her Confirmation name. I could feel Big Matty smiling too as the Verrazano-Narrows Bridge loomed over our shoulders and we turned toward home.

"Maybe St. Fi's isn't so bad after all," I told her.

MAGIC MAN

Under no circumstances were we allowed to go to Harold Hall. Ever. Not even when we needed to find the perfect hiding spot when we were playing Ditch. That's what my mother told me and Laura. Not even for trick-or-treating. And Laura had turned trick-or-treating into an art form. She would go to the butcher and he would give her a slice of bologna because he didn't have any candy. Then she would go to Kentucky Fried Chicken, which also didn't have any candy. The counter workers would feel sorry for her and give Laura a dinner roll. Then she'd make a sandwich.

But my sister would hit the Halloween jackpot when she snuck over to Harold Hall on Fort Hamilton Parkway. That was the name carved into the concrete archway, like it was someplace elegant. But it was actually a big, looming, spooky-looking orange brick apartment complex with an inner courtyard where any number of fiends could lurk. Especially fiends like the Magic Man. "Who's the Magic Man?" Desi wondered on the walk back from St. Fi's one day.

"No one really knows," I began.

"Is he a ghost?"

I shook my head. "Just your friendly, neighborhood pervert. He lives around the corner from us in Harold Hall. You know, that huge building that takes up half the block."

"Why do they call him that?" Desi gulped.

"Because he runs around in a magician's cape and hat."

"How come?"

"You'll have to ask him," Laura piped then snickered at Desi's fearfulness.

"Hey, mind your own beeswax," I told her. Laura stuck her tongue out at me but kept her trap shut.

By this time, we were walking down Shitty Gelston. That's what my father called the stretch of Gelston Avenue after ours. Why? Because it was shitty. It was lined with broken-down apartment houses. There were a few private homes on the block but they were rundown, too. Then there was the dilapidated house with the big yard and the even-bigger German shepherd who barked at you every time you passed, whether he knew you or not.

The only good thing about Shitty Gelston is that besides the Alladice Boys, my third-grade teacher Mildred McVay lived there with her spinster sister Dottie. Mrs. McVay was gruff but loving and fair. Sometimes we still walked to or from school with her if we happened to meet her on Shitty Gelston.

"So, tell me more about this magician," Desi pushed.

"The Magic Man," I corrected her. "The Magic Man likes scaring kids. He jumps out at them from dark corners. And Harold Hall is filled with dark corners. One time, he even flashed a couple of girls."

"No!" Desi shrieked.

"Yes! He asked them if they wanted to see a card trick. They said 'yes,' and the next thing they knew, his wiener was hanging out of his pants."

Desi gasped. "What happened after that?"

"Nothing," I told her. "They ran away. No one knows where he lives. If the super does, he's not talking."

"Maybe the Magic Man *is* the super," Desi said.

"I never thought of that."

All of a sudden, Athena screeched. No warning whatsoever. "What?" Desi yelled.

"Stop!" Athena shouted. "You're scaring me!" We stopped but Athena lunged at Desi and grabbed the mushroom hat off her head.

"Give it back!" Desi ordered.

"Only if you stop!" Athena challenged.

"We stopped...we stopped..." I told her.

But Athena didn't seem to be listening. "Why did he give you that hat?" Athena bellowed. "Why didn't Daddy give me a hat?"

"It was the time I got that bad haircut. Remember?" Desi said, trying to soothe her sister. "You never got a bad haircut."

"He never gave me anything," Athena whined. "You were always his favorite."

"Don't be stupid. Daddy gave you lots of stuff."

Matty was ignoring us, as usual, in his own, private world. It sounded like he was humming "Ring, Ring" by ABBA. I hated ABBA.

Athena threw Desi's hat into the middle of 92nd Street, right in front of the crossing guard. Desi tried to grab the hat but the crossing guard held her back. A purple Gremlin ran over her poor mushroom hat, leaving two black stripes on the fluffy beige yarn. Desi picked it up and held it to her chest. Athena bolted across the street, toward home. "No wonder she was his favorite!" I yelled after her.

But Athena didn't turn back and call me out. She just kept going. Matty followed Athena like a dumb lamb while Laura went home without me.

The public-school kids had just been let out of PS 104. As Desi and me made our way down Gelston, we had to battle through the squish of bodies, which all seemed to be going the opposite direction. "I feel like we're salmon swimming upstream," I said to her as we were being jostled.

Desi smiled, momentarily forgetting her flattened hat. "You have a unique way of looking at things, Cici. Maybe that's why I like you so much."

I felt my olive skin blush. "Uh, thanks," I told her. "I think you're pretty cool, too."

Relieved that my house key was still in the milk box in the hallway—this meant Laura remembered to put it back and John Rubio across the street hadn't taken it just to get me in trouble—I shut the door quietly and slipped down the hallway to the basement. The door was propped open, which signified that my grandfather was down there, sewing at his ancient Singer sewing machine.

I was lucky that all of my grandparents were still alive and that one set of them even lived in the same house as us. This grandfather, who'd been born in a small town in Calabria called San Vincenzo, was super-nice. His name was Antonio and he'd come to the US alone, when he was only 22, on a steamship called the Giuseppe Verdi. Even though he'd been in America for over 50 years, he still spoke English with a heavy accent. But I liked the way he carefully weighed every word when he talked, like he was tasting it, savoring it.

Grandpa Downstairs (which we called him to distinguish him from our other grandfather) had all sorts of great stories. He also had this hearty way of saying "hello" and making you feel important. He was always giving me special gifts, like the worn red and green phrase book that helped him learn English and a tiny snapshot he'd bought from a photographer the minute he stepped off the Ellis Island ferry. It was of the New York City skyline when he got here in 1921. (I still have it.)

When I introduced Desi to Grandpa Downstairs, he took her hand in both of his and shook it gently, smiling and saying, "Hallo, hallo." I told him about Desi's hat, which he took just as softly as he'd shaken her hand. He examined MushroomHat thoughtfully, turning it over in his palm. The pom-pom was loose, something we hadn't noticed before. *"Permesso?"* he asked as he reached for a needle. Desi nodded.

Grandpa Downstairs had a rainbow assortment of threads. He picked out one in pale beige which matched Desi's mushroom hat perfectly. Ancient as he was, he threaded the needle on the first try, first wetting the thread in his mouth then biting it off with his front teeth, which were still his own. Desi sort of held her breath watching my grandfather sew her hat. He did it with love and tenderness, silently sensing how important this silly cap was to her. It only took a few strong, steady stitches. "There, good as new," he said when he was done. I kissed Grandpa Downstairs on the cheek, which was always clean-shaven, soft and smelled like home to me.

Desi stammered out a "thank you," then we set to washing the hat in another part of the basement, down near the row of washing machines. Four of them for each of the apartments and one dryer for my Aunt Bernie (born

Bernadine), who thought drying clothes on a clothesline was beneath her, something only peasants like my mother and grandmother did. The rest of us used one of the lines in the basement or in the backyard. I liked the smell of sunshine that soaked into our clothes in the summer months when Tessie hung them outside.

I showed Desi where the slop sink was, grabbed the box of Tide and a bucket to soak the hat in. Desi looked grave and serious, probably secretly wondering what she would do if the black tire track stains didn't come out. I filled the bucket halfway with warm water and added a touch of detergent powder as the faucet streamed. The water bubbled up. "Tide's in... dirt's out," I told Desi. That was their slogan.

At first, she didn't get it. But when I pointed to the blue writing on the orange and white cardboard crate, she smiled. "Well, it is 'America's Favorite Detergent.' Just like the box says," she added.

We took turns plunging our hands into the water, mimicking the washing machine's agitator. I told Desi about my grandpa: how he came to the United States from Italy on a boat when he was little more than a teenager. How he settled in Harlem in a community with other Italian immigrants. How he got a job making men's suits, which was seasonal. How his friend Enrico found him work making costumes for showgirls, which was steadier work. Desi was interested, asked questions as we plunged and agitated. "How'd he meet your Grandma Lou?" she wondered.

I added a touch more hot water. "His friend Carlo was keeping company with this woman named Barbara in Brooklyn. One day, Grandpa came along and met one of Barbara's sisters, Louisa. And that was that."

"It sounds like a setup," Desi commented.

"We call it *mooshada*," I conceded. "Italian/English for 'matchmaking.' It probably was. Both of them were pretty shy."

"Tell me more," Desi pushed.

Our hands stirred up the soapy water. "Well, they say my grandfather was very handsome. When he was young, he looked a lot like that silent movie actor Rudolph Valentino."

"I can see that."

"He really did," I told her. "I'll show you a picture. A few years after my grandfather came here, Valentino died. People went nuts. There were

100,000 in the streets and fans supposedly killed themselves over it. When they saw my grandfather, they freaked out. They thought he was the ghost of Valentino."

"No!" Desi shrieked with laughter.

"It's true!" I giggled. We glanced over at Grandpa Downstairs, happily sewing one of my grandmother's old dresses and giggled some more. "He barely spoke English so he had no idea what was going on."

Our washing was working. The water soon turned gray and Desi's beloved MushroomHat was bright beige again. We changed the water twice then were satisfied and shook hands on it. "Well done, miss," she laughed. I could see the relief in Desi's face as she squeezed the extra water out of the hat. I also gave it a squish for good measure. From all of the stoop-ball playing and sports, I think my hands were stronger than hers were.

Desi swore she would clobber Athena when she got home and thanked me again for my help. "That's what friends are for," I told her. She left with her soggy hat in hand, happy, and thanked my grandpa again.

That weekend, Athena, Matty and Laura went sledding at the golf links. All the neighborhood kids snuck in through a hole in the fence at the Dyker Beach Golf Course (PS, there was no beach), down near Poly Prep. Years ago, a kid had drowned in Poly Prep's pond when he fell through the ice. It happened when I was in second grade and walking past it still creeped me out. To this day, I can remember how Father Parsons said that maybe God needed a little drummer boy in heaven, maybe that's why he took Salvatore Angarri at age 10.

Even in second grade, I knew this was a load of shit. And by the way she was sobbing, so did Sal's mother. Although my sister Laura was too young to remember it, she remembered the stories and always wanted to cross the street and walk in front of Victory Memorial Hospital instead of passing the murderous pond. Laura thought Sal's ghost lived there. I bet Athena and Matty were too haunted by their own ghosts to argue and gladly crossed the street with my sister when she insisted. (Laura could be very persuasive.) Even though I wasn't there, I pictured the three of them doing this, dragging their sleds across the avenue.

Despite the fact that we liked sleigh-riding as much as the next girl, Desi and I went on another quest while our younger sibs went sledding. Ever since she'd heard about the Magic Man, Desi was hell-bent on seeing him so she wanted to go to Harold Hall. Even though both of our moms had forbidden it. This puzzled me about Desi—why she wanted to disobey our mothers on this one. She was always the "good girl" even more so than me. "Why are you so obsessed with this guy?" I asked.

"Not obsessed, just curious," Desi told me. "Besides, I don't feel like going sleigh-riding. It's for babies."

We had turned 13 the previous October, Desi on the fourth, me on the ninth. We were infinitely more mature than our sisters, wore training bras and were finally permitted to tweeze our monobrows, which I immediately overdid and looked like an Egyptian in mourning. (I'd read somewhere that the ancient Egyptians shaved their eyebrows when someone close to them died.)

Desi and I still weren't allowed to wear makeup but had chipped in to buy yet another greasy array of eyeshadows from Woolworth's. This one came in a white plastic strip and looked like a kids' watercolor set. That's pretty much the way it looked when we put it on—like a five-year-old had gone nuts on our faces with a paintbrush. We hid our makeup stash in Desi's dresser drawer and only used the war paint indoors, scrubbing our faces raw before we went outside.

That snowy day, Desi and I were brave/dumb enough to try and go out wearing makeup. Raffi stopped us in our tracks with a raspy "Hold it!" We cringed and listened to her. "You two look like clowns," she said, inspecting our rainbow-colored faces closely.

But instead of chewing us out, Raffi made us wash the makeup off and showed us the right way to apply it. Her fingers felt like fairy wings and lulled me into a quiet, mellow place. When Raffi was done, I had to admit that we looked much better. Natural, but prettier, more grown up. "But *mijas*, you're still not allowed to wear makeup," she laughed, then turned back to her world-shaped mug filled with God knows what. "Just this once..." she conceded and went back to watching her Spanish soap operas on *Telemundo*.

We slinked past Raffi and down the chipped, marble steps the super was constantly cleaning with Spic-and-Span yet always seemed dirty. I knew where we were headed, didn't even have to ask. "What does *mijas* mean?" I wondered.

"My daughters," Desi told me. "It's Spanish slang." I flushed with pride. Raffi saw me as one of her own. I was like Desi's sister, only better.

Desi and I crossed Fort Hamilton Parkway stealthily, passing Met Foods, hoping Mrs. Dunphy wouldn't see us. She was always so nice, with her big, toothy smile and a Parliament eternally perched between her lips. Because we didn't want Mrs. Dunphy to tell our moms she had seen us walking toward Harold Hall, we kept our heads down. We motored past the laundromat where Mrs. Yaccarino was folding sheets. Luckily, she didn't see us either. Our target was only a few steps away.

My knees felt weak as we passed under the huge arch that had "Harold Hall" etched into it. The contents of my stomach (a bunch of White Castle sliders and a chocolate thick shake) turned to water. I grabbed Desi's arm. "You sure?"

"You scared?" she wondered. I didn't answer. "Yeah, me, too," she admitted. "But let's go anyway." We did. Holding each other's gloved hands, wearing Raffi's lovingly-applied makeup.

Past the archway, Harold Hall had the look of a brokedown palace. Like the one the Grateful Dead sang about. Or like an ancient woman, like Big Mami, who you knew was stunning once (from all the faded, scallop-edged pictures she liked to show us) but now was just wrinkled and shrunken and tired. There was a courtyard in Harold Hall with crooked paving stones coming up in spots. It had been shoveled mostly clear of snow. There was a large concrete fountain in the middle of the courtyard with no water in it, no ice, no icicles hanging from it. Just a pile of old snow. I had the feeling water hadn't gurgled in it for a long time, that it was broke, too.

Four smaller hallways fed onto Harold Hall's courtyard. The building itself was six stories high. Grandma Lou said it was built in the 1920s. It took up almost half the block, had fire escapes in the front and three turrets. Harold Hall definitely looked haunted, me and Desi agreed. I immediately had to pee, just like I did when we played Ditch and was close to being found. "Me, too," Desi admitted. "But hold it in."

For some reason, Desi chose to go through the archway to our right. Maybe because we were both righties and the right side is the best side, as we both knew. There was a heavy steel door and the hallway was dim, even though there were lightbulbs burning. But it reminded me of some old folks' places, where they used the lowest wattage bulbs possible which barely penetrated the darkness.

There was an elevator with a flaking painted door which had been painted and repainted many times over the past 50 years. We didn't take it. Instead, we opted for the staircase of polished concrete which went up and up, two sets of stairs between each landing. At least they were out in the open and lit by big windows at every floor. It was sunny out since the snow had stopped but you couldn't tell by the light that filtered in through the street. "What are we looking for?" I asked Desi.

"We'll know when we find it," she told me. But we both knew: we were looking for the Magic Man.

We went to the top floor and worked our way down. Each hallway looked the same. Welcome mats stood in front of some of the apartment doors, others were bare. Some said "WELCOME" in plastic, others in coir, which was made from coconut shell fibers, I'd recently learned. Each floor was a symphony of smells which told of the tenants who lived beyond the tightly-sealed doors: curry, garlic, savory meats ("That's *pernil*," Desi said knowingly. "Pork roast. Yummy."), and cabbage, always cabbage. We climbed down from six to the lobby level. Some doors were decorated with Christmas wreaths, but it was way past December. Others had scribbly drawings Scotch-taped to the surface, so you knew that kids lived there.

It was weird that we didn't run into anyone in Harold Hall, though it was the middle of the afternoon on a Saturday. We figured people were holed up inside because of the snow or else out sledding or doing errands.

By the time we got to the ground level, we were disappointed our visit was so uneventful. Then Desi suggested going downstairs to the laundry room. "No!" I told her. "Only bad things happen in the basement." All the horror movies we loved/hated warned, "Don't go in the basement," only some idiot always did. So did we.

Desi pulled me by my jacket sleeve. We tiptoed past the super's apartment and made our way toward the laundry room. She said the laundry room was always in the same place in all of these buildings and that Harold Hall was a lot like her building—but on steroids like Mr. Olympia, Arnold Schwarzenegger.

Sure enough, right in front of us was a door marked with the word "LAUNDRY" in peeling blue paint. Desi shouldered her way through it, dragging me along with her. An old, white Whirlpool churned its way through the "wash" cycle while the others sat dormant. Two dryers shuddered and crashed like demons jangling mini chains, their button-flies and zippers clanking against the dryer drum. I loved the smell of clothes being cooked in a dryer: to me, it was warm and comforting. Was it the scent of heated fabric softener, the scent of detergent or both? It lulled me into a snuggly, soft place.

When I told this to Desi, she laughed, "Maybe that's because you don't have to do the family's laundry!" It was true, Raffi made Desi and Athena clean the whole family's dirty clothes once a week while my mom did ours herself, like she did everything else: cheerfully. It made me despise her even more.

Being in the bowels of Harold Hall's laundry room was comfy and cozy. The gentle hum of the machines muffled all other sounds. Maybe that's why we didn't hear the door creak open and thump closed until it was too late. But when we turned around, there he was: the Magic Man in all his glory. Me and Desi gasped and grabbed for each other's hands. All the Magic Man did was smile an oily grin.

He looked just the way the other kids had described him: slightly shiny black suit complete with bow tie, slicked-back dark hair, pasty white face (possibly from makeup), lips too pink to be natural, especially on a man. ("Maybe it's Maybelline," Desi and I remarked later.) The Magic Man wore a black satin cape with a red underbelly, a black top hat cocked at a jaunty angle and spotless white gloves. He even had a white-tipped black wand tucked under his arm. "Greetings," he said.

"Um, hi," Desi and I stammered in unison. We hadn't even rehearsed it.

"Do you want to see a trick?"

We couldn't find our words, so we nodded. Even though we knew what would happen next.

The Magic Man smiled theatrically and pulled a deck of cards out of his breast pocket. He fanned them expertly like they were sewn together. (Maybe they were.) Back and forth. Forth and back. It was mesmerizing. Even the sound captivated us. The cards moved from one hand to the other, floating in the air.

Finally, the Magic Man held them in front of us. "Pick a card. Any card," he commanded. I nudged Desi to do it. She wiggled out the King of Hearts. "Don't show me," he warned. She didn't. "Now…" he cooed. "Slip it back into the deck." She did and the Magic Man followed up with more hand flourishes, shuffles, flips and card-cuts. All the while talking in a pleasant, slightly shivery voice. "The Kings in a deck of cards represent real kings throughout history. Did you know that?"

"No," I managed to say. 'How nice of him,' I thought. 'Taking the time to show us card tricks. Maybe they're wrong, all the things they say about him.' But my knees were still shaking. I could feel Desi tense up standing next to me, ready to spring like a scared stray dog.

"It's true," the Magic Man told us. "The King of Diamonds represents the very wealthy Julius Caesar." And with that, he flipped the King of Diamonds onto the lint-flecked floor. "But that's not your card. Am I right?"

"Yes," Desi said.

The Magic Man smiled. "Ah, I thought so. Now, the King of Clubs is the brutal Alexander the Great. Maybe you've heard of him." The King of Clubs fluttered to the ground. "But also not your card."

"Right again," I told him.

"Of course. That's why they call me 'the Magic Man.'" He continued shuffling until he flipped over the King of Spades. "This fellow represents the kind but strong King David of Israel. Perhaps you've heard of him."

"In religion class," Desi said.

"He killed Goliath," I added, not to be outdone.

"Precisely," the Magic Man continued. "King David was a nice, Jewish boy…like me." The Magic Man bent the back of the card, propelling it toward the ceiling. We watched it spiral down. "Not your card either, though."

Although we knew what was coming, we were still glued to the spot. "There's only one king in the deck without a mustache," he said. "Did you know that?"

"Uh-uh," Desi told him.

"It's true," the Magic Man admitted. "The King of Hearts, sometimes known as the Suicide King." He continued to shuffle. "Do you know why they call him that?" Again, we shook our heads, mesmerized by the movement of his hands. "No? Because he has a sword through his head. But like most things, it's an optical illusion."

The Magic Man flipped over the King of Hearts. Desi and I leaned in closer. "It sure looks like he's stabbing himself in the head," she told him.

"Looks can be deceiving," the Magic Man conceded. "But it's actually just the result of a bad copying job. Centuries of it. An error propagated over and over again throughout the ages. Blame it on English card makers, where the sword, or ax, appears to disappear in the poor King's head."

"Who is it?" I wondered.

"Oh, King Charles the Seventh of France. A good man, but emotionally disturbed. Quite mad, you see. Like me."

The Magic Man held the cards in front of him, with the King of Hearts on top. He moved the deck lower and lower. "Take a closer look," he urged. "Charles the Seventh's visage was put on the card at the beginning of his reign. Some time later, he became ill and was bedridden for the last two years of his life. That's when he became obsessed with cards. Especially those in his likeness. In a fever, he rambled on about the king being the 13th in a suit of cards and how that number kept popping up everywhere, how it was bad luck."

The Magic Man continued to move the cards down lower and lower so that Desi and I had to lean in deeper and closer to see them. "His son Louis the Twelfth took over the throne when his father, the King, became too insane to rule. Not long after, Charles's physician went into his chamber and found him raving, standing in the middle of the room, waving a large sword. Do you know what he was saying?"

"No, what?" we gasped.

"'Ils m'ont montré la vérité de treize, et il n'est pas signifie pour les yeux mortels.' How is your French?"

"Not good," Desi admitted.

"Then I shall translate. It means, 'They have shown me the truth of 13, and it is not meant for mortal eyes.'"

"We're both 13 years old," I told him.

"Ah," the Magic Man remarked. "An unlucky age."

"What happened next?" Desi whispered.

"Without a moment's hesitation, the King proceeded to ram the sword's blade into the left side of his head, between his ear and temple. It came out the other side. He wavered a moment before collapsing to the floor, dead."

"Wow!" we both gasped.

"Wow, indeed," the Magic Man said, satisfied that he'd scared the tuna salad out of us. "His likeness as the King of Hearts was altered to graphically depict his taking his own life, thus earning it the nickname 'the Suicide King.'" Desi and I were speechless. "You know, girls, there are other things besides the number 13 which are not meant for mortal eyes," he offered.

"And what's that?" Desi ventured.

"This!" The Magic Man moved the deck of cards away from where he held them, which happened to be at his crotch, and there was his Johnson, exposed. With sleight of hand, he must have unfastened his zipper when Desi and I were focused on the cards and caught up in his story.

The two of us screamed; the Magic Man laughed, propelling the deck of cards at us in what is commonly known as "52 Pickup." All of the remaining cards cascaded to the floor. Desi fumbled with the laundry room door, opened it and flew through it. I ran out behind her. We didn't stop running until we reached the basement door that led to the street. Then we kept running until we were at the corner of Fort Hamilton Parkway.

Mrs. Yaccarino was gone from the laundromat but Mrs. Dunphy was still manning Met Food's cash register. She waved, causing a long ash to fall from her Parliament. We waved back.

I didn't know exactly what had happened with the Magic Man but one thing I did know—I would never trust another man again. Not for a very long time.

DESI'S ROOM

Desi and I were sweaty messes by the time we crossed the street and dashed up the three flights of double stairs to the Ruiz place, convinced the Magic Man was following us. We were sure he would pop up at every landing, crouched under the steps, ready to jump out with his thing dangling. The memory of his penis became more horrible, more huge, more oddly fascinating with each step. "It looked like a white mouse," Desi gasped. "You know, a newborn white mouse, all squirmy and pale."

"But it was much bigger!" I cried out. "More like an albino snake."

"Like a turkey neck," Desi said.

"You stole that from *The Bell Jar*," I told her. We'd both read Sylvia Plath's book feverishly to each other the month earlier, having snuck it out of the Fort Hamilton branch of the Brooklyn Public Library without (gasp!) checking it out. It was the first time either of us had done such a thing. And it felt so deliciously wicked that we might actually do it again, maybe with a Bukowski book.

"So what if I did," Desi countered.

Out of breath, we fell onto the cold, dirty steps, giggling. "What's all this racket?" Mrs. Prill yelled, opening her door a crack. We could smell the fishy baby powder essence of her and caught a glimpse of her heavily-rouged cheeks, her old white lady afro, through the door slit.

"Nothing," we told her.

"Ha," Mrs. Prill said, not even offering us an ancient Werther's which she seemed to have an endless stash of in her housedress pocket. She slammed the door, muttering something about "those noisy, rotten PRs."

Desi and I got up and kept running to the third floor. We could hear the music before we opened the door to Desi's apartment. Maybe that's what Mrs. Prill had been complaining about: Raffi's music, not us. When we opened the door to Casa Ruiz, we saw Raffi and Stefan dancing, doing some kind of Latin hustle to a Tito Puente song that was blasting on the stereo. It was so loud, they didn't even hear us come in.

Now, Raffi was barely five-foot tall while Stefan was over six. She barely reached his shoulder. Umbe sat watching them from one of the green, crushed velvet bucket chairs which matched the green crushed velvet sofa. Also in the living room were also two lamps with ceramic bases shaped like a matador and a flamenco dancer plus another light that hung from a chain over the octagonal dining room table that was shoved into the corner. Raffi's decorating sense far surpassed my mom's Guinea sensibilities—which was plastic slipcovers on the couch, dark wood furniture from some dead maiden aunt in Queens and Venetian glass knick-knacks scattered all over the place, like dust.

Umbe had a half smile on his face watching Raffi and Stefan glide across the worn parquet wood floor. Despite their height differences, the dancers were as graceful as gazelles. It was a pleasure watching them move, so fluid, so natural. I wondered if I would ever move like that with a guy. Probably not, I decided.

Umbe cradled an earthenware coffee mug that had a burnt orange interior. I figure it held rum which was his beverage of choice, though in a pinch, beer would do. Looking at Umbe sip his drink, I realized that even Raffi's dinnerware was way cooler than my mother's. No cornflower blue, unbreakable Corelle dishes for this chickie! For Raffi, it was the cheap, unpredictable, threatening-to-shatter nature of earthenware all the way.

Now let me back up. Umbe was Humberto Tripas, Stefan's boyhood friend. They'd grown up together in Ponce, PR. Umbe contacted Stefan before he came to New York and asked if he could crash with Stefan until he got settled. Like his friend, Umbe was tall, lanky, sleepy-eyed and dreamy but way handsomer than Stefan. Desi and I both had mad crushes on Umbe, but to him we were nothing but cute kids. Couldn't he see that we were almost women?

Raffi and Stefan wiggled their way across the living room floor. It looked like they were doing the *merengue* but it was nothing like the way Umbe had taught me to do the dance. (When Umbe had taken me in his arms and showed me the step-drag, I beamed when he proclaimed that I had "Puerto Rican feet.") Stefan had his knee wedged between Raffi's slightly-spread thighs. She moved down, down, down on his leg until she was perched on it, rubbing slightly against it, then worked her way up again. Umbe threw back his head and laughed, only nothing came out of his mouth because the music was turned up so high. Then he got up to join them on the living room floor. The three of them huddled together for a moment.

When Desi saw this, she turned bright red and darted across the room, seeking the shelter of her bedroom. I started to follow her. That's when Raffi saw us. "Desiree!" Raffi screeched, turning down the music. "Desiree Rebecca Ruiz!" Desi stopped moving. Stefan and Umbe stepped away from Raffi. "What are you doing skulking around like fucking James Bond?" Raffi wondered.

"Nothing," Desi said. "We were just going to my room."

"Well, go there and stay there and quit spying on me."

"I wasn't spying on you," Desi said to a wooden square on the floor. 'Girl, shut your mouth and just go!' I wanted to tell my friend. Didn't she hear the slur in Raffi's voice, the cottony thickness that *ron y Coca-Cola* gave her tongue? I knew it all too well and Mrs. R wasn't even my mother.

Stefan was whispering to Raffi, trying to get her to calm down but even he couldn't help. Umbe had the sense to keep quiet. Raffi pushed Stefan away with her elbow. "You trying to tell me how to raise my own kid?" she yapped like a pissed-off Chihuahua. "You some kind of expert, Esteban? Huh? Where's your kid? Huh? With his *mami* who has an order of protection against you, right?"

Once Raffi started there was no stopping her. She had reduced a grown man who towered a full foot over her into a silent, cowering child. "Can I go now?" Desi wondered in a tiny voice.

"Get out of my sight!" Raffi screamed. "And take off that stupid hat. I told you not to wear it in here."

Desi just stood there, choking back tears of anger and humiliation. I slipped the mushroom hat from her head. It was damp with sweat from our block-long run from Harold Hall (and the Magic Man's dick!) and charging up six flights of stairs. "What are you waiting for? Go!" Raffi yelled.

As we went, I heard Umbe coo to Desi's mother, "Rafaela...*chica*..."

Athena and Matty still weren't back from sledding, which meant we had Desi's room all to ourselves, at least for a little while. We shed our winter skins in layers, peeling off our gloves first. "They must be icicles by now," Desi laughed, though she looked like she might cry any minute. She was referring to our younger siblings, of course.

"I wouldn't mind that one bit," I admitted.

"Me neither," she said. Then Desi held her breath and listened. The music in the living room had gotten lower and we could hear three voices tangling together, though not loudly. She got up and closed the door, made sure it clicked. There was no lock. "Do you want to?" Desi asked.

"Your mom will get mad if she catches us," I warned her.
Desi shrugged. "So what. She's already mad. Seems like she's always mad about something these days."

With no encouragement from me, Desi headed for her dresser. It was white and tall and must have been nice once but the paint was chipped in spots from where Athena had kicked or slammed it. She had the bottom three drawers and Desi had the top three.

To take attention away from the scars, the dresser was spattered with stickers—"Can You Dig It?" peel-offs as well as Topps Wacky Packages. But even colorful, silly stickers couldn't cover the fact that Athena had a nasty temper, a lot like her mother's.

Like I always did, I tried to make things better with words. "It must be hard for her," I started. "Raffi must miss your..."

"We all miss him," Desi told me. "Being mean won't bring him back." She went to pull open the highest drawer. It stuck so she yanked again. "She just can't stand that I look like him."

There was a framed picture of the five of them on the nightstand. I knew it had been taken the summer before Big Matty's accident. They all looked so happy and Desi wasn't wearing MushroomHat. I guess she didn't need it then.

As I studied the photo, I knew that Desi was right; she *did* resemble her dad. "You look like both of them," I offered. "But mostly, you look like you."

"You suck at lying, Celeste," Desi said, digging through her underwear drawer.

"Don't call me that. The nuns call me that."

"No, they don't. They call you 'Celestine' even though that's not really your name. Because Celeste is technically not a saint's name."

"And neither is Desiree," I countered. We both laughed.

"But I like the story of your name," Desi said. "Your real one."

As a girl, my mom had loved the song "Tubby the Tuba," especially the part when the celeste came in. (AKA, a celesta. It's a keyboard that looks like an upright piano and has a pretty, glittery sound.) When I told this to Desi, she couldn't get enough of it and made me tell her the story over and over.

"I think I might have been named for the Desiree potato," Desi countered.

"Stop," I said. "You know it was because of the movie. Marlon Brando made a good Napoleon."

"Big Matty and Raffi saw it on their first date," Desi admitted. "They were teenagers, just a couple of dumb kids." In the drawer, she moved aside her training bras and days-of-the-week panties. Finally, between "Sunday" and a pile of Kotex, Desi found it. The Box. That's what we called it: "The Box."

What was inside The Box was a secret known only to me, Desi and Mary (she of the dress shop downstairs). Mary was an unofficial auntie to Desi, the kind of aunt who gave her things she wasn't supposed to have: hanging earrings, Bazooka Bubble Gum and this. This, being a plastic, teal case containing 40, count 'em, 40 Avon lipstick testers. They were tiny, half the size of our pinkie fingers, and we treasured each and every one of them. Even the slutty reds we wouldn't dream of wearing. Yes, in addition to being a cool aunt, Mary also sold Avon products.

The lipstick testers were intended as samples for prospective beauty-product buyers so they could try out a shade before they bought it. Except Mary had given Desi the entire kit on her 13th birthday. She'd managed to slip it to Desi on the sly without Raffi seeing. Whenever Desi needed a lift (like today!) or when we were feeling especially wicked, Desi pulled out the mint green box.

Our favorite shade was called "Deep Carnation." The pale whisper of pink was worn down to a waxy nub. "Deep Carnation" was closely followed by "Instant Mocha." Colors like "Peach Surprise" didn't work with our dark complexions and looked like we'd taken a swig of Milk of Magnesia when we tried them on for size.

Desi unsnapped the box's top and selected "Full Stop." Like its name implied, it was the shade of a stop sign. "No!" I told her. She ignored me, steadied her hand on my chin and went for it. I tried to protest, holding back the giggles.

"Shush or you'll look like Mrs. Prill." That made laugh from deep in my gut. Mrs. Prill always applied her lipstick outside her thin lips and thought no one noticed that it made her look like a circus clown. We both agreed that "Full Stop" was a terrible shade. I wiped my mouth on a Kleenex, the lipstick staining it like blood. Desi tried again, this time with "Pastel Peach." Her touch was soft as rain. Then I did her: "Caramel Ice." We tried a few other colors before she slipped the box back into its hiding spot. If Athena found it, she definitely would have told on Desi or smashed it. Or both.

"Oh, we almost forgot!" Desi said, opening the nightstand drawer and extracting a frayed yellow cloth tape measurer. (My grandfather was getting rid of it so I glommed it from the top of the basement trash when my mom sent me down to get the laundry one day.) "You first," she said. "I went first last time." I lifted my shirt and my thermals underneath it. "Everything," Desi said. I rolled my eyes and wriggled my arms out of my tops. "Or else we won't get a true reading."

I sat there on the edge of Desi's bed with my clothes up around my neck in my lacy training bra from Century 21. Since the bra didn't even have hooks, I slipped it down to my waist. My nipples were pale and puffy. "Baby bottle nips," my sister Laura teased when she got a glimpse of them once.

But Desi didn't make fun of me. Instead, she screwed up her face in concentration and wrapped the measuring tape around my chest. "Still 28," she said. I barely filled out an AA cup.

Desi didn't have to be coaxed out of her clothes. She stripped off the layers quickly, revealing her B cup-sized boobs to me proudly. "I feel like I've grown," she announced. "Or maybe I'm just getting my friend."

Her bra was white cotton with an eyelet pattern. A grown-up bra with clasps, adjustable straps and everything. Desi's chest was almost twice the size of mine: round, apple-shaped, topped with dusky, flat, large-areolaed nipples which barely stood out, even in the chill of the room. "Still 30," I told her. "But they do look bigger," I agreed.

Desi was built like her dad: strong and solid. Not fat but beefy. And she wore it well. I was painfully thin no matter how much I ate. My hip bones scooped in like sharp, dangerous weapons.

"They hurt," she said, hugging herself. "They feel lumpy."

"My period just started this morning," I admitted.

"Then mine isn't far behind," she laughed. Soon after Desi and I began hanging out together, we began menstruating together. It was both weird and wonderful.

"Imagine what Umbe would think if he walked in on us right now," Desi gasped as she started getting dressed.

"Imagine!" I pulled up my bra and pulled down my shirts.

"But he might like it," Desi sighed. "He might fall for us." We'd already agreed that if Umbe had a crush on either of us, the other one wouldn't be mad. We were best friends, after all.

"I bet he'd go for you. Guys don't like me."

"Yet..." Desi reminded me. "Remember what Mami always says. 'The most beautiful thing about a woman a man can't see with his eyes.'"

"It sounds better in Spanish," I told her.

"Everything sounds better in Spanish," she laughed. It was true.

Then we did our second favorite thing next to staring at Umbe when he wasn't looking. Which was *talking* about Umbe. We even had a list of things we liked about him, which was practically everything. Our Umbe List included:

- The way he held his Marlboro;
- The way he wrapped his lips around his Marlboro;
- The way he blew smoke out of the corner of his mouth so he wouldn't blow it into our faces when he smoked his Marlboro (Umbe was such a gentleman!);
- The way his bell bottoms curled up at the hems where they met the ground;
- The way his t-shirt hugged his chest;
- The way he said the word "turquoise;"
- The way he said our names;

- His laugh;
- His pinkie toes (Umbe liked to walk around barefoot, even
  in the winter.);
- The little mole above his mouth; and
- His mouth.

Desi kept the list in a notebook in her nightstand drawer and she wrote each entry backwards so Athena couldn't read it if she found it. Sister Vivian (aka "The Lip") had once told us that Leonardo da Vinci wrote backwards and we thought this was super cool. Besides, Athena hadn't learned about da Vinci yet so we were safe, at least for a couple of years.

"Sometimes it makes me feel funny 'down there' when I think about him," Desi admitted, putting the notebook back into the drawer.

"Me, too," I told her. "All shivery and tingly. Like it's swallowing."

"Swallowing?"

"Don't you feel that too?"

Desi thought about it. "More like…shining…"

"Shining…I like that. It sounds pretty."

Desi threw a pillow at me. "It feels pretty! It feels great."

"What do you do about it?" I wondered.

"Sometimes when I'm in bed, I squeeze my legs together. Tight. Over and over again. Then I fall asleep."

"Sometimes I do the same thing but with a pillow."

"And?"

"And it feels good. Too good."

Desi sighed. "There has to be something else. Something more."

"What?"

"I don't know yet but when I find out, I'll tell you."

At 13, Desi and I were dumb when it came to sex. When we heard that Andy Mangano had fingered Annette Ryan in the corner of the schoolyard, we couldn't understand why. What did he get out of it? What did she get out of it? We had no one to ask. We knew this was something we couldn't ask our mothers, no matter how cool they thought they were.

"And if I figure it out, I'll tell you, too," I promised Desi.

Two rooms away, we heard the front door thump closed, Raffi yelling, Athena stomping, Matty crying and Mrs. Prill banging on the ceiling below the Ruiz living room with her broom handle, yelling for everyone to shut the heck up. All hell had broken loose in a matter of seconds. But that was just life as usual at Casa Ruiz.

Athena burst in through the bedroom door, red-faced from the cold and sweaty from her winter clothes. Her brown cheeks were so pink it looked like she'd been slapped. "What were you two doing in here?" she asked.

"Nothing," Desi told her.

"Just talking," I told her.

"Ha," Athena responded. She whipped up the tape measurer from Desi's bed. "What's this for?"

"Math homework," Desi said, snatching it back.

"Ha," Athena said again.

"You'll see when you have Miss Quincy," Desi added. Miss Quincy was homely and hole-faced and liked to rock back and forth on her toes when someone puzzled over a math problem. The boys swore she did this close to the edge of their desks, dry-humping the corner as she went up and down from heel to toe. I didn't know what "dry-humping" was and neither did Desi.

Matty sashayed into the doorway, his coat and hat off but his scarf still tied around his neck at a jaunty angle. His face was puffy from his crocodile tears released at the mere thought of the destruction Hurricane Rafaela might unleash. This time, the storm was avoided, probably because Umbe and Stefan were there. *"Arroz con gandules,"* was all Matty said before he disappeared.

"Pigeon peas and rice," Athena piped then darted out of the room.

Matty popped back into the doorway. "What happened to the picture?"

When we looked at the family photo on Desi's night table, it was the wrong way. Raffi, Big Matty, Desi, Athena and Matty smiled at us upside down at the Catskill Game Farm. It looked like they were standing on their heads. I tried to turn the frame right-side up but it kept falling over. "That's weird," I said. "The picture's upside down in the frame."

"Why would you do that?" Matty asked. "That's messed up."

"I didn't do it," Desi told him.

"Neither did I," I added. "I just looked at it, then put it back."

"It's him," Desi said.

"Him who?" Matty wondered. But he knew. He just didn't want to know.

"Promise not to cry if I say it," Desi warned him.

"Say what?" Matty squeaked.

"Daddy," Desi whispered.

Almost on cue, Matty started to cry. He hadn't promised he wouldn't. He was so predictable.

"Shush," Desi said. "Don't let her hear you. She'll get mad. Madder."

But Matty didn't stop. He couldn't. He just cried softer. Desi put her arm around her brother's shoulder, led him into her room and guided him toward her bed. He plopped down between us and rested his head against mine. I could feel his tight, wiry curls, slightly damp from his winter hat. "Don't be scared, Matty," Desi cooed.

"I'm not scared," Matty insisted. But I could tell he was. Scared and sad.

"Daddy just wants us to know that he's still here, that he's still looking out for us," Desi tried.

But Matty just cried harder, silently, snorting on the tears and snot. His whole body shook. "Maybe that's why he's crying," I told Desi.

I felt Matty nod against my head. Desi and I wrapped our arms around him and let him get it all out. When I told him that he was the center of our Matty-filled donut, he started laughing and choking on his boogers. Desi handed him a tissue.

Raffi's voice cut through our laughter. All three of us stiffened. "Dinner! I'm not gonna call you again." We didn't want to get Hurricane Rafaela raging again.

I grabbed my stuff and started putting it on as I walked with Desi, Athena and Matty to the living room. The table Raffi had wedged into the corner was already set. Trivets waited to be covered by steaming pots. Stefan bustled around the narrow, galley-type kitchen, happy, in his element. Small as the kitchen was, Stefan worked magic in it. Raffi too, when she cared enough to cook.

"*Mija*, you're not staying?" Raffi called to me.

"Thanks, I wish I could," I told her and left.

AT THE KITCHEN TABLE

In the Piccolo House, all the important stuff happened at the kitchen table. We were Italian American, after all. The kitchen table is where Laura and I did our homework. It's where our mom made our meals. It's where our dad was the most relaxed. That is, after he had his two Manhattans when he came home from the Ratings Department of Yale Transport Corporation. Probably a pretty boring job but Phil seemed to like it okay. My father was a numbers guy while I was not a numbers gal in the least. At that point, I wasn't exactly sure what I was or what I wanted to be but I was sure it didn't involve figuring out the cheapest way to get a shipment of tulip bulbs from Holland to a nursery in Middletown, New York. That was my dad's department.

My mom's department? It was making sure my dad was happy. This might include: making one of Phil's favorite meals, making love to him twice a week (Wednesdays and Saturdays), making sure the apartment was clean and tidy, making sure Laura and I did our homework (and didn't ask Dad anything within five minutes of his coming home from the office—and having his first Manhattan). Tessie always said that if Dad was happy, then everyone was happy.

What made Tessie happy? I don't think she asked herself that question, so I didn't have the nerve to ask her myself. But my guess is that it was probably food. Which is probably why she was so big.

I'd seen pictures of my mom before she got married, before she had Laura and me. She definitely was pretty. Willowy, slender, like a young tree about to flower. Maybe a cherry blossom or something like that. Wide, open smile, a deep dimple, intelligent, friendly eyes. Desi thought I looked a lot like Tessie but I couldn't see it.

And my dad... When Desi got a peek at the snapshot of Phil in his Korean War uniform, him in a low crouch, elbow casually resting on his knee, cap in hand, hair lightly tussled, she said, "Dang, Cici, your dad was hot!" I gave her a little shove and told her she was crazy but actually, Phil wasn't too bad back then.

I wondered what happened to my parents since those pictures had been taken. But then I realized that me and Laura was what happened to them. They had kids and we sucked the life out of them.

Tessie's kitchen was her domain. It was the only place she truly looked comfortable. She could make something delicious out of a hunk of cold, raw meat and a few spices, and did. Where Raffi hated cooking—she said it was because she was forced to feed her whole family at age 12 (her mom was a drinker and her dad had walked out on them by then), and more than 20 years later, she was tired of cooking. But Tessie thrived in the kitchen; she shined there.

As I did my homework on the Formica tabletop, out of the corner of my eye, I would see my mom moving gracefully from sink to stove, happily stirring, tasting and humming to herself. It made me feel warm and safe—the thought that this big, almost-beautiful woman took pleasure and pride in taking care of me. Of us. Tessie could sit at the table for an hour, patiently trimming the gristle from a cheaper cut of veal because even on his salary, my dad preferred veal stew to beef stew. And my mom liked giving people what they liked. But again, what did Tessie want? That seemed to be it: making people happy. And she was good at it.

If someone was in the hospital and Tessie knew they liked cheesecake, she brought them a slice. (And a plastic fork.) If a relative in Florida pined away for pickled pigs' feet, which they didn't have in supermarkets there, she'd remember to pack a jar when we drove down to Delray Beach. She remembered people's birthdays and anniversaries—and sent thoughtful Hallmark cards for each occasion. She remembered the names of pets—and even brought catnip or doggie treats when we went to visit.

My mom was such a *nice person*. Then why did I hate her so much? Maybe because I was afraid that I might be her someday. Okay, maybe hate isn't the right word. But I didn't like her very much and I was mean to her a lot. "If eye-rolling was an Olympic sport…" she'd often say to me, "then you would have a chest full of medals—just like Mark Spitz." I was embarrassed by my mother's thick, varicose-veined legs, her dry heels, her unpolished toenails and her unworldly ways. Why couldn't Tessie be "the groovy mom?" Why couldn't she be more like Raffi?

Back to the kitchen table. The center of Tessie's universe. The four of us had supper there together every night. It was one of the Piccolo House rules, one of many. Like taking those terrible chewable fluoride vitamins every morning. Or having to dry the dishes every night. Only the "eating dinner together" rule wasn't so bad. The food was great and my dad always seemed to be in a good mood, especially if it was Wednesday or Saturday.

At 6 PM every night, Laura slid into her place against the wall because she was the smallest, while I squished into the spot near the Frigidaire. Phil was at the head of the table and Tessie had her back to the stove and sink, giving her easy access to serving us.

While lots of families took their plates and ate their supper in a rec room or in front of the boob tube, we ate facing each other. (Besides, we had no rec room.) There was a lot of laughter and sometimes we even played "20 Questions" and "Name that Tune" when other families barely spoke, shoveling forkfuls silently into their faces. Desi loved having supper with the Piccolos: she thought it was exotic and fun, while I thought the same of the rough-and-tumble, thrown-together meals at her place. I guess we always want what we don't have, right?

Sometimes my dad would tell us stories about his childhood, growing up a few miles away in Borough Park, in a rambling house with cheerful grandparents who almost made up for his drunken father and cowering mother. Or he'd talk about being in the Service. Not the shooting part or the working in the ammo dump part but traveling to Tokyo on leave and having the same pork curry in the same restaurant every night for a week. Or the doe-eyed girl named Mariko who wanted to marry him. (Phil still had letters from her in his strongbox—next to Mariko's signature were faded pink lipstick prints.) My dad came alive then, when he was talking about the Korean War or his grandparents Mike and Bridget. It was like he was onstage, performing.

When Desi came by for dinner, she was in awe of my dad, maybe because she missed her own father. Afterwards, she would make me tell her stories about growing up with Phil. Over and over. Like how he used to put the *1812 Overture* on the Decca record player and we would act out the music. One part, we called "We Have No Water," because the music sounded like someone dragging themselves through battle, foodless and fluidless. When the cannon parts came, we'd pretend to get wounded.

Or else, Phil would act out scenes from *Chiller Theatre* movies like *The Hunchback of Notre Dame*. One time, he jumped up on the coffee table and a leg snapped off underneath him. He crashed to the living room floor laughing, with my mother screaming. "Did your dad do things like that?" I asked Desi once.

"No," she said. "But he did other things." Only she was too sad to tell me what those things were. That's how much she missed him. So, I let it go.

Then, when Desi was leaving my house that night, she smiled sadly and told me, "He taught me how to do the *merengue*. My dad. He put my feet on top of his and led me around the room. That's how I learned."

"Sounds nice," I said.

"It was," Desi answered, her lower lip quivering, her voice shaking. She looked like an abandoned puppy standing there in my doorway. I didn't know what else to do but hug her. "Thanks, Cici. You're a good friend," she told me, then mashed her mushroom hat onto her head and went down the stairs. A better friend would have known what else to do. I should have made Desi stay for dessert. I should have made her have a Ring Ding and a glass of cold milk to calm her down. I should have done something more than just hug her. But sometimes a hug is all you've got.

Sure, there was lots of joy around the Piccolo kitchen table but the apartment was also too close for comfort. There wasn't much besides those four miniscule rooms. There was no place to hide, no place to be alone. At least Desi's apartment had all of these nooks and crannies. Even Matty's closet/

bedroom was his own personal space. But I had no place that was just mine. Which is probably why I spent so much time in the bathroom.

I liked to take long, luxurious baths, just lying there in the steam, adding more hot water when I needed to. We had an old-fashioned claw-footed bathtub. Its feet kind of looked like lion's paws. Squished into the cramped bathroom, it was chipped, stained, but deep and comfortable. It almost felt like you were being cradled in an enamel palm when you laid in it. I liked to just lie there and daydream: what I would look like when I grew up, if anyone would ever love me (I mean, totally-seriously-forever love me) and if Umbe even knew I existed. Stuff like that.

Laura had this little, blue, plastic hairbrush for her Thumbelina doll which she sometimes left in the bathroom. One time, I just started brushing my hair "down there" with it. I don't know why. But it felt good. Relaxing. It got so that I would seek out that little, blue, plastic doll hairbrush, even if Laura hadn't left it in the bathroom. It became "a thing," a bath time ritual for me. I could get lost in the brushing, feeling myself go all soft in the legs and breathless. Then once, when I was sitting cross-legged in front of the faucet, adding more warm water, the gush parted my hair and made me shiver with a gasp of pleasure. I sat straight up, swearing I'd never do it again while simultaneously wanting to do it again.

Before I realized it, I was lying flat on my back in the tub, hair floating, face just above the water line, scooting my butt up against the bathtub wall. When the water stream hit me, my lips fluttered and an electric shock zapped through my body. My legs shot straight up into the air as I scooched closer to the flow. I felt my crotch spasming and spasming, like a fist opening and releasing real fast. It felt good yet it felt terrible. I never wanted it to end yet I couldn't wait for it to be over. I wanted to laugh. I wanted to cry. I did start crying but then my face went underwater and I swallowed a mouthful of soapy liquid. I sat up, sputtering above and stuttering below, coughing and gasping, and wondering what the hell had just happened.

Then there was a loud banging on the bathroom door. "What's going on in there?!" my mother bellowed. "Your father has a hurry call!"

"I'll be out in a minute," I told her, pulling out the plug and standing on rubbery legs. I burned my behind on the silver-painted heat pole which brought steam up from the basement to the radiators in the other rooms. My father glared at me when I passed by, wrapped in my towel. He disappeared into the bathroom, wielding the *New York Daily News*, ready to settle down for a nice, long crap. Did he have a *Playboy* magazine hidden in the *News*, too? I couldn't bear the thought, just crept guiltily into my room, shut the door tight and slipped into my granny gown.

As I drifted off to sleep that night, I was convinced that I was the only one on the whole entire planet who did such filthy, nasty things in the bathtub. And that no one would ever want to be my friend if they found out, not even Desi. Did *anyone* do things like this? No, I doubted it, especially not Desi. Not with Big Matty always spying on her from heaven or wherever he was.

I fell asleep with both hands nestled between my thighs, squeezing, squeezing, squeezing. I dreamed that Laura screamed when she discovered my pubic hair in her doll brush, bringing my parents and my entire class at St. Fi's (plus the nuns and lay teachers!) into our small bathroom, which was as crowded as one of those clown cars at the Ringling Bros. and Barnum & Bailey Circus. And there I was in the middle of it, cowering in the cold bathwater, the tiny, blue, doll hairbrush tangled in my pubes.

Nope, I would never do it again. And I would never tell Desi about it, who I told just about everything. I was a disgusting freak, a pervert, a sex maniac. There was nothing more to say.

"ROCK THE BOAT"

"Chinga, la merengue," Umbe told us in Desi's living room. Which basically meant, "Screw the *merengue*."

Apparently, the *merengue* and all other Latin dances were dead. There was a new *baile* in town and it was called the Spanish Hustle. Everyone was doing it. The Spanish Hustle was born in the South Bronx in 1972. Puerto Rican teenagers had invented it and now, Umbe was going to teach it to us. Raffi was working downstairs at Mary's Dress Shop, Stefan was chefing at the Museum, and Athena and Matty were at friends' houses, so we had Casa Ruiz all to ourselves.

Umbe had brought his battery-operated Philips cassette player/recorder for the occasion. He made the best mix tapes and already had this one cued up to the perfect song to teach us the Spanish Hustle. "Rock the Boat" by the Hues Corporation came on when he pressed the "Play" button under the Philips arrow.

The song had come out last year but it was still going strong. Desi and I had seen the group lip sync it on both *Soul Train* and *American Bandstand*. In our twisted teenage minds, "Rock the Boat" was about our unrequited love for Umbe. It was all about a voyage of love starting, a touch that thrills like the rush of the wind, safe arms and a quiet place to harbor. All that and a cargo full of love and devotion. Tender lips…the strength that flows from you…and the fear of it all slipping away. But how did Umbe know? Did he feel the same way about us, too?

"Come on, *chica*." Umbe stood there with his hands outstretched, his worn-out bell bottoms hugging his hips just so. Desi shook her head, blushing and hurled herself into one of the velvet bucket chairs, crossing her arms and legs emphatically. Maybe dancing with Umbe reminded her too much of learning the *merengue* with her feet on top of her father's to dance with another man.

"That leaves you," Umbe drawled to me. "Come on, Cici, don't leave me hanging." I took his hand.

Umbe closed his long, slender fingers around mine. "It's a lot like the *merengue*," he explained, "but not." I hoped he didn't feel my body trembling when he rested his hand lightly on my waist. It tingled where he touched me. "Just follow me," he said. "Do what I do."

When Umbe spun the two of us in a wide circle, I thought I'd pass out. I had to keep reminding myself to breathe. Then he twirled me like the ballerina in my jewelry box—twice. I somehow managed to keep my footing. "Good," he told me. "Good. Now, like this." The next step was turning our feet to the middle, kicking into each other. Kind of like a sliding step Gene Kelly might do in a movie but to a disco beat. Full of kicks and turns and half turns. Once, I actually kicked Umbe in the ankle, but not too hard. He didn't seem to notice or mind.

Desi watched us with a slight smile on her face, her eyes half closed. *"Our love is like a ship…"* the Hues sang as Umbe turned and stepped and led and twirled. *"So I'd like to know where…"* went the song. Umbe's hand on the base of my spine felt fine and right. When he looked at me, the zit in the middle of my forehead felt like an angry, red mountain but he didn't seem to notice that either. He was so into the music, the Hustle…and me? No, it wasn't possible. But still… Dancing with Umbe didn't make me feel like a kid. *"Don't tip the boat…"*

After "Rock the Boat" came "Jungle Boogie," which you could also Spanish Hustle to, but it was harder, at least for me. Desi still wouldn't switch partners and try dancing with Umbe. But when "Shambala" came on, Desi didn't fight when both of us pulled her up to the middle of the living room floor. It was such a happy, joyous song, she couldn't resist. We did crazy, freestyle moves. Desi had a thing for Three Dog Night and so did I.

We were all laughing and howling to the part in the chorus that went, "Aah, oooh, oooh…yeah, yeah, yeah, yeah, yeah" when Raffi walked in with Athena and Matty. I guess they'd met their mom at Mary's Dress Shop after their play dates and came up together. The music was blasting so we didn't hear the door open. Suddenly, there they were, ripping off their coats and hats and mittens, peeling off their snow boots and joining us in the dance.

We flailed our arms up around our heads and shouted/sang about brothers and sisters with flowers in their eyes, everyone being lucky, helpful and kind, washing away troubles, pain, sorrow and shame. Raffi and Umbe exchanged knowing glances at the part that talked about everyone being high. But at that moment, we all were high, and not from something you smoked or drank, but from the sheer joy of being in each other's presence. And from music. Always from music. It amazed me how the right song could magically transport you to a different place, good or bad. How the songwriter knew exactly how you felt, how you wanted to feel, how you needed to feel, good or bad or ugly.

Like:
- Roberta Flack's version of "The First Time Ever I Saw Your Face" – the first time ever I saw that angelically-handsome John Williams at St. Fi's;
- "Precious and Few" by Climax," "Natural High" by Bloodstone, "Close to You" by the Carpenters played in my head whenever I saw John Williams in the schoolyard;
- "Killing Me Softly," when the cherubically-perfect John Williams ignored me and didn't even know I was alive. Again, by Roberta.;
- The tragic beauty of Don McLean's "Vincent." (Although I was afraid I'd end up tormented, alone and unloved like van Gogh, my favorite artist of the moment.); and
- I longed to be cherished like the women in "Your Song" or "Tiny Dancer" (which Bernie Taupin, my # 1 lyricist, wrote for his beloved Maxine). Would anyone ever love me like that? I doubted it.

But dancing in the Ruiz living room—something that would never, ever happen in the Piccolo living room around the corner on Gelston Avenue—I felt cradled, happy, and yes, loved.

When "Soul Makossa" came on, the moves got wilder and we got sweatier. During "Dancing Machine," Matty, Jr. treated us to his slide-across-the-floor robot moves, lifted directly from Michael Jackson on "Soul Train," minus the afro and sparkly powder-blue vest. We all roared with applause, not caring if Matty was a *mariposa* or *maschio-femme* or anything else but Matty.

By the time the song ended, we were all flushed and falling all over each other, laughing. Umbe and Raffi hugged, maybe a little too long. Just then, Stefan slinked in, carrying a battered pot of what I later found out was *moros y cristianos* (black beans and white rice, roughly translated to "Moors and Christians"). He put the pot on the table and joined us on the makeshift dance floor.

The funky keyboards in Stevie Wonder's "Superstition" was next. We rocked out, still laughing. The lyrics talked about writing on the wall, 13-month old babies, broken mirrors. It said that when you believed in things that you don't understand, then you suffer. Desi and I stared at each other, suddenly serious, silently thinking about Big Matty, then looked away.

"Who wants *pasteles*?" Raffi asked. We all did. "Good," she told us. "Mami just made a batch this morning."

Pasteles were Puerto Rican manna from heaven, really complicated to make. They involved an outer layer of grated green banana, potato and tropical pumpkin (called "masa") wrapped around a savory meat stew which usually included some combo of raisins, ham, bacon, chickpeas, olives and loads of other spices which never showed up in Italian cooking. Stuff like *adobo*, *annatto* and *sofrito*. The meat was put inside the masa, wrapped in a softened banana skin, tied with kitchen twine, then gently boiled to deliciousness. Mami was the expert maker of *pasteles* and other Puerto Rican delicacies. I bet she and Aunt Cassie made a few dozen *pasteles* together, sitting elbow to elbow at Mami's worn wooden kitchen table, grating, rolling, stuffing, wrapping, and gossiping in Spanglish. This made the *pasteles* taste even better.

"You staying, Cici, right?" Raffi told me as she went to the kitchen to heat up the *pasteles*. I knew my mom was making veal and peppers for dinner but could probably manage a *pastele* without spoiling my appetite.

A few days later, Desi and I found ourselves in the apartment, struggling to keep up with *Lilias, Yoga and You* on Channel 13. Athena and Matty were battling their way through Candyland while Raffi was out doing errands. There was a knock on the door, then the sound of it pushing open without waiting for a response, followed by Umbe's familiar "It's me." My heart did a backflip hearing his voice and I'm sure Desi's did, too. Unrequited crushes suck and are pretty awesome at the same time.

There Desi and I were in our Danskins and tights, trying to cover up and make ourselves look small. Umbe didn't take note of our embarrassment. "*Chicas*, what's up?" he drawled, stroking the thin beard tickling his chin. "Yoga," Desi said. "We can't seem to get the headstand."

"It's easy," Umbe told us, sucking his teeth. "Look." With that, he kicked off his sneakers and folded himself down onto the middle of the living room floor. Up went his long legs, straight as a bone. "See," he said, much to our wonder, then unfolded himself just as easily.

Whenever Desi and I tried this, we toppled over, thumping our knees, our feet, and bruising our bones. When Umbe saw how hopeless we were, he laughed and shook his head. "Let's try it against something first," he suggested. He picked up one of the velvet chairs like it weighed nothing and moved it to the side. I couldn't help but notice how Umbe's arm muscles rippled.

Desi took off her glasses and put them on the coffee table. Next to each other, with throw pillows cushioning our heads, we tried and tried to do headstands, but kept falling into each other like dominoes. I thought I broke Desi's nose when my foot cracked into her face. Luckily, I didn't.

"How about one at a time?" Umbe sighed. Desi went first, butt against the wall, slowly raising her knees, then her feet. She held the position for about three seconds, then crumbled. "Good," he said. "Now, Cici."

If Desi could do it, I knew I could, too. I was up for only a millisecond when my feet started sliding down the wall. Umbe grabbed hold of my ankles to steady me. The feel of his hands on my legs had me shaking like a newspaper in the breeze. I couldn't wait for it to be over…and yet I didn't want it to end. When I started to get woozy, I came out of the headstand.

We practiced some more, one at a time, then all together with Umbe beside us, uneven pickets in a not-so-white picket fence. When we got nauseous from being upside down too long, we stopped. Umbe cracked a Corona from Raffi's stash. He gave me and Desi a Coke to share. "I got something to tell you, *chicas*," he began.

'Here it comes,' I thought. 'Umbe is going to declare his undying love for us and tell us that he's willing to wait five years until we're legal.' But instead, Umbe told us that he'd met someone. "Her name is Sylvia," he beamed. "We've been going out for a few weeks. She's pretty cool. I think you'd both like her."

Umbe had a girlfriend! And she wasn't me! Or Desi! I already hated this Sylvia chick, whoever she was.

Desi and I listened to Umbe politely as he told us everything we didn't want to know about his new girlfriend. He'd met her through Mary downstairs. Sylvia was one of the women who not only designed but sewed the dresses Mary sold. It was serendipity, he said, destiny that he happened to be down there, helping Mary bring in a delivery when Sylvia showed up. "She's really nice, ask Raffi," Umbe said. "And Raffi doesn't like anyone," he reminded us. "But she likes Sylvie." Oh, so now it's Sylvie!

I tried to seem interested but bit by bit, I was dying inside, Desi didn't try to hide her disappointment. I saw her lower lip wobbling as she held back her tears. I didn't want her to start bawling in front of Umbe, so I suggested we go to her room to do the homework we didn't have. She agreed, scuffing her feet.

"How could he?!" Desi whined after she shut the door. At least we had some privacy since Matty and Athena were playing games—now it was Battleship, I could hear their cries of "You sunk my battleship!" coming from his postage stamp-sized room. I just shrugged at Desi's rhetorical question. I couldn't imagine why Umbe needed a girlfriend. Weren't we enough for him?

"I guess he sees us as kids," I offered.

"But we're not," she countered.

I looked down at my almost-flat chest. "We kind of are. And it's a lot to ask of him to wait until we turn 18. Five whole years."

"Four years and eight months," Desi pointed out. "But we're worth it!"

"I know that and you know that…" I started. But I didn't know how to finish.

Luckily, Athena and Matty bounced into the room, him clutching his blue Battleship board to his chest, and she with her red one raised above her head, ready to clock him with it. "You cheated," Athena snarled through her teeth.

"Did not," Matty told her. "Desi, help!" Desi and I managed to wrestle both Battleship boards from each of them without any of the red and white pegs that rattled inside falling out. But not before Athena gave her brother a nice crack with hers.

"Let's listen to some music," Desi suggested, rubbing Matty's head. Reluctantly, her siblings plopped themselves onto opposite beds, crossing their arms over their chests, glaring at each other.

"You know what they say…" I offered as a peace pipe. "…that music soothes the savage breast."

"You said 'breast'!" Athena barked. "I'm telling Mom!"

"Mom's not home," Desi told her. "Breast! Breast! Breast!"

Even Athena laughed at this. Desi found WPLJ on the clock-radio dial, turning it to 95.5. It always came in slightly fuzzy but we still liked it, mostly because of Jim Kerr. Not only did their new DJ sound like a sweet guy but he spun the best tunes. He was midway through "Drift Away."

Desi took her tape deck off the bookshelf. Knowing her, she wanted to be ready to record a depressing song or two because of this recent development with Umbe. There's nothing like a sad song to make the lovelorn even sadder. She unwrapped a fresh cassette tape and popped it into the player. To test the batteries, she pressed "record" and "play" but her finger slipped and the blank tape started to play. At first, there was just scratchy nothingness. Then we heard a voice.

"That's impossible," Desi said. "It's a new tape. I just opened it."

Athena turned down the radio while Desi played back the tape. The voice was low, whispery, weak. "We went camping and…" it said.

"What?" Athena asked.

Desi played back the tape again. "We went camping and…"

Matty's face went white. "That sounds like Daddy," he gasped.

"It can't be," Athena told him.

Desi played the tape one more time. "We went camping and…"

"It's like…it's like…he's trying to tell us what happened."

"We didn't go camping, but. We went hunting," Matty stammered.

"You guys were going to pitch a tent, though, right?" Desi asked him. Matty nodded. He and his dad hadn't had a chance to set up camp.

Athena said, "I want to hear it again," and moved to press the "rewind" button.

"Noooo!" Matty wailed.

"Yes!" Athena snapped. "Stop being such a baby."

"He's not being a baby," I told her. "He was there." Even though she was younger, I'd never stood up to Athena before. Her face looked as shocked as I felt but the words had just uncontrollably shot out of my mouth. I didn't know much about the day their father had been killed in that hunting accident but I did know that Matty saw the whole thing and that their uncles had to get him drunk to calm him down. Drunk until he passed out.

Desi grabbed the tape recorder and made like she was going to tape some music. She turned up the volume on the radio as Jim Kerr was announcing the next song, "Bad, Bad Leroy Brown." There was no way Desi wanted to tape that. Jim Croce's "Time in a Bottle," maybe, but not "Leroy." Still, Desi fiddled with the tape player, then opened the cover and took the tape out. One finger hooked around the brown tape and yanked. It snapped like a rubber band. Her eyes met mine. I knew she'd done it on purpose.

"Hey!" Athena yelled.

"Hay is for horses," Desi told her. "Not for me." She threw the mangled cassette tape in the garbage can.

When "Pillow Talk" came on by Sylvia (Sylvia!), it was too much for Desi. She turned off the radio.

It was time for me to go.

MORE MAGIC

Desi and I never breathed a word about our tangle with the Magic Man at Harold Hall but it seemed like every week there was a report of another creepy sighting. With or without his ding-dong hanging out. Whether this was fact or fiction, no one knew. But whenever the cops tried to find the Magic Man, they couldn't. No one in the building had ever seen anyone who fit his description. The super claimed he never saw anyone running around the hallways in a tuxedo, tall hat and cape, let alone waving around a magician's wand. But every few days, St. Fi's was all abuzz about the Magic Man: someone had either seen him or knew someone who did.

During recess one day, Sister Paschal Marie demanded to know what we were talking about and no one spoke up. This infuriated the crusty old nun's already short fuse. She was known for taking boys out into the hall, screaming at them and roughing them up. You could hear their heads bouncing off the wall as Sister Paschal Marie "interrogated" them. Never the girls, for some reason. But we were so scared of her that many of us (like me!) sobbed silent tears whenever she brutalized a boy in the corridor.

"Not telling the truth is as bad as telling a lie," Sister PM reminded us in her trademark snarl. It was one of her favorite sayings and one we hated with a passion. She walked up one aisle and down the next, her white robes brushing against our desks, her black veil trembling in her wake. I made sure never to look her straight in the eye but dared to occasionally glance up at the pale wimple that choked her fat neck like an attack dog's collar. Maybe that's why she was so cranky—her too-tight wimple cut off the oxygen supply to her evil brain.

With each step, Sister Paschal Marie smacked the wooden pointer into her open palm. "The truth shall set you free," she added. "No? Don't believe me? Well, in my classroom it will. It will set you free from detention. It will set you free from a punishment assignment…"

Everyone hated Sister Paschal Marie's punishment assignments. They ranged from secular torture like writing the names of all fifty states fifty times to religious tortures like writing the Ten Commandments ten times and giving an example of each transgression. She took sick joy in ruining weekends as well as ruining lives.

For some reason, Sister PM harbored an unnatural hate for poor Tommy Sica. Tommy wasn't an angel but he still wasn't nearly as bad as Marco DeVeltri, who'd been left back more times than anyone could remember, had a driver's license and even shaved. Marco was bigger than Sister Paschal Marie, who was no lightweight. Maybe this is why she picked on Tommy instead of Marco—Tommy was doughy, dumb, docile and easy to bully. We all cringed when she bellowed, "Thomas…."

Tommy Sica stood at attention beside his desk like a soldier. He'd been through this drill many times before. "Yes, Sister."

"Tell me what everyone was talking about," she commanded. Tommy said nothing. Sister Paschal Marie's face burned scarlet as she grabbed him by the ear and yanked him out the door to the hallway. We heard raised voices, muttering and the whoosh of her wrathful pointer stick. Desi tapped me on the shoulder. I turned around in my seat to see her eyes large with fear. "Should we tell her?" Desi asked.

"No, never," I said. "You never tell." Desi was relatively new to this. Maybe nuns at St. Francis-Assisi in the Bronx weren't this mean so Desi didn't know the caliber of cruelty she was dealing with.

"But she's hurting him," Desi said. Her eyes were already filled with tears. Then there was the sound of a hollow head hitting a painted concrete wall. Three times. Followed by a deafening silence.

"Tommy can take it," I pressed. "He's used to it."

Across the aisle, Betty Dunphy nodded to Desi that Tommy could definitely handle it. Judy Yaccarino seconded the motion. "See?" I told Desi. Her mouth fell open and her eyes got even bigger. I looked up to see Sister Paschal Marie looming over my desk, casting a great, penguin-shaped shadow over it. I turned around in my seat.

"See what?" the nun wanted to know. Sister PM was a larger-than-life version of the beloved cartoon character Casper the Friendly Ghost, only there was nothing to love about Sister Paschal Marie. I doubted that even Jesus Himself loved her and He supposedly loved everybody. Hint of a mustache, snaggle-toothed, the acrid air of vinegar about her... I glanced to my right to see Tommy Sica stumbling back to his seat, his cheeks splotchy where the Sister had smacked him, his shirt untucked, his clip-on tie crooked.

"Nothing," I whispered.

"Nothing what?"

"Nothing, Sister," I said, a bit louder.

"Are you raising your voice to me?" Sister Paschal Marie growled. 'Please God, strike her dead,' I prayed silently. "No, Sister," I said out loud.

Sister Paschal Marie tugged my arm. Hard. She dragged me out from behind my desk. I stood up straight, as straight as I could on my turned-to-jelly legs. I looked down at my fuzzy Catholic school shoes and thought, 'No way am I going to Catholic high school. And Jesus, please kill Sister Paschal Marie. Smite her right here, right now...'

Out of the corner of my eyes, I saw a tear slip out from under Desi's glasses and drip onto her desk. She gripped its sides tightly, white-knuckled. Sister Paschal Marie roughly tilted my head up with the tip of her dreaded pointer stick. I prayed she wouldn't whack the back of my thighs like she'd done to Beatrice Garvey for wearing her skirt too short. I was afraid I'd cry or piss myself or both. Just as the nun-troll raised her whooping stick over her head, out in the hallway I saw sainted Sister Helena pass by the open classroom door. Then she took a step back and entered the room.

Sister Helena had taught me how to write script, and not only how to read but how to love reading. She always gave us stars, whether our work was perfect or not, blue and green for just trying and silver and gold for exemplary work. She also encouraged my first feeble attempts at poetry. Yes, Sister Helena knew many things about me, but mostly she knew that I didn't deserve to be beaten and humiliated in front of my eighth-grade class. "What's shaking, Sis?" she asked Sister Paschal Marie, who bristled, but lowered the stick.

While all Sister Paschal Marie could manage was a grimace, Sister Helena smiled widely. She was too pretty to be a nun: *café con leche* skin the color of mine and Desi's but with impossibly kind green eyes. "What's shaking..." Sister Paschal Marie grumbled, "is incorrigible children."

Sister Helena laughed...laughed...in Sister Paschal Marie's ugly face. "Oh, they don't seem so bad. I had most of them in second grade. Right, Mr. Sica?" Tommy Sica nodded. "Not a bad one in the bunch."

Sister Helena looked at me with such fondness, I almost burst into tears. I wanted to kiss the hem of her frock, just like Mary Magdalene did with Our Lord. "And how about you, Celeste? Still writing?" (I loved that she didn't need to call me by a saint's name.)

"Yes, Sister," I managed to respond.

"Good," she smiled. Then to Sister Paschal Marie, "Keep your eye on this one, Sister PM." At being referred to by letters instead of her nun name, Sister PM winced. But Sister Helena went on, undaunted. "Cici is going to grow up to write important things someday." With a swish of her robes and the faint scent of lilies, Sister Helena was gone, taking all hope with her.

Sister Paschal Marie glared at me. "I have no doubt that you're going to write important things," she spat. "Starting right now. All of you. Ephesians 4:29. Write this down in your religion notebooks." She cleared her throat. "Do not let any..." She stopped abruptly. "I don't see any pencils moving, people." We clutched our pencils tighter. So tight, I heard one or two lead points snap off. Then Sister Paschal Marie began again:

> *"Do not let any unwholesome talk come out of your mouths, but only what is helpful for building others up according to their needs, that it may benefit those who listen."*

The raging nun looked out over us, ready to swat anyone who wasn't paying attention. "Got that?" We nodded in unison. "Good. Recess is over. I want you to start writing the verse now in class, then continue it at home. One hundred times in all."

Sister PM gave a self-satisfied smirk then added, "And I don't want to get any notes from your parents about how much your hands hurt, how hard you cried or how unfair this assignment is," Sister Paschal Marie droned. "You know what's unfair? The fires of Hell. That's unfair."

Sister Paschal Marie took a step toward her desk, then whirled around to face us, her head whipping like Regan's in *The Exorcist*. "And no visits to the convent or the rectory either," she added. "I don't care how much your family donates to this church."

Everyone was too scared to groan but we let out a universal sigh. Which thankfully, Sister PM didn't notice. She was too busy lecturing Robert Tarpey about personal hygiene and how God doesn't like children who don't clean behind their ears.

No one blamed me for the punishment assignment. They knew no one was to blame for the Wrath of Paschal. Like a tornado, it was a force of nature. Sometimes a cyclone picked up your house and flung it; sometimes you got through it unscathed. Sometimes you got a punishment assignment; sometimes you didn't. We were all in the same boat. But I think the boys in class had a newfound respect for me. Not only didn't I cry or pee but I didn't cave under Sister Paschal Marie's scrutiny. In a way, I was one of them. And in another way, I wasn't—nothing could save me from being a gawky girl with braces, someone they still didn't want to kiss, no matter how brave I was.

At St. Fi's, the best/worst things happened during recess, especially when they let us go outside. A few days later, I overheard Michael Pollock and James Casey holding court in a corner of the half-frozen schoolyard. They were just out of earshot but judging by all the sneaky laughter, it sounded like something good.

When I moved closer to their Alpha Male circle, the laughter stopped. Desi tried to hold me back but I kept going. Cool boys like them always made her nervous.

"What's happening?" Michael asked. I shrugged.

Just as he always did, James Casey burst into the chorus of "Cecilia," even though he knew that "Cici" stood for "Celeste," not Cecilia. When I reminded him for the millionth time, he said, "Are you sure?"

"Of my name? Sure, I'm sure." But this didn't matter to James. He started singing the verse in the Simon & Garfunkel song about how the guy got up to wash his face and came back to find someone else in Cecilia's bed. The other boys joined in on the chorus about how Cecilia was both breaking their hearts and shaking their confidence. Daily. I rolled my eyes and waited for them to finish while Desi blushed crimson. "What were you talking about just now?" I probed the boys.

Michael's face lit up wickedly. I knew enough to brace myself for something really disgusting. "Oh, poetry. You like poetry and stuff, don't you, Cici?"

"I do," I told him.

Well, what do you think about this poem?" Michael looked around to make sure no nuns were within earshot. He cleared his throat and began talking so quietly, I had to lean forward to hear him in the noisy schoolyard. Here's what he said:

I got an invitation
from the Board of Education
to perform an operation
on a girl.
I stuck my dickitation
up her lower ventilation
to increase the population
of the world.

I didn't get it. And by the expression on Desi's face, she didn't get it either.

"She doesn't get it. Neither does her friend, Mushroom," James Casey announced. He was so cute with his blue Noxzema bottle-colored eyes, white blonde hair that stood on end, small chip on one of his slightly-crossed front teeth, so freaking cute that Jamie got away with murder. He was excused by even the most evil nuns and the most prudish girls let his indiscretions pass without telling on him. Desi adjusted MushroomHat. "I get it," I told him.

"So do I," Desi echoed. But they still knew we didn't.

"It's about sex," Michael Pollock said. "How people do it."

"Do it?"

"Do sex," he sighed. "Don't you know?"

I didn't. Catholic schools didn't teach us about sex. To supplement my non-sex ed, when I was 12, my mother gave me a pamphlet from Kotex called "How Shall I Tell My Daughter." It sounded like you were trying to hide a serial-killer past from your kid instead of telling her where babies came from. But after reading the booklet from cover to cover, I still had no clue. Whenever I asked Tessie something remotely sexual she always said, 'Read the book.' Well, I *had* read the book. Three times. From cover to cover. While I knew how chickens and dogs did it, I was still sketchy on how humans made babies.

"Of course, I know," I stammered.

"Doesn't everyone?" Desi said.

"But that poem..." I insisted. "My parents didn't do that."

"They had to," Michael pointed out. "At least twice."

I considered the logistics. Even with the flick of the Zippo on Wednesdays and Saturdays, I still didn't think they did that. Hugging and kissing, maybe, but no dickitations in lower ventilations. Raffi and Big Matty, though? Hmmm. Maybe.

While my mom reluctantly admitted that women had a "special opening," I never imagined *this* was what she was talking about. That wasn't a special opening at all, but the same, old, tired hole. The place I peed from. What a letdown.

"Mine did it five times, at least," James Casey announced proudly, because he had four siblings. His hands were buried deep in his pockets when he said this, which is why he had earned the nickname "Pockets Casey." Jamie always moved his hands around like he was jangling invisible change, but no coins ever made a sound. Weird.

Desi puffed out her chest. "Only three for mine but one of those times was twins."

"Whoa!" the boys informed us. "Twins means they did it in both holes."

"Ieeew, gross," Desi and I said together. That was our cue to leave the circle of schoolyard boys.

On the walk home, Desi and I puzzled over the possibilities. It still didn't make sense to us. In my room, we pored over "How Shall I Tell My Daughter," reading the pertinent parts out loud to each other, but even this did no good. We were more confused than ever about sex and where babies came from.

I couldn't ask Tessie anything and Desi couldn't ask Raffi. As cool as Raffi was as a mom, she'd slapped Desi across the face the first time she got her period. (Desi told me that this was a Jewish tradition Raffi got from her sister Elsie, who'd married a Jewish guy and converted. A Puerto Rican Jew? Who ever heard of such a thing?) It was all downhill from there.

Could we ask Umbe? Too embarrassing. And what if he offered to show us like he'd shown us how to do yoga headstands? No, thanks.

So, like many other things, Desi and I just suffered in silence. We wondered and daydreamed and tried to figure it out for ourselves. Failing every time.

SYLVIA

The way Umbe talked about her, you would think Sylvia had found the cure to cancer or at least walked on water. But no such luck. Sylvia was just a seamstress. But if you made the mistake of calling her that, Umbe would correct you. "She's a designer, too, you know," he was quick to point out.

"We know, we know…" Desi or I would sigh.

None of us had met the mysterious Sylvia, except for Raffi, who'd seen her briefly in the dress shop. When me and Desi grilled her about Sylvia, Raffi was non-committal, shrugging while she heated up the pot of *arroz con pollo* Mami had made earlier that day. Raffi stirred it with a wooden spoon, breaking up the clumps of rice. "Sylvia's very nice," she said. "Maybe too nice," she added after a pause. But by the way Raffi said it, we knew that was all she was going to say.

Umbe was dying to get "his girls" to meet Sylvia. He came up with what he thought was the perfect plan—taking all three of us to a poetry reading. It was the worst idea in the history of bad ideas.

Although I'd been writing poetry pretty much since I learned how to write, I had never been to a poetry reading, let alone an event in the City. Yes, Umbe and Sylvie wanted to take me and Desi on an excursion to Manhattan.

Greenwich Village to be exact. Or, Greenberg's Village, as Diane Keaton mistakenly referred to it in *Sleeper*, which Desi and I had seen at the Dyker Theatre the year before. (We were still trying to figure out what the Orgasmatron actually did.) "It'll be fun!" Umbe said. We doubted this but agreed to go with them.

Since Sylvia didn't live nearby, Umbe said we would meet her in the City. The three of us took the RR together from the very last stop, which was 95th Street, to West 8th Street in Manhattan.

It was a long ride on the local train, so we passed the time doing what we did best: making fun of people. Without them knowing, of course. (That would be mean.) You know, stuff like asking each other which breed of dog the woman across from us resembled—a Pekingese, with her over-teased reddish-brown hair which was dyed a color not found in nature. Whispering about the man with his back to us who was holding onto the pole. The cuffs of his high-water pants hovered three inches above his shoe-tops. The rhyme went:

> *The rain is over.*
> *The streets are dry.*
> *Then why-oh-why*
> *Are your pants so high?*

Umbe laughed out loud when I finished the poem. (I guess he'd never heard it before.) He snorted through his nose—"the Snort of Sincerity," our friend Maureen called it. Desi felt sorry for the guy, pointing out that maybe he was too poor to buy new pants. "You can take the fun out of anything," I told her. "Even making fun of people."

I'd dressed carefully that morning, choosing my navy blue Danskin, which I imagined made my boobs look big (in retrospect, nothing made my fried-egg sized chest look big), my baby-blue bell bottoms from Alvy's Dungaree Outlet and my Olaf Daughters clogs, a splash of Tigress between my nonexistent boobs. Desi and I took turns doing each other's makeup from our secret stash and made sure not to run into Raffi when we left. She would have forced us to wash it off. Umbe noticed but didn't make a big deal about it. He smiled and said, "You two look...very grown up." If I died right then and there, I would have died happy.

We waited for Sylvia on the corner of West 8th and Broadway, near a pizza place. Sure enough, a slim brunette arrived a few minutes later. She was tall, with long legs and even longer harem pants that scraped the sidewalk. Her hair was pulled back into a tight ponytail which made her look slightly Chinese. Her chest was flatter than mine. Big tortoiseshell glasses were perched on the bridge of her nose, which was larger than mine. This couldn't be her.

PS, it was her.

I was shocked and a little disappointed when Umbe introduced the woman to us as his main squeeze Sylvia Silverstein. My heart sunk. I wanted better for Umbe.

After polite hellos to us kids, Sylvia hugged Umbe for a long time, probably longer than she should have. While they smooched, Desi put her finger into her mouth, pretending to gag. I did the same back to her.

When Sylvia finally let go of Umbe, I noticed that she was few inches taller than him in her buffalo wedges. She was probably taller than him barefoot. It just wasn't right.

As we walked down to MacDougal Street, passing gypsy shops with rings and amulets studded with glass eyeballs in the windows, I felt like we were on a field trip, following our hip but mismatched parents. I liked thinking of Desi as my sister but not Sylvia as my mother or Umbe as my father. Gross.

There was a cute shop called Reminiscence. It sold vintage clothes and other neat stuff. Sylvia complained that we would be late for the reading but Umbe said those things never started on time. (Had he been to poetry readings before?) "Poets are always late," he reminded her. "Too spaced-out from smoking pot." Sylvia laughed along with us, realizing it was true. She barked when she laughed. And she had these big, horsey front teeth. Double gross.

Umbe bought Sylvia a pretty lacy blouse and told us girls to choose a pair of barrettes each. They were all so nice that it was tough to decide but I ended up picking ivory flowers while Desi chose ones made of colorful Guatemalan fabric. We promised to share them because we liked them both a lot. When Sylvia kissed Umbe thank-you, I saw her slip her pink, snaky tongue into his mouth. Was there no end to her grossness?

We hurried down MacDougal to Minetta Lane, past a string of comedy clubs where barkers constantly tried to entice you inside. Outside the Café Wha? Umbe told us that Bob Dylan had played here the second he came into

New York from Michigan. "He asked if he could do a few songs," Umbe continued. "It was Hootenanny Night, so anyone could play a few songs. January 1961. He did some Woody Guthrie tunes. The crowd went wild. And the rest is history."

As Sylvia hustled us along the curved street, Umbe said that everyone who was anyone did the Wha?...Jimi Hendrix and comics like Bill Cosby, Lenny Bruce and Woody Allen. Then Sylvia stopped abruptly in front of a worn out-looking tenement that was connected to a row of other worn out-looking tenements. She checked the address against the one she'd written on a scrap of paper. "This must be the place," she said.

"You sure?" Umbe asked. "Looks more like a shooting gallery." (I'd read *Go Ask Alice*, so I knew what a shooting gallery was—it was a seedy place where junkies injected heroin into their veins.)

Sylvia ignored him and said, "Downstairs." We stepped over bits of trash, paper cups and food wrappings. I thought I saw the glint of a needle and syringe on the ground but I couldn't be sure. We were moving too fast.

The place was packed. Hot and stuffy from all of the bodies, it looked a lot like my basement but smaller and narrower and filled with people. There were a few rows of folding chairs but they were filled. We made our way to the back of the room where there was a cement ledge. Umbe boosted us ladies up so we could sit while he stood nearby, leaning against the cinderblock wall, keeping watch over us. They were handing around a sign-up sheet on a clipboard. I passed it along without adding my name. "This could be your big Greenwich Village debut," Umbe said. "Like Bob Dylan." I shook my head and turned away, blushing.

"Come on," Desi pushed.

"Humberto tells me you're a great writer," Sylvia told me, trying to get on my good side. But right then, I didn't have a good side.

"I'm okay, I guess," I shrugged. Wait? Humberto? Nobody called him 'Humberto.'

"She's better than okay," Desi said. "Miss Coughley picked one of her poems to represent St. Fi's in a diocese competition." I elbowed Desi hard in the ribs. "Ouch!"

"Tattletale."

The microphone screeched, heavy with feedback, as the audience groaned. The first reader was announced, an old woman who was obsessed with birds and wrote boring sonnets about them. Umbe almost fell asleep. His head nodded down to his chest but bobbed back up again when a bummy-looking guy took the tiny stage. He read an okay freestyle piece about the City, overly dramatic, instead of letting the words speak for themselves. When he got to the line, "And a truck farted..." we all lost it, painfully holding back our laughter. Which was a lot like holding in a fart. Thankfully, that was the last line of the poem.

Then the next reader was called. And called again, "Celeste Pico...is there a Celeste Pico in the house?" I shot Umbe an angry look. "I didn't know how to spell 'Piccolo,'" he shrugged. How could he have added my name to the sign-up sheet without me seeing it? Dirty sneak.

"But I don't have anything to read," I whispered.

"I do," Desi told me, and took a wrinkled sheet of loose-leaf paper out of her shoulder bag. "I keep everything you write."

"Traitor!" I said through my teeth. But inwardly, I was flattered.

"Three times and you're out, Celeste Pico." I raised my hand and made my way to the stage.

I was afraid that I would cry, puke, faint or all three. But I didn't do any of the above. I reminded myself of what Sister Joelle told us when we had to give an oral report in front of the class:

1) Make eye contact with your audience.
2) Use your finger to keep your place so you don't forget where you are when you make eye contact.
3) Remember to breathe.

I guess the third one was the most important because without breathing, the other two didn't matter. The MC handed me the mike. Unfolding the piece of paper Desi had given me, I looked out into the crowd. Everyone was waiting for me to start, even me. I took a deep breath and began:

I always thought that we were Space Children
Because we were so unlike anyone here on Earth...

After the first word, I knew I had it, that I had them. That I wasn't going to choke or trip or embarrass myself. Desi and Umbe were smiling at me; she mouthed the words along with me. She knew the poem by heart because it was about us. Forever friends who felt they didn't belong anywhere until they met each other.

Sylvia wore a strange expression on her face. Like up until now, she'd thought I was a goofy, clumsy kid but maybe, just maybe, I might be a real writer. Someday, at least, if not today.

I felt powerful. I felt important. I felt like I mattered. Some people leaned forward, hanging onto my words. I read slowly but not too slow. Measured. Like the words tasted good in my mouth. In a way, they did. I'd worked hard on crafting them, making sure they were perfect. Crossing out the wrong ones and exchanging them for the right ones, then changing them again.

Sister Joelle had told us that a dude named Paul Valéry once said:

"A poem is never finished; it is only abandoned."

And it was true. Every time I reread one of mine, I could change a comma or a tense or a phrase.

At the Village poetry jam, I kept reading, one side of the loose-leaf paper and then the other until I got to the end. I tried to keep in mind what Sister Jo said about remembering to breathe.

I always thought that we were Space Children,
Swinging from a star,
Deep inside, that we were Space Children,
And now I know we are.

The room went nuts. I tried to leave the stage right away but the MC held my wrist and kept me there. He raised my arm above my head like a prizefighter, like I was Muhammad Ali at the end of a match. "How old are you?" the MC wanted to know.

"Uh, 13," I told him.

"Let me guess…Catholic school girl?"

I felt like he'd stripped me bare in front of everyone. "How did you know?"

The MC shrugged and looked at the paper in my hand. "Your penmanship, maybe." He finally let me go but not before saying to the crowd, "Celeste Pico... Remember that name, guys. She's going places."

Desi and Umbe hugged me and kissed me on the head. Sylvia patted my shoulder and said, "Good job. I'm impressed."

A couple of other poets followed until the MC announced that there would be a short, experimental film coming up next. It was called *Rock and Roll and the American Experience*. "Sounds promising," he admitted.

It wasn't.

We were all treated to a scratchy, black-and-white movie that jumped and skipped so much it made me dizzy. There were clips of Jimi Hendrix playing guitar with his teeth and then...and then...

A big, dark-eyebrowed blonde without her shirt and floppy, water-balloon boobs topped with saucer-sized nipples flashed onto the screen. Just for a few seconds, then back to Jimi. Then the movie hopped back to the woman, who was now joined by a skinny, black-haired guy who was naked except for tube socks. You couldn't see his thing, only his pimply, hairy butt.

As Jimi Hendrix became lost in his guitar solo, the skeleton dude became lost in the blonde's hair down below, which didn't match the hair on her head. "The curtains don't match the rug," Jamie Casey might have commented.

The cuts between the music and the couple were so fast, you didn't realize what you were seeing...at first. But when Umbe finally did, he grabbed me and Desi by the hand and started leaving. Sylvia followed. The MC was trying to shut off the projector. "*Pendejo*," Umbe yelled at him. "Asshole. My kids are here."

His kids! Umbe just called us his kids.

"Sorry, man," the MC stammered. "Sometimes art isn't pretty."

Although I was slightly grossed out, I still didn't want to go but Umbe dragged us away. So, this was what Michael Pollock was talking about in his nasty schoolyard limerick. I would definitely have to do more research.

It was dark outside when we hit the basement steps and cool, easier to breathe than in that crowded basement. Umbe looked like he'd seen a ghost, a big-haired, big-boobed ghost. "Sorry, girls," he apologized. Then all four of us cracked up. "But did you see the size of her *chocha*? It was as big as the Grand Canyon!"

"His left sock had a hole in it," Sylvia pointed out. "And her stockings had a run..."

"Whatever you do, don't tell Raffi," Umbe begged. "She'd never let me take you guys out again."

"Tell her what?" Desi smiled, already in on the joke.

Umbe said he was going to take us somewhere special for dinner. His favorite restaurant in the Village. Was it Mamoun's Falafel, the place he always raved about? Nope. We went down Minetta toward Avenue of the Americas, AKA Sixth Avenue to natives like me. I was half expecting some fancy Spanish place—and wondered how Umbe could afford it on his bike messenger salary. But we passed Café España on Bleecker Street without going inside. What did he have in store for us?

Desi and I laughed when Umbe stopped in front of Papaya Dog and announced, "This is it."

Meanwhile, Sylvia looked horrified. She just didn't "get" Umbe's sense of humor and probably never would. Witch.

"What?" he told her. "Julia Child says this place has the best hot dog in New York," Umbe added, pointing out the sign that said the exact same thing in orange neon.

There wasn't even a place to sit. The tables were all tall, standing perches, I guess to discourage the bums from parking their butts there all day and never leaving. Another sign said they were open 24/7. There was no menu, per se, just posters all over the walls. Although you could order chicken strips and cheeseburgers at Papaya Dog, what they were famous for were their franks. Umbe refused to get us anything else.

Even though they had Coke, Sprite and Dr. Pepper, their papaya drink was the bomb, Umbe said, hence the name of the establishment. So, it was dogs and papayas all around.

While Umbe got our food, Sylvie inspected the yellow and red tiles, which were surprisingly clean. To avoid talking to her, Desi and I occupied ourselves by reading the funny signs out loud to each other. They said things like:

Coconut…good for your kidneys.
Let's be frank…we want you to buy our _urters.
Papaya…good enzyme supplier…helps digestion.
A tropical oasis in the concrete jungle.
and
Recession Buster! 2 dogs & small drink, 99¢

Umbe returned with a cardboard tray filled with franks and drinks
in bright yellow waxed cups printed with Papaya Dog's wacky smiley-face
logo. Even Sylvia had to admit that those dogs hit the spot. She liked the way
the franks popped when you bit into them. Washed down with frothy papaya
nectar (think Tang on steroids), they were perfect, sweet marrying salty. I'd
never tasted papaya before. It had a pukey aftertaste, which Desi said was why
they called it "puke-paya" in her house. But we still liked it. We liked anything
Umbe thought was good. Except maybe Sylvia.

It was getting late, so we headed for the subway. Umbe suggested we
take the D or the B to the RR. On this route, the train went over the Manhattan
Bridge instead of bombing its way through the Joralemon Street Tunnel.
Besides, the City looked pretty in the dark, he said.

As usual, Umbe was right. Up until then, I'd never been on the train
at night. Looking back at Manhattan from the bridge took my breath away. It
was like a glittering jewel. The midtown skyscrapers were sharp against the
dark blue sky. The Empire State Building's top glowed like a white hypodermic
needle as the Chrysler Building competed for attention. And downtown stood
the boxlike Twin Towers.

Even Brooklyn didn't look too bad: the Williamsburg Savings Bank
building, whose red-handed clock told the wrong time. The shadows of
Prospect Park and Green-Wood Cemetery beyond it. The crooked rooftops,
water towers, Red Hook docks, fire escapes, Old Law Tenements, housing
projects, brownstones, and far off in the distance, the specter of the
Verrazano-Narrows Bridge, which was practically in our backyard. Its two
strands of lights looked like electric pearls.

By day, the City was a big, hot mess, a mishmash, but by night, it was magical. When the B train bounded back into the tunnel at the other side of the Manhattan Bridge, the magic disappeared.

I closed my eyes for a second, my head pressed against Desi's as we sat squashed together in the light blue seat at the end of the car. Her mushroom hat felt like a pillow against my cheek. Umbe and Sylvia sat across from us, smiling slightly. I studied the graffiti on the double doors next to them and felt my eyes grow heavy. 'This isn't a bad place to be…to live…' I thought to myself.

Before I knew it, Umbe and Sylvie were shaking me and Desi awake as the B rolled into the 36th Street station where we would switch for the RR and get back to our boring, little lives.

Somehow, though, I knew that things were about to change for us, and that it would never be the same, that we would never be the same, again.

PAPO, DUSTED

There was always an endless stream of relatives waltzing through the Ruiz apartment. I tried hard to keep track of them but kept messing up who was related to who and how. I knew Mami, Aunt Elsie, Aunt Cassie and Jacinta were on Raffi's side of the family, and that *Abuelita* (real name: Raquel) was Big Matty's mother, but after that, I was lost. Once Desi even drew a family tree for me but when I tried to read it, the branches looked hopelessly twisted and I still couldn't figure out who belonged where.

As far as I could tell Papo (real name: Arturo) was a cousin on the Ruiz side (Desi's dad's), not the Santiago side (her mom's). Papo was Uncle Ernesto's son, who, in turn, was *Abuelita's* son. But not one of the uncles involved in Big Matty's hunting "accident" upstate.

Since I'd lost Umbe to Sylvia, I settled for having a crush on Papo. Desi said I was boy crazy; Athena said I was just plain crazy. Looking back, I was probably somewhere between the two.

Papo was a bad boy as far as I could tell. And I thought I liked bad boys back then. He had an edge of meanness, a slight sneer to his pouty lips and oily, curly, black hair. Papo should have spelled trouble, but to me, he just spelled c-u-t-e. To him, I was just a scrawny, braces-wearing kid who stared at him like a lovesick puppy dog. At first, I thought he liked me. You know, liked me liked me. Instead, it turned out that he just *liked* having me make a fool of myself for his amusement.

For instance, Papo would ask me to get stuff for him: a glass of Mountain Dew, a postage stamp. And I would. Once, he told me that his birthday was the following week and if I sent him a card, he might consider going out with me. (PS, I did; he didn't.)

As nice as she could, Desi tried to explain to me that Papo was only messing with me. She did this even as I coerced her to come with me to the Hallmark store on 86th Street to find the perfect happy-birthday card. I was in such a good mood that we split a chocolate parlay from Loft's Candy Store next door, my treat. For days, I was walking on air, but the next time I saw Papo, he didn't even mention the card—or taking me out. In fact, he snickered and made fun of me to his other cousins, thinking I wouldn't notice. But I did; I noticed everything.

I thought, I hoped, I prayed, that maybe one day, Papo would see the real me, would realize how special I actually was. Like Prince Charming seeing the beauty of Cinderella underneath all that soot and ash. But that was just a fairy tale, a kid's story. It wasn't real life. Sometimes real life sucked.

I think Uncle Ernesto could see how sad I was about how mean his son Papo was to me. I wouldn't crack a smile when Uncle Ernesto told his stupid jokes about a wooden whistle that *woodn't* whistle and a steel whistle that *steel* woodn't whistle. That's how hard I was trying not to cry.

Uncle Ernesto felt so sorry for me that he gave Desi $10 to take the littler kids (us included) downstairs to Vito's Pizzeria for a small pie and sodas. If we only had one slice each there might be enough money left over to have iceys afterwards. Yep, Vito carried Italian ices even in the winter. That's one reason we loved him. Another was his amazing hero sandwich, called the "Vito's Special," made with every cold cut under the sun plus provolone, shredded lettuce, and oil and vinegar dressing to make the bread the perfect balance of crispy and soggy. But whenever I ate pizza at Vito's, I felt like I was cheating on Pizza Wagon.

Desi thought it was a good idea to get a 64-ounce bottle of Coke, which would cost less than six smalls. When Matty insisted on opening it, the brown liquid shot all over us like a rusty fountain. Since I was sitting next to

Matty, I got the worst of it. We cleaned up as best we could and had our pizza anyway.

After our iceys, we raced each other upstairs. I won and got up there first. Papo was nowhere to be found—Desi said that he and her other cousins smoked, and not Marlboros either. The women were in the kitchen, as usual, and only Uncle Ernesto was in the living room. We thanked him again for the pizza money and told him about the exploding soda. "I'm soaking wet," I giggled. Then the others ran into the girls' room to play Mystery Date. Even Matty liked playing that one—he thought the "Dud" was the hunkiest one, and so did I.

Before I could leave the living room, Uncle Ernesto came up to me. "You said before that you got wet," he whispered. "Let me feel how wet you are." Then he touched my damp thigh.

I was only 13. Nobody had ever touched me like that before. Or looked at me like that. As much as I daydreamed about Umbe and Papo, this was different. This didn't feel right. This was Uncle Ernesto: funny, chubby Uncle Ernesto who drove a bus in Sunset Park and gave us money for slices and Goobers and Starbursts. He would never do anything to hurt me, would he?

Uncle Ernesto moved his hand up my leg, worked his fingers into the crease of my thigh. I put my hand on top of his and dug my nails into it. "Hey!" he said.

I plucked his hand off my leg like it was a mosquito. "No," I said, and went into Desi's room. I thought I heard him call me "Bitch!" as I walked away but I didn't care. I didn't want him to touch me like that. Period.

Sex and drugs seemed to be everywhere in 1974. But me and Desi were too young to be interested in either. We were very immature 13-year-olds, mentally as well as physically. (Yes, we were both born in 1960 but we wouldn't turn 14 until October.)

At St. Fi's, there were hushed whispers about sniffing glue, about how kids who were never into building model airplanes before suddenly were—and it had nothing to do with being creative. The kids were getting high from the glue and paint fumes. We found plenty of empty spray paint cans in the corner of PS 104's schoolyard. And we knew the canisters weren't from tagging— that's graffiti talk. They were from huffing—sniffing the fumes from spray paint and gasoline canisters to get high. It felt like being drunk, they said.

Drinking was something me and Desi didn't do either. We were having enough trouble being regular teenagers without throwing drink and drugs into the mix.

The worst thing me and Desi ever did was duck out of Sunday mass early and use the second collection-plate money to go to White Castle. I felt really guilty about this—Desi, too. But not so guilty that we didn't want to escape Father O'Reilly's foaming at the mouth during his sermon. He was always condemning "these kids today" and sometimes even brought random items like a coat hanger or a chisel with him to the pulpit to make a point. (Don't ask!) When Father O'Reilly said mass, Desi and I couldn't get out of church fast enough. A large Coke and a sack of belly-bombs beckoned us to the gates of sin and damnation like the evil apple in the Garden of Eden.

Our mothers didn't like us going to White Castle. Or "the White Tower" as my Grandma Lou always called it, no matter how many times I corrected her. It wasn't because White Castle was fast food but because of the before-mentioned junkies. Junkies were always being found passed out in White Castle. Just about every time we went there, someone was nodding out at one of the aluminum tables or was found curled up on the bathroom floor. Once a junkie who was refused a cup coffee waited for a server in the subway station and slashed her before she could make it through the turnstile to the RR.

Although junkies scared and shocked us, Desi and I were still seduced by White Castle. We loved their oniony, little, square burgers (square!) with holes punched into them whose cheese became one with the pillowy soft buns. We wanted to "buy 'em by the sack" and did.

Yes, we were good girls. Except for skipping out on mass. But nobody knew, except maybe Big Matty, who Desi was convinced knew everything, even what she thought. She swore her dead dad saw everything that went on in the Ruiz apartment. When Desi said that, I got a chill remembering Uncle Ernesto. I didn't want anyone to know how he had touched me. Somehow, I thought what he'd tried to do to me was my fault. I felt so embarrassed about it that I didn't even tell Desi—and I told her everything. Except about my love affair with the bathtub faucet. I would take that one to the grave.

If Big Matty knew everything, then he should have warned the family about Papo. Not only wasn't Papo smoking cigarettes but he wasn't just smoking pot either. He'd graduated from joints to angel dust, apparently. Desi and I weren't exactly sure what angel dust was, only that it was really bad. And that Art Linkletter's daughter Diane died from it. Or from LSD. Neither of us could remember. But Diane Linkletter had jumped out of a sixth-story window in West Hollywood and even her rich, straight-laced father couldn't help her.

This story scared the bejesus out of us. Desi and I vowed never, ever to do any drugs. We also swore off certain sexual acts which we were sketchy about (i.e. blow jobs) but sounded gross regardless of our confusion.

"Even when we're married?" Desi wondered.

"Especially when we're married," I told her. I'd given up all hope of marrying Papo, or anyone, and was bitter.

Winter was almost over and you could almost taste spring in the air. It tasted like warmth and rain and smelled of fresh, clean earth in Brooklyn front yards where the crocuses were peeking up through the remnants of dirty snow. Like the season, Desi and I were also in between—not quite kids, not quite women. We felt like our bodies were betraying us: our chests hurt, our nipples were sore, our ovaries throbbed, our bellies ached, hair was springing out everywhere. On our upper lips, between our already-thick brows, and coming in even thicker below our waists…

Desi and I weren't very good at depilatory methods either. Glancing at my botched brows, *Abuelita* Raquel rolled her eyes, sighed, "*Ai, chica*" dramatically and made us promise never to tweeze our eyebrows again without supervision. She also made me swear to let mine grow in. I did.

Abuelita also showed us how to use Jolen Crème Bleach on our upper lip fuzz but it burned and smelled like chlorine and took our breath away. Besides, it gave us blonde mustaches instead of dark ones. The two of us never did Jolen again.

Whenever Desi and I felt like homely, hairy losers, we did a few things to make ourselves feel better. Sometimes we shuffled through the stack of Polaroids Desi had of Big Matty. But instead of brightening our moods, this could backfire and make us feel even worse. Desi convinced me that we wouldn't feel so sad and out-of-place if her dad were here. Big Matty always had the gift of making people feel good. Even misfits like us. "But we're not really misfits if we found each other," I would tell her. "With each other, we fit, right?"

"Right," she would say.

Other times, Desi and me would go up 86th Street, window shopping mostly. Neither of us got much of an allowance and Desi did way more chores than I did. I think money was tight at Raffi's place but she tried hard not to show it and not to let her kids go without. If I could scrape together a buck and change, I might get a 45 at the Little Record Store. But it was always the same kind of song, lovey-dovey music, usually by the Spinners or the Stylistics. "You Are Everything" or "Betcha By Golly Wow" or "One of a Kind Love Affair." I was convinced they were written about a made-for-each other couple like me and Papo, who weren't really a couple. Desi was a saint, listening to these songs over and over again on the black-and-white Decca in my room until we knew all the sappy words by heart. That was a true friend.

If the weather was nice, sometimes we would go for a long walk, down the Shore Road Bike Path. We'd head toward the Verrazano, and if we felt particularly adventurous, we'd climb over the low sea wall and nose around the rotting pier. It was always wet, always damp and slippery, even when the Narrows was calm. Big chunks of the pier were missing so we had to step carefully. There was a certain dangerous delight we took in exploring here, a wickedness in doing what wasn't allowed. There wasn't much to see on the pier, just a slightly better view of Fort Wadsworth across the way and the murky shores of Staten Island itself.

After the pier, Desi and I might go off to our favorite tree. It was on a small hill just past the bike path. I don't know what kind of tree it was but it had strong, thick branches that stood out like arms. They were just low enough for us to reach without much trouble, without even boosting each other up. This tree was perfect for sitting and contemplating and looking. Sometimes I even went there alone but it was much more fun with Desi beside me. Just about everything was more fun with Desi there.

Desi herself liked looking up at the underbelly of the Verrazano. We would try to figure out exactly which block of cement Big Matty had scribbled her name into on the day she was born almost14 years earlier, five days before I was born.

Desi loved to hear my story about the first time I ever crossed the Verrazano. I was only four years old and it had opened a few weeks earlier. Grandma Lou took me, my cousin Gino and my sister Laura, who was just two, on the B79 bus. We caught it at the corner of 92nd Street and Fort Hamilton

Parkway, took the bus over the bridge's two-mile span and got off at the first stop in Staten Island. Holding the girls' hands tightly (not Gino's, who was two years older than me and thought he was practically grown at six), Grandma Lou crossed Narrows Road North and went along Fingerboard Road to Narrows Road South to the bus stop. All four of us caught the B79 going in the opposite direction, back to Brooklyn.

"What was she wearing?" Desi asked, though she knew. That's how often she made me tell the story.

"Oh, Grandma Lou was all dressed up like she was going to church," I smiled. "She had on her good coat, the black one with the real fur collar, a black pillbox hat with netting and rouge on her cheeks."

"Like Mrs. Prill?"

I thought for a second. "Not exactly," I told her. "More blended. I used to love to watch her put it on. The rouge came in a little brass compact. It said 'Lady Esther' on the cover with a tiny bow."

I don't know why Desi liked this story so much. Maybe it gave her a sort of comfort. Maybe she liked hearing about how people traveled across the bridge her father helped make, that there were happy memories associated with this thing that he helped build. But whatever the reason, I told Desi the story whenever she asked. We were usually sitting in our tree-perch when she did.

"Grandma Lou put on lipstick, too," I recalled. "Red lipstick. But on her, it didn't look trashy. It looked good. Especially when she smiled. And she smiled a lot that day. It was a miracle that even Laura behaved on our bus trip because Laura never behaved, especially when she was two. I remember looking at Grandma Lou sitting next to Laura, the slight smile on her face as she stared out the window at Brooklyn coming into view. I remember thinking how beautiful Grandma Lou was and how I could feel her love for us, for all three of us, coming off her skin."

"Are you sure it wasn't her perfume?" Desi teased.

"Grandma Lou doesn't wear perfume," I told her. "She always wears Avon's Roses Roses Talcum Powder. In fact, she got a little of it on the front of her dress."

"You left out that part," Desi scolded. "That's almost the best part."

The tree's bark was starting to dig into the backs of my legs. I shifted my weight. "What about you? When was the first time you went across the bridge?"

I knew this story too, but I loved it. I loved the way Desi's face got all soft and serious when she told it. I felt like I was right there in the car with the kids, squashed into the back seat with them. I could just picture Raffi's face as she turned back to yell at them to be quiet, stern but smiling. I could just see Big Matty's face as he drove, beaming that something he created stood so tall and true and strong. The bridge linked families together. It helped people get to work easier. Instead of taking a slow, lazy ferry from the 69th Street Pier or from Manhattan, they could drive across this beautiful blueish-gray, record-breaking bridge.

"We went the day it opened," Desi said. "My dad was so proud of it, he couldn't wait. Before the Bridge was done, sometimes we'd park at one of those rest areas along the Belt just so we could look up at it."

As Desi continued the story, I followed it in my head, traveling to the wilds of Staten Island to get a large pie at Lee's Tavern near Hylan, which was worth paying a toll for. The kids all fell asleep on the way home to the Bronx.

Desi got a faraway look in her eyes when she was done telling the story. "Will I ever stop missing him?" she sighed.

"Probably not," I told her. "You'll just miss him different. It will still hurt but not the same way."

"I guess I can live with that," she said.

A tugboat led a big barge out of the harbor and toward Coney Island. "How's Papo?" I wondered.

"Not good," she told me, looking at the tugboat. "He tried to bite a cop last night."

"Why?" I gasped in disbelief. "He thought he was a dog?"

"He was so dusted that he didn't think he was a dog; he *was* a dog," Desi explained.

"What happened next?"

"They took him to Bellevue. He's still under observation."

I wanted to cry. I wanted to laugh at my dumb luck, having crushes on people who were uncrushable. First Umbe, then Papo. And forget about John Williams. He still didn't know I was alive even though I'd been in his class since second grade. Instead of crying, I watched the barge grow smaller and smaller.

Desi smiled and nudged my shoulder. I nudged her back. "We're like sisters, aren't we?" Desi said.

"Better than sisters," I told her. "We don't fight."

"You're the we in me," she said out of nowhere.

"I like the way that sounds," I admitted. "But I don't know what it means."

"I heard it somewhere. I can't remember where, though. But it reminded me of us. Of our friendship." Desi jumped down from the tree branch and landed soft on the ground. I followed. "I think it means that you make me feel like a whole person. At least that's what it means to me."

I thought for a second. "Hmmm. I like that. I like that a lot."

Desi and I started walking toward the path that led to the stone overpass which went across the Belt Parkway and led to 101st Street. We went past Cannonball Park, whose real name was John Paul Jones Park. (But no one called it that.) There was a sealed-up cannon from the War of 1812 and a line of huge cannonballs that looked like a painted black caterpillar. A few kids were leap-frogging across them while others were climbing the other cannonballs piled up in little pyramids. Desi and I were quiet, just enjoying each other's company. That is, until we got to Pigeon Park, one of Bay Ridge's many "triangle parks."

"Don't worry," Desi told me. "I have a lot of cute cousins."

"Who says I'm worried?" But I was worried. It's like she read my mind.

We just looked at each other and smiled, passing Grand Union, Engine Company 242's firehouse, coming to Kentucky Fried Chicken, breathing in the greasy pepperiness of its exhaust fans, turned down the block and went home.

ASK THE DUST

It seemed like Ash Wednesday just happened and there was Easter, right around the corner. Although even in April, I still felt like I was scraping ashes out of the pores in my forehead. Desi and I had the misfortune of Father O'Reilly giving us our Ash Wednesday ashes. Instead of painting a neat, little cross on our heads like Father Parsons did, Father O'Reilly smeared his entire fat thumbprint onto our skulls like he was mad at us as he droned:

Remember, man, that thou art dust and unto dust thou shalt return.

Yeah, thanks for the reminder that I'm a piece of crap, *Padre*. Dirt. Lower than dirt. Ashes. For a fleeting second, I thought Father O'Reilly might know about my boyfriend: the bathtub faucet (and occasionally, the showerhead). But he couldn't possibly have known, could he? Although I always promised myself that I'd never, ever do it again, I always did. Maybe Father O'Reilly was right. Maybe I was lower than dust.

The eighth graders at St. Fi's practiced our Confirmation walk once a week, on Friday afternoons, with Sister Paschal Marie's obnoxious clicker teaching us when to stand, when to kneel, sit and when to kneel again. If we didn't move fast enough, she screamed at us. It didn't matter that we were in church or that old biddies were trying to say the Rosary. Sister Paschal Marie yelled at us just the same and made us go through the motions again, like circus animals in training.

I think I already mentioned that in 1974, a double class of seventh and eighth graders were making their confirmation because of Father Mulvaney's tragic motorcycle accident the year before. (Thanks again, Father M!) So, it was double the kids, double the unruliness.

All of our practices were pretty awful but this one practice was the worst yet. We were grateful to be off for Good Friday and the week after Easter. But this meant there'd be no rehearsal for two weeks, even though Confirmation was only a month away. And as Sister PM constantly reminded us, "hopeless heathens" like us needed the practice.

In between family suppers, Desi and I hung out as much as we possibly could when we were off for spring vacation. I tried not to moon too much over Papo. When I saw him after he'd been in Bellevue, he seemed really out of it, barely talked to anyone, hardly even made eye contact. He was a mess—somewhere else, not in the room with us, eating red beans, yellow rice and *tostones*. It's like Papo somehow had become invisible in Bellevue's psych ward and was slowly becoming visible again. Though I didn't think he'd ever be the same Papo who'd goofed on me mercilessly with Desi's older cousins. I kind of missed the mean Papo. He was so much better than this Papo.

I made a point of never being alone in a room with Papo's father, Uncle Ernesto, again. Even though he always tried to be super nice to me.

After I saw Papo that first time following his angel dust freakout, I made Desi come with me to the Little Record Store to get "Have You Seen Her." I was lucky they still had a copy of that Chi-Lites hit which was a few years old but was timeless to me. In my twisted teen brain, the lyrics were all about a lost love that never came to be, an unrequited love like Papo's and mine. Of course, this wasn't true, but I believed it at the time so it was true.

When I sang along with the Chi-Lites, I changed the "her" to "him." I don't know how Desi never lost her patience with me but I guess that's what friends are all about, right? Being patient instead of punching you in the face or telling you to just get over it and get on with your life.

Stefan was still in the picture. I'm not sure if he and Raffi were still seeing each other (or if they were ever seeing each other) or if they were just friends. But Stefan went out of his way to be good to all of us, especially me and Desi. Stefan was a sweet guy. And he really liked kids. (Though not in the same creepy way that Uncle Ernesto did!) Maybe because he missed his own son so much. Stefan couldn't afford to pay child support so his ex didn't let him see his kid.

In the middle of Easter break, Desi and I were starting to get bored with going to see movies (*The Sugarland Express* at the Dyker and *Blazing Saddles* at the Harbor), watching the *Million Dollar Movie* on TV, spinning endless Elton John records (I wanted to grow up to be EJ's new lyricist…screw Bernie Taupin!) and taking aimless walks through the hood. We were running out of stuff to do.

That's when Stefan suggested that Desi and I jump on the train and go visit him at the Met. Not only was the museum practically free—a lot of people didn't know that the Metropolitan Museum of Art had a "pay what you wish" entry fee so you didn't have to pay more than a quarter to get in—but Stefan promised that he would cook for us and serve us lunch in the Met's fancy dining room for free.

We were stoked. All we had to do was get to the Met, way the hell up on 5th Avenue and 86th Street in Manhattan. To us, that was a million miles away from Bay Ridge, but Stefan was confident we could get there on our own. (Raffi, not so much.) Stefan made the commute five days a week and he knew we could do it.

This would mark the first time Desi and I would be taking the subway without grown ups. Her mom talked to my mom and explained that Stefan was a friend of the family and that he was good people. It was a quick call, Raffi and Tessie having nothing in common except the fact that their oldest daughters were best friends. Stefan wrote down the directions to the Met on a sheet of paper from a pad that actually had a drawing of a bare butt on it…with a hand scratching the butt. Next to the scratched butt were the words "Scratch Pad." (Get it?) At first, Stefan didn't understand the joke but when Raffi explained it to him in Spanglish, he laughed. Desi slipped the directions into the back pocket of her Levis. We were all set.

On Thursday, she and I caught the RR at 86th Street, making a slight detour so we could make a pit stop at Your Baker. I couldn't believe Desi had never had a Napoleon before and Your Baker's were the best. We tried sharing one on the subway platform but it made a mess, its thin layers of puff pastry crumpling to the concrete. Desi's favorite part was the creamy filling while mine was the chocolate and vanilla fondant topping. Stefan told us later that Napoleons were also known as *mille-feuille*, which meant "thousand-leaf" in French. "In the kitchen, everything is better in French," he laughed.

Still choking on those flaky layers, Desi and I stepped onto the RR. We'd been warned not to get off until Lexington Avenue. We knew it would be a long ride but Lexington never came. I mean, ever. Already, we were at Steinway Street, which is in Astoria. Which is in Queens. I thought. "Toto, I don't think we're in Brooklyn anymore," I told Desi. "Or Manhattan either," I added.

We jumped off the train and got on another. I think it was the M. Then another. Back and forth, Desi and I went on the MTA to stops I never heard of. Somehow, we ended up at Grand Street, which I knew was in Little Italy. But Little Italy was really far from the Upper East Side where the Met was. The signs above the subway platform said we were heading back toward Brooklyn. "Let's just go home," Desi suggested.

"No!" I snapped. "They thought we were old enough to do this and we're going to do it! We're going to get there, no matter what." Desi unfolded Stefan's scrap of paper again. His neat, schoolboy handwriting made no sense to me. "We didn't pass any Lexington Avenue, did we?" Desi shook her head.

We weren't supposed to talk to strangers so we weren't comfortable asking anyone. After our encounter with the Magic Man in Harold Hall, the both of us were spooked. Who knew what kind of crazies rode the trains? Well, we *did* know because in the two hours we zipped back and forth through the New York City subway system we crossed paths with:

- four hobos who didn't smell human;
- a three-legged Chihuahua in a knitted cap;
- two singers, one of them so-so, one of them amazing;
- a self-proclaimed outer spaceman who played terrible saxophone;
- a blind man who sang a song called "Little Girl" which was great;

- a mob of kids who danced, flipped and climbed the poles;
- a supposed Vietnam vet who didn't look old enough to be one;
- a real Vietnam vet who beat up the fake one;
- an old lady who picked the skin off one hand and flicked it onto the floor (once she even ate a chunk of her dead skin—yuck!);
- an old man whose shoes flapped like flags in the wind;
- a boy who ignored the "No Spitting, No Smoking" sign and did both; and
- a man in a suit who stood in front of our two-seater and kept clearing his throat so we'd look at him, then nudged his chin down toward his crotch (which was eye level) so we'd look down there— PS, we didn't.

I loved this human comedy; Desi hated it. She swore she was going to move out of the City the second she was old enough. Not me, though. To me, the City and the subway was life. Manhattan, the crazy swirl of it, the stench of it…it all added up to the reason why people came here from Ohio and Iowa… because New York was so unlike Ohio and Iowa.

New York City was *The Odd Couple* meets *Bridget Loves Bernie* meets *The Honeymooners* meets *I Love Lucy*. And us native New Yorkers liked it that way! At least I did. But I could see how nervous being lost underground made Desi. True, the heat was blasting in the train car but she was sweating bullets. Although rivers of perspiration came down from under her mushroom hat, Desi refused to take it off. It was her security blanket, especially in times like these.

By some miracle, we found our way back to the RR. "We've got to check the map," I told Desi, gesturing to the closest one, half blocked by a ghetto kid's head.

"I can never read those things," she said.

"We have to at least try," I pointed out. I opted for another map next to a little girl who was sleeping/drooling on her mother's shoulder. At least her head didn't block the transit map, even though her mom gave me the stink eye. I gave it right back to her.

I managed to find the yellow ribbon that represented the RR on the map and followed it up from Brooklyn, across the East River and north to midtown. I made Desi look too. Sure enough, there was a spot where the RR and the 6 train crossed but at the RR station, it said "59th Street" and at the 6 train's station, it said "Lexington Avenue."

As the train doors banged open, I glanced at the black-and-white sign on the subway platform. "This is it!" I told Desi and yanked her out the doors just before they slammed closed.

"Are you sure?" she asked as the RR pulled away.

"Pretty sure," I admitted. A sign on the platform had a number six in a green circle. We followed the stairs that led up to it and waited for the 6 that was going uptown, not downtown. I was determined to show our folks that we could find our own way without help from anyone else. The IRT trains seemed narrower, older and more rickety than the others we'd been on. It was only three stops to 86th and Lex.

Even out on the street and in the cold daylight, I could tell that Desi was still nervous. "Which way now?" she asked. I showed her the trick my dad had taught me so I could tell the difference between uptown and downtown, the East Side and the West Side. "See the Empire State Building?" I pointed slightly to the left. "That's on 5th Avenue." Then I gestured to the southernmost tip of Manhattan. "See the Twin Towers? That's downtown. My father says as long as you remember that, you'll never get lost."

"Your old man's pretty smart," Desi admitted.

"Just practical. Phil is a numbers man," I told her. By the faraway look in her eyes, I could tell that Desi was thinking about her own dad. "If Big Matty was still here, I'm sure he'd show you plenty of neat things," I said. I don't know if this made Desi feel better or worse but she started walking in the right direction, using my dad's trick. I followed her.

Although both of us had lived in New York all our lives, we had never been to the Metropolitan Museum of Art before. It took our breath away. There were three sets of double doors between four sets of double columns. The roof was lined with haloed heads. Even though it was pretty chilly outside, people still sat on the wide staircases. We had arrived! The sun was shining hard and the sky was the exact same shade as John Williams's eyes. (Yeah, after Papo, I was back to crushing on JW.)

I turned to Desi. "We did it!"

"We did," she said. The two of us shook hands in one quick, sharp movement, like businessmen did. Then we looked up at the huge building looming in front of us. Even though we were over an hour late to meet Stefan, she and I were hesitant about going inside. It was like we were imposters, pretending to be grown ups and doing grown up things. The museum was so humongous, it looked like a monster, something that could swallow us up and never let us go. Like a granite version of the whale that swallowed Jonah. Or the Blob.

But finally, our hunger won out. "I'm starving," Desi said and we started climbing the stairs, weaving our way around the people sitting on them. Even without seeing any art, we were blown away. Just the Great Hall—with its scooped-out ceilings, cutouts in the walls with floral arrangements tucked into them (which stood as tall as we did) and a fountain bed that contained a tree—was something else. Me and Desi rushed up another staircase, barely glancing at the religious paintings and crosses in a darkish area that was made to look like a church. Man, it even smelled like church, heavy on the incense and ashes. Stefan had told us how to find the restaurant and at least this part, we remembered.

Desi and I didn't even have to go inside the Dining Room—I don't know if we would have had the guts to anyway—because Stefan was looming at the entrance in his kitchen whites, waiting for us. He sprung at us like a Puerto Rican mother hen. "I was so worried about you guys," he said, his Spanish accent turning the "y" in "you" into a hard "j." He ushered us to a table for two in the large room which had a skylight that was bigger than my whole apartment. Practically every seat was taken and suit-wearing waiters and waitresses were rushing around, delivering food, writing down orders. Desi and I sat up straight in our chairs and tried to look elegant. I don't think it worked, especially with MushroomHat being there, too.

Before Stefan disappeared, he whispered to a waiter, who nodded. His name tag read "Alex." With a fancy flourish, Alex poured water into wineglasses but didn't bring us menus. He put small dishes and a basket of bread and butter in front of us. The bread was still warm. The butter was carved into rosettes. "Do you have any money?" Desi whispered to me.

"Just a couple of dollars," I told her. "You?" She shook her head.

"We should leave Alex a tip," she said.

In a few minutes, Stefan reappeared with a couple of plates and a clean kitchen towel over his arm. "I made these for you myself. Special," he smiled.

The dishes held juicy jumbo shrimp wrapped in bacon and creamy coconut rice studded with raisins.

A man in a suit at the table next to us craned his neck to look, taking his attention away from his lettuce wedge. "I didn't see that on the menu," he said.

"It's not, sir," Stefan told him politely, then rushed back through the swinging kitchen doors.

"Special treatment," Suit Man huffed.

Desi shrugged. "He's our dad," she lied. This seem to satisfy Suit Man.

Next, Stefan came out with little wooden skewers of marinated pork and a peanuty dipping sauce. It melted in our mouths, no comparison to the meat Tessie got from A&S Pork off 86th Street, which was pretty good. The sauce had a slight kick to it but was still yummy. Desi and I were starting to get stuffed.

When Stefan brought us porcelain bowls of an ice creamy thing that he set on fire, Suit Man turned away, disgusted. "Baked Alaska," Stefan told us. Underneath the browned topping was chocolate, vanilla and strawberry ice cream in a checkerboard pattern. It tasted amazing but we felt like we were going to explode.

After Alex whisked away our dirty plates, Stefan told us not to leave a tip. "We did this for Alex's wife and kids last week," he explained.

Stefan had to work till three, so he told us to nose around the museum for an hour or so. He'd meet us in the American Wing, at the Frank Lloyd Wright Room, when he was done with his shift.

Desi and I didn't know where to begin. We walked through the Medieval Sculpture Hall, which looked interesting but also looked like a big church, which turned us off, so we kept walking. We had enough of churches in Catholic school. Stefan had said that "Arms and Armor" was his favorite section. But it wasn't ours. Apparently, it was also James Earl Jones' favorite because Stefan had told us the story of a docent who'd taken *The Great White Hope* actor and his wife on a tour, and how they'd spent hours and hours looking at armor. Until Mrs. Jones gave the docent the high sign that she'd had enough. So Desi and I passed on the armor, too.

Wandering around, we came upon a large, long sculpture gallery bathed in sunlight from above. Statues of people we'd heard of from mythology and history were there, and they were larger than life. For some reason, me and Desi were drawn to the nudes, in bronze and in marble: a woman covering up with a towel, another resting on a stone slab, looking ready to run, a naked guy holding a sword and a severed head. (But we were most interested in Sword Guy's naughty bits, which looked like a seashell and was even tinier than Little Matty's.)

Desi remembered that there was an Egyptian section that was supposed to be even better than the Brooklyn Museum's, so we headed there next. We had to go back down through the Great Hall to get there but it was worth the trip. The gold jewelry especially. We didn't stop to look at the mummies and the painted coffins, which I was afraid might remind Desi of her dead dad—everything did. The signs took us past large sculptures from one of the Ramesses fellow's temples.

"The same Ramesses from *The Ten Commandments*?" Desi wondered. We'd both watched it on Easter Sunday. Ramesses was played by Yul Brenner, wearing a snazzy diaper.

"Probably," I told her.

We looked around some more. Man, the Egyptians sure liked their gold. There were earrings, breastplates, rings, necklaces. Desi and I walked through the rooms, reading the placards and talking about what we saw. A small, painted wooden statue caught our eye. It was of a woman on her knees, her hand in front of her face. She wore a red skirt and nothing on top, just had little black dots for nipples and a bricklike thing on her head. "It's called 'Mourning Isis,'" Desi read. "She's a goddess."

"What's she mourning?" I wondered. "Her husband? Her boyfriend? Maybe the fact that she has no shirt?" Desi laughed; she was my best audience. I looked at the printed card next to the case. "Oh, some dude named Osiris."

"Hey, I know about them," Desi told me. "They were brother and sister. Then they got married."

"Yuck," I interrupted. "Could you imagine marrying Matty?"

"No," Desi admitted. "Anyway, another brother killed him, cut him up into little pieces and scattered his body parts all over Egypt."

"How many pieces?"

"Forty-two, I think. Isis cried so much, she flooded the Nile," she continued. I wondered if Desi had cried that much when her father was killed, enough to flood the Hudson or the East River or both. But I didn't ask. Desi leaned closer to me and talked in a whisper. "The goddesses managed to find all of the pieces, all except for his penis. They put him back together, minus his thing. And...here's the grossest part..."

"More gross than putting a dead body back together again?" I wondered.

Desi nodded. "Much more gross. His sister Isis made a phallus out of gold..."

"What's a phallus?" I wondered.

"A dick," Desi said. "So, Isis brought Osiris back to life, got pregnant and had Horus, who was both their son and their nephew."

"Weird," I admitted.

"The Ancient Egyptians were weird people," Desi said knowingly.

Even without the incest angle, it was a wild story. Full of death, drama and pissed-off family members. It was better than Phoebe, Ruth and Erica on *All My Children*, our favorite soap opera.

According to my Barbie wristwatch, it was almost 2:45. We knew it would take us at least 15 minutes to find the American Wing, if we could find it at all. "We should get going," I told Desi. "We don't want to give Stefan another heart attack."

"I guess," she said.

Back up the Great Hall's staircase we went. We tried to count all the steps but lost track after 56. Luckily, Desi remembered the way and took us through Medieval Art, making a right through Medieval Treasury and Secular Works, neither of which interested us. But we loved the beautiful double set of cast-iron stairs from the Chicago Stock Exchange and the gorgeous Tiffany glass windows. We paused to look at them and agreed that the Wisteria Window was our favorite. But the magnolias and irises were pretty, too.

Desi said that she liked the Frank Lloyd Wright Room from the Little House. It was full of warm wood (oak, I think), built-in comfy couches and chairs, and lots of stained glass, only not as fussy as Tiffany's glass was. "Why is it your favorite?" I asked her.

"Because it looks like nothing bad would ever happen in a room like that."

Before I could ask her more, Stefan showed up, but I knew what she meant. The Frank Lloyd Wright Room was so sunny and cheerful and comforting. I wanted to curl up and read *Slaughterhouse-Five* or *In Cold Blood* there. (My reading preferences back then were shocking rather than cuddly, fuzzy Judy Blume books.) I wanted to have endless cups of Swiss Miss hot cocoa in the cradle of Frank's sturdy beige armchairs.

But before I could jump the ropes into the room, Stefan said we should get going. Only not before exiting through "Arms and Armor," which we had tried to avoid like the plague. It wasn't that bad, especially Henry VIII's "fat" armor, a child's set of armor and the horses in armor, set up like a parade.

Lucky for us Stefan was tired from work and didn't want to stay long. He'd smuggled out two huge chocolate chip cookies for us, wrapped in a cloth napkin that he'd return the next day. Since it was still light outside and not too cold, Stefan suggested we walk down 5th Avenue to the RR's 59th Street stop. "Which way?" he asked, quizzing us.

Before I could answer, Desi looked at the skyline, spotted the Empire State Building as her marker and pointed south, "This way," she said confidently.

Me and Stefan followed her, smiling our way down 5th Avenue.

A ROOM OF ONE'S OWN

There was no doubt about it, I needed my own space. The apartment I shared with my family was cramped and the room I shared with Laura was even worse. Besides being annoying, my sister was a slob and noisy. I couldn't even concentrate enough to do my homework when Laura was around, especially if she was playing Barbie Dolls with Carolyn Russopietro, the Queen of Coochie Farts. Plus Laura was always going through my stuff, looking for the key to my hot pink diary. (I kept it hidden in an o.b. Tampons box. Nobody ever looked for anything in a tampons box.) Like there was anything juicy written in there. My life was far from juicy.

And forget about being able to write poetry or short stories in that apartment. I mostly wrote when I was daydreaming in Religion class or during mass. Or the rare times I went down to the Shore to think: alone.

Desi was always with me, wherever I went. We were like glue. We were together so much that sometimes my mom would start humming "Me and My Shadow" when Desi came to the apartment, but always with a smile on her face. I think Tessie was happy I had found a good friend like Desi. Tessie had a friend like that growing up named Grace Sforza. Not only was Grace my godmother but she had also had been my mom's maid of honor. She was still

Tessie's best friend. They saw each other a few times a year and talked on the phone a lot. And when they did, Tessie would giggle like a schoolgirl on the other line. I hoped it would be like that with me and Desi when we got to be their age. Which was really old.

When I told my mom and dad that I needed more space, they said it was impossible. We couldn't afford to move so I could have my own room. (But I think the real reason was that my mom couldn't bear the thought of not living in the same house as her mom. I would *never, ever* be like that, I swore. I couldn't *wait* to get away from my mother!) My folks said they would see what they could do about getting me a writing nook. Which usually meant they would do nothing.

But a few days later, my mom said she'd talked to Grandma Lou and they'd created the perfect place for me to write. They'd gotten it ready while I was at school and couldn't wait to show me. I couldn't imagine where it might be. A secret corner in the house that I didn't know existed? Not possible because I knew every nook and cranny, every cobweb in the dusty hallway and every dust bunny on the ladder that led up to our tarpaper roof.

My heart sunk when my mother led me to the cellar. She was smiling so wide, I thought her face would break. I had to bite my lower lip to keep from crying. My family was banishing me to the basement! I'd never be able to write down there!

Past my grandparents' old mahogany bedroom dresser (which was piled with paper A&P shopping bags filled with junk), right across from the cinderblock prison of the boiler room, my mother and grandmother had set up a bridge table. Then they shoved a discarded dining room chair in front of it. This was to be my office.

Propped in the middle of the table was a Smith Corona manual typewriter. "I got it from SteMar Business Machines down on Smith Street," my mom said proudly. "Took it home on the subway in the shopping cart." A bulletin board was propped against the whitewashed cement wall, supported by a cardboard Ronzoni box overflowing with cans of Tuttorosso crushed tomatoes. "What do you think?" my mother wondered, her voice shaking slightly with excitement. "The typewriter's your Confirmation present."

I could tell that Tessie and my grandmother had worked hard to move the bags and boxes to make space for me but the place was awful. Terrible. Just then, the boiler kicked in and roared. "I think it's great," I told my mom and hugged her. "Thank you."

Tessie's eyes filled with happy tears, mine with tears of disappointment. "Well, I'll leave you to your writing," my mom beamed, her lone dimple popping through her chubby cheek. Instead of writing, I sat down and sobbed. A good, snorty, snot-filled cry. I wished my mother had thought of bringing down a box of Kleenex in addition to a notebook and pencils. I rubbed my teary, boogery face on my sleeve.

"This place has potential," Desi proclaimed when I showed it to her.

"Potential?! For what? Potential to be haunted?"

Desi ignored me. "It's yours. It's nobody's but yours. And they cared enough to make a special space for you." I stared Desi down, unconvinced. "Besides, you know you can write anywhere, just so long as it's quiet. In a tree, on the train…"

As usual, Desi was right. Thanks to her, I began to see the promise, the love in the room, instead of just mouse droppings, clotheslines and dust. That's why it was so good having Desi around: she found the best in even the worst situations. Except, of course, her own.

Things weren't great for Desi at home. Raffi seemed to be in a bad mood all the time and picked on Desi constantly. Even if she didn't do anything wrong. Sometimes it seemed that Desi just *being there* was enough to annoy her mother. "*Ai*, you're just like your father, so stubborn," Raffi would say. Or "Your pops didn't like *yucca* either. Well, screw you, it doesn't taste like old gym socks. Just eat it!" I rarely had dinner there anymore. Not because they didn't invite me but because it was so emotionally intense at the Ruiz place. It was good that the weather was getting warm and that it stayed light later because Desi and I could stay outside longer. My house wasn't a picnic either with the evil gnome Laura sharing my room but at least it wasn't as volatile as Desi's place.

I know Raffi was mad at Desi because she was so much like her father. I saw in pictures that she looked a lot like him. Desi was a young Big Matty in a plaid Catholic school skirt. I bet every time Raffi saw Desi, she saw Big Matty, and it killed her. But hopefully, it wouldn't kill Desi.

Raffi's extreme moodiness seemed to have started when Umbe told us about Sylvia. Did Raffi and Umbe have a thing? All this time, I thought she had a Jones for Stefan. Or at least that he had one for her. Were both guys hot for Raffi or vice versa? Thinking about it made my head hurt.

When I wasn't hanging around with Desi I spent time in my basement office, despite it being so damp and dingy that it gave me the creeps. I wouldn't be surprised if Johnny from *Night of the Living Dead* was waiting for me down there. ("They won't stay dead!" the movie poster said.)

A couple of years earlier, my grandparents had the boiler bricked into its own cinderblock room—I guess boilers started exploding so the city passed this crazy law that said all boilers had to be enclosed. My card-table desk was right outside that boiler room and the door was always propped open. So much for protecting me if it blew up. I would be a goner. Me and Johnny, the Zombie, would be pulverized.

As much as I complained about being banished to the basement, it didn't mess with my creativity. When Desi came to call for me, my mom would buzz her in then yell into the hallway, "Desi, she's in the basement" then shout, "Cici! Desi's here!" as if I hadn't heard. That's Tessie for you. Always stating the obvious. It made me want to choke her sometimes. Okay, almost all the time.

Besides lovesick poetry I never showed anyone, not even my best friend, I'd started writing short stories. Pretty good ones. I was working on a fiction piece called "Retfa," which was "after" spelled backwards. "Retfa" was about a man who finds out that he's reincarnated and what happens to him when he does. It still needed some work, though, but it wasn't half bad.

I didn't think the nuns at St. Fi's would like the theme of "Retfa" because the only person Catholics admitted had come back from the dead was Jesus. Oh, and Lazarus. Jesus brought Lazarus back while Jesus was responsible for doing His own hocus-pocus sleight of hand. I might get punished or else kicked out of Catholic school for writing a story they saw as sacrilegious. So, I kept "Retfa" to myself at first. Besides, like an Easy-Bake Oven cake whose lightbulb had gone dead, it wasn't ready.

Most of the time, I was still scribbling my musings in a wire-ringed notebook and my most private thoughts into my diary. But more and more, I was able to transfer my thoughts from head to hand to the Smith Corona. At this point, I could almost type as fast as I could think and was getting better every day.

When I got pulled out of Mrs. Rizzi's math class, I couldn't imagine what I'd done wrong. All Margaret Pietanza, the hall monitor, told me was that I was wanted in the principal's office. My knees were shaking so hard, I didn't know if I could stand. I turned around to see Desi's worried expression then faced front and followed Margaret, who we'd nicknamed "Pigeon" (because she was pigeon-toed). Pigeon was sworn to secrecy and couldn't tell me why she was walking me to Sister Regina's office. Pigeon looked concerned, too, but then again, she always looked like that—as though she was astounded by life in general, no matter what was happening, good or bad.

Waiting for me at Sister Regina's coffin-like wooden desk were Miss Coughley and a guy I didn't know. He had a steno pad in his hand and a big camera around his neck. Whatever I had done, it was about to be documented. "Am I in trouble?" I asked Miss Coughley.

"Should you be?" Sister Regina wondered.

"It's about your poem," Miss Coughley smiled.

"Which one?" I asked.

Sister Regina piped up and told me that "Space Children" had come in first place in the diocese-wide poetry competition and was going to duke it out with the other parishes in the city-wide contest. Well, she didn't exactly say it like that but it's what she meant. Miss Coughley was beaming, making her ruddy complexion even ruddier.

The guy in the suit was introduced to me as Todd Generali from the *Home Reporter,* our local paper. He had a column called "Generali Speaking" and was writing up something about my poem being picked to represent the diocese. (A diocese, we were forced to learn and repeat in Religion class, was a district under the pastoral care of a bishop. The Diocese of Brooklyn included Queens and more than 180 parishes. Yeah, they made us memorize that, too.)

The reporter asked me a bunch of questions and wrote down what I said. It felt odd. Nobody had ever done that before. Paid that much attention to what I said. Then Mr. Generali posed me in between Miss Coughley and Sister Regina. I felt like the center of a Catholic sandwich. Like an Oreo but not. The reporter said he wasn't sure what issue the article would be in but told us to keep an eye out for it.

When I went back to class, I could see that everyone was nervous. I could feel their eyes all over me, checking to see if I had any bruises or marks from being swatted with the ruler or if I had blood dripping down my legs. But there was none of that drama. A few of them looked disappointed that I was still in one piece. Not Desi, though. She poked me between the shoulders with her pencil eraser the second I sat down in front of her. "What happened?" she whispered.

"Nothing bad," I assured her. "I'll tell you later."

Mrs. Rizzi was in the middle of one of her "no tickee, no shirtee, no money, no paper" rants. I was relieved that there were no Chinese kids in our class because it always made me feel uncomfortable when Mrs. Rizzi put on her fake Asian accent to berate one of us. Just like the laundromat wouldn't give you your clothes if you couldn't produce your ticket, Mrs. Rizzi wouldn't give kids back their tests if they didn't pay the fine she charged for bad behavior. It didn't seem fair to me even though she supposedly donated the money she collected to the Little Sisters of the Poor.

I also didn't like the idea of Mrs. Rizzi's "June Box." This was where she put all the things she confiscated from students during the year: packs of Trident chewing gum, boxes of Tic Tacs, cigarettes, Spaldeens, Frisbees and the occasional girlie magazine. The last one always came from Joey Santino or Rick Collins. They not-so-secretly sold dirty magazines in the schoolyard.

And why did Mrs. Rizzi call it a June Box? Because you wouldn't get your stuff back till June. (Except *Playboys*. You never got those back. I figured Mr. Rizzi had quite the collection.) To me, putting something in a June Box was basically stealing, even if you were a parochial school teacher.

Unable to contain her joy, Desi jumped up and down when she heard about "Space Children" winning first prize. I thought this would be her reaction so I waited until recess to tell her. Desi said my poem would kick butt in the diocese contest and that she couldn't wait to see the article in the *Home Reporter*. "I'm so proud of you," she smiled, and hugged me around the shoulders.

I blushed, "Thanks. Now quit being so ridiculous."

We managed to scrape together enough change to share a White Castle chocolate shake and a raised glaze donut. Chocolate was the only shake flavor worth anything in our book. We split the donut down the middle. Desi gave me the slightly bigger half. The shake was so thick our cheeks caved in trying to drink it through the straw. A nice older girl behind the counter whose nametag read "Elaine" gave us two spoons without complaining. A junkie snoozed at one of the aluminum tables. Some guy was ranting about how the burgers were made of dogfood. To prove his point, he started barking. "Man, everything your mom says about this place is true," Desi said.

"Grandma Lou, too," I added.

"Don't go into that dag-blasted White Tower," Desi mimicked, sounding just like a wrinkled Italian lady in a housedress and orthopedic shoes. *"I once went in there for a hamburger and the flies were as big as zeppelins."* The thick shake would have gone shooting through my nose if it wasn't so thick. The shake, I mean, not my nose.

It was good to see Desi making jokes and laughing. Even though I knew she liked spending time with me, all too often she was sad. I could see it between our words, between the smiles, in the silences. Her eyes would get this lost look and they seemed darker, deeper. During these times, I knew Desi would retreat, remember her father and think of the terrible way she lost him. One day, he was buying them Junior Mints at Ann and Harry's Candy Store and the next, half of his head was blown away and he was gone. Something would remind Desi of her dad, a song on the radio like "Honey," which had been one of his favorites, or "Black Magic Woman," which Big Matty swore was written for a woman like Raffi with inky-black eyes. And then Desi would get all sad and low…and hard on herself for feeling so sad and low.

And when she did, I would remind Desi that her father hadn't even been gone two years so the scar from losing him was still fresh and raw. This seemed to make her feel better, at least for a little bit. I tore out an article from one of Tessie's *Family Circle Magazines* about how grief was like an ocean wave. You could go on for a while feeling nice and good, then all of a sudden, out of nowhere, you get hit with this big surge of grief, which knocks you off your feet like a big wave.

Desi read the article slow and serious, like she was rolling every word around in her head. She bit her lip and when she finished reading, she said, "Thanks," then folded the magazine article into the pocket of her Levi's.

"Make sure Raffi doesn't find it," I told her.

"I will."

Raffi always got really pissed off when she thought the kids were mooning over their father. "Get over it!" she'd yell at them. "I have." Then, as an afterthought she'd sometimes throw in, "Face it, he ain't coming back!" This would usually get them even more upset, especially Little Matty, who cried if you looked at him crooked.

Every week, I checked the *Home Reporter* to see if Mr. Generali's story about me was in it. I felt a mix of excitement and dread about the whole thing. I got into the habit of going out early on Saturday mornings to check the newsstand. Then, one week, there it was. Me stared back at me, looking all smeary in the dark newsprint, except for my braces, which caught the flashbulb's glow. Miss Coughley looked blotchy, boxy and Scot-like while Sister Regina looked stern and pissed off, which was pretty much the way she normally looked.

The article was pretty good, short but sweet. But they spelled my mom's name wrong in the caption (Tessa instead of Tessie) and messed up the title of my poem ("Spaced Children"…what the hell was that?) But all in all, it was good to be mentioned.

Despite how I looked or what it said, I bought five copies of the paper with my allowance money. One, I slipped under the Ruiz apartment's door with *"Mira, mira…Celestina"* written across the top of the page. I hoped they'd like it and that they'd be proud of me.

It was too early to call for Desi, before nine. I knew not to ring the bell so early. Raffi needed her beauty sleep no matter who was in the *Home Reporter*. Even if Julio Iglesias was banging on the doorbell, she wouldn't answer it before 9 am.

Back on Gelston Avenue, Tessie was so proud it bordered on annoying. I thought her dimple would pop. She hugged and kissed me and made me my favorite breakfast, digging the waffle iron out of the food pantry that was stuffed with stuff we never ate. My mom was a child of the Depression and lived in fear that there wouldn't be enough when there was always enough. More than enough.

JUNIOR

Just as Desi promised, she *did* have a parade of cute cousins. I gave Papo the cold shoulder even though he tried to be super nice to me. I could never forgive the way he humiliated me and my thankless devotion. Besides, he wasn't all there since they let him out of the Psych Ward at Bellevue. Although Desi's *primo* Chulo was handsome, he was fresh from San Juan and barely spoke English. And her other cousins looked at me cross-eyed because of the whole Papo thing.

But then Junior started coming around.

In a rare mood of forgiveness, Raffi made up with her cousin Roberto, who was married to Junior's mother Estella. Supposedly, Roberto and Raffi had been feuding for almost seven years and Desi barely remembered Junior, whose real name was Luis. But no one called him that. Not even his mom, Estella, who everybody called Mimi. Mimi was a short, round meatball of a woman with close-cropped curly Peroxided hair and gold rimming her two front teeth. It was hard to believe that such a homely woman could have a son as *guapo* as Junior. Or that Roberto was so stupid in love with Mimi. I mean, Roberto looked at chubby, little Mimi like she was Cheryl Tiegs or something.

Not that Roberto was such a prize either but he was definitely better looking than Mimi.

At first, I thought Junior hated me but it turned out he was just really, really shy. He barely said two words to me. But when I would glance at him, I'd catch him staring at me then looking away. "Trust me, he likes you," Desi swore, but made me promise not to say anything because Junior would deny it. If he even uttered a word at all. Junior was so bashful I hardly heard his voice at all.

Matty, who at just shy of 10 by this time, lacked social discretion. When we were all playing Monopoly in the girls' room, Matty asked: "Hey, Junior, do you like Cici?"

In response, Junior burned bright red which was noticeable even with his *café con leche* complexion. Junior abruptly left the room, his Monopoly money in neat piles, sorted by color. "You'll lose your turn," Matty called after him, but Junior still left.

I was confused by his behavior. Did this mean that Junior liked me? Or that he didn't? Probably the second one, I figured. I was used to boys not liking me.

Desi just shook her head and rolled her eyes. "Matty, when are you ever going to learn to keep your big trap shut?" Matty thought about it, weighing his options. "It's a rhetorical question, stupid," Desi added. It wasn't like Desi to call anyone stupid, especially her baby brother. But sometimes the younger kids got on her nerves. Mine, too. Even Matty, who was a usually a sweetheart. At our age, sometimes everyone got on our nerves. Except one another.

For some reason, Junior didn't get on my nerves either. He and his family began coming over to Desi's almost every weekend. Junior was a few months younger than me and only in the seventh grade, but unlike most boys, he was taller than I was.

You see, after a lifetime of being a shortie, I'd suddenly started shooting up. Desi didn't, though. I was probably about six inches taller than her but still skinny and an A-cup, while Desi was getting rounder and curvier, but not fat. She was growing into the kind of girl guys dug while I just looked like I was being stretched. My nose was getting bigger, if that was even possible. (Desi swore I was imagining it, as any best friend would.) I had a pronounced

Roman honker like practically everyone in my family while Desi had a cute, turned-up thing, like everyone in hers. Even Junior.

But Junior didn't seem to mind my nose or anything else. Yep, I caught him sneaking peeks at me when he thought I wasn't looking—but I was always looking. Junior…he liked wearing carpenter jeans. You know, the kind with that loop on the side for a hammer and the slot for a ruler. Except Junior actually used the loops and slots. Plus his butt looked so nice in those carpenter pants.

What else about Junior? He liked building things, making carved wooden boxes and picture frames, Athena said. He went to a special middle school in Queens that specialized in practical skills like carpentry. Junior wasn't too muscly but he had strong arms and a solid chest. He wore mostly t-shirts and leaned toward the rock-and-roll variety. The Rolling Stones tongue. The Grateful Dead tie-died flowered skull. But on him, they worked.

Junior's hair was longish, not quite to his solid shoulders. It was honey brown and slightly kinky. I later learned that it was soft to the touch. His eyes were hazel, light for a Puerto Rican, the color of caramel and ringed with olive green. Junior also had a good mouth for a guy, nicely-shaped with fullish lips but not too girly. He was smart but not show-offy and he was kind to the littler kids, more patient than Desi and I were, maybe because he was an only child.

I almost died when, one Sunday night, Raffi suggested Junior walk me home. "It's only around the corner," I shrugged.

"But still," Raffi said, trying not to smile. She was doing a terrible job of hiding her feeble attempt at matchmaking.

To my surprise, Junior agreed, even after Athena and Jacinta moaned, "Oooooh," in unison. He blushed but he still followed me down the apartment building stairs to the street. He asked if I wanted a slice when we passed Vito's—I said no. He asked if I wanted anything from Penner's Grocery Store—I said no again. He asked if I liked school—I said I didn't but he did. He told me about his favorite classes which were plumbing and welding. He asked my real name, even though he probably already knew it. I liked the way "Celeste" sounded in his mouth. I asked his real name even though I knew it. He made me practice saying "Luis" so it didn't sound like "Louis," which was *not* his name. He was named after his father Luis, which is how he got the nickname "Junior."

For once, I wished I lived further away. Junior and I walked as slowly as possible but were still in front of 126 Gelston in less than five minutes. I had to be inside the house by nine and it was already 8:55. Older kids were in the schoolyard, playing basketball by the light of the lamppost. Junior took my hand. My heart hurt in my chest. Would he try to kiss me? Feel me up? Both? Neither? "I can't..." I stammered.

"I know," he said. Junior raised my hand to his lips and kissed it. My heart-shaped rose zircon ring with the arrow going through it brushed his mouth. I hoped it didn't cut him. He dropped my hand, smiled, turned and was gone. I watched him go for a minute, then bounded up the stairs. I was in by 8:58.

True to form, Tessie stuck to her "one party a year" rule. But Raffi had no such sanction. For Raffi, everything—even weekends—were an excuse for a celebration. Desi's Confirmation, and a month later, her graduation from St. Fi's, were no exception. Besides, Raffi did parties different than Tessie did. Raffi's were free-for-all potluck, BYOB celebrations. Tessie had to do everything herself, from soup to nuts. She always got herself into a tizzy, bent out of shape that she might run out of Fritos, Fresca or Cheez Whiz, but it never happened. And so what if she did run out of something? Would the world fall off its axis is she didn't have enough Cool Whip? According to Tessie, it just might.

Although cold cuts and salads were ordered months in advance from Andre's Catering (who also catered my parents' wedding), Tessie was responsible for everything else: lugging the beer and soda home in her shopping cart, getting all the chips and dips, doing the decorating, picking up the paper goods, ordering the cake. (My dad would have to pick it up at the Golden Loaf the morning of the party.) For every get-together, my Aunt Jean would say, "I'm not driving in from Valley Stream for cold cuts." (All of 30 miles.) But she'd occasionally end up coming in anyway.

I'd have to wait for my combo Confirmation/graduation party until June but at least I had Desi's to look forward to. For her parties, Raffi flew by the seat of her pants, sending Matty or Athena across the street to Penner's if she ran out of anything...and a relative usually ended up digging into their pockets and throwing the kids a $20 to cover it, so this "running out trick" was genius on Raffi's part.

Besides divvying up the duties, everyone brought a dish to Raffi's soirees. Who brought *pernil*. Who brought yellow rice and red beans. Who brought fried plantains. Who brought *croquettas*. No dish was ever repeated and it was all delicious, even if they just brought a salad and dressing like Sylvia, who wasn't much of a cook.

A Ruiz Family gathering was no fuss and no bother. None of the drama that always happened when my family got together. Let me take that back… there was still drama but it was a different kind of drama. Puerto Rican drama versus Italian-American drama. To me, PR pathos was much more entertaining. Desi thought just the opposite but maybe that's because the other family's theatrics was so new for each of us.

For example, at Raffi's shindigs, someone always got so drunk that they either:

1) fell down;
2) puked;
3) peed;
4) crapped;
5) cried; or
6) all of the above (accompanied by a smorgasbord of English and Spanish phrases).

At my house, a poker game (because every family gathering seemed to morph into a poker game except maybe funerals) could easily turn into World War III and have my father yelling, "Why don't you just make the whole freaking deck wild!" He'd been known to shout this almost on cue whenever my Uncle Fred suggested they play deuces wild.

In Desi's house, somebody always had a concealed weapon that couldn't seem to stay concealed (possibly two): a gun (not loaded) or a knife. Then someone would faint. PHR, Junior called it. Not-so-secret code for "Puerto Rican Hysteria." For someone so quiet, Junior was pretty funny.

In contrast, no one ever passed out at my parties. Cursed someone out, yeah. Stormed out, sure. But passing out's a lot more memorable. Even if it's only PRH.

Before you knew it, Desi's and my Confirmation day rolled around. It fell on a pretty Saturday in May, no rain, not a cloud in the sky. The Confirmation ceremony itself went on without a hitch, despite all of the nuns' warnings about us screwing up, kneeling at the wrong time and worries about us forgetting to renounce Satan since we were all going straight to Hell anyway.

Even Desi taking a boy's name as her Confirmation name turned out to be no big deal. Since we had a double class being confirmed (seventh and eighth graders plus public school kids from CCD), Father Parsons helped out Monsignor Wiest. (Yes, the very same one who cut the album "A Priest with a Song in His Heart," which featured such all-time favorites as "Bill Bailey" and "Yankee Doodle Boy.")

As luck would have it, Desi and I got on Father Parsons's line, so we got a beneficent smile and a gentle tap on the cheek to signify that we were now soldiers of God. (The smack was supposed to remind us that our faith might cost us something, that being a Christian might cause you some pain. The dreaded face-whack was later replaced by a hearty handshake.) Gentle as he was with the smack, Father Parsons was heavy-handed with the chrism. I could feel the sacred oil drooling down my forehead, threatening to drip into my eyes. "Don't wipe it," Desi warned me. "It's a sin."

Sin, schmin. I wiped.

After we took pictures in front of the church and near the rectory by that marble statue of Jesus hanging out with some lambs, we were free to go. I introduced my parents to Desi's mom. (Our moms had spoken on the phone once in a while but they'd never met in person.) Despite how different they were, Raffi and Tessie were very polite to each other and exchanged niceties about the other one's daughter. Even my father, who hated being in church and was grateful it didn't fall down whenever he went inside, admitted that Desi was a "great gal."

Raffi even invited Phil and Tessie to Desi's Confirmation get-together that night. I was relieved when they said they already had plans—watching the CBS Saturday night comedy lineup was more like it. They had a long-standing date with Mary Tyler Moore, Bob Newhart and Carol Burnett. The last thing I needed was them embarrassing me in front of Junior. Thank God, Laura had a sleepover at Carolyn Russopietro's so she wouldn't be able to humiliate me at Desi's party either.

In spite of myself, I was able to enjoy being the token white girl at Desi's Confirmation party. I didn't even mind when someone put on Eddie Palmieri and Umbe led me into the middle of the living room floor to show off the dance skills he'd taught me. The singers kept yelling *"Azucar!"* which means "sugar" in Spanish. The beat was a lot different than "Rock the Boat" but I could still follow it. Especially with Umbe's hand in mine and his other hand cradling my waist. Sylvie was smiling but Junior looked weird. Jealous, maybe, to see another man touching me? I was glad Uncle Ernesto wasn't there because he might have gotten the wrong idea from the dance. It was just a dance, nothing else.

Eddie Palmieri was accompanied by claps and calls of *"Ai, chica"* from Desi's family. Was I like an organ grinder's monkey, performing for oglers? I didn't care because it felt so good to dance like that. I think I was pretty okay at it because nobody made fun of me or laughed. They cheered us on, a gawky girl with braces and a grown-out London shag haircut and a handsome, sloe-eyed Latino who was even cuter than A Martinez from *The Cowboys*. Most of Desi's relatives were so drunk I think they would have cheered on a kitten and a puppy doing the *merengue*. But I still think Umbe and I did a great job.

Despite the party, Tessie still wouldn't budge my crappy curfew of 9 pm. There was no way of getting around it. Once, I tried messing with my watch and lying that it was slow. To check out my story, my dad took my Barbie watch overnight. When it kept perfect time, I was grounded for a week. I didn't want to risk that happening again.

So, reluctantly, I said my good-byes and left at 8:50. When Junior offered to walk me home, I immediately wished I'd done an "Irish good-bye"—which is slipping out without saying good-bye to anyone—and left earlier.

For a second time, Junior and I took the long way home: down 92nd, along Fort Hamilton Parkway, then up 90th to Gelston instead of just up 92nd Street. When we passed Harold Hall, I told Junior about the Magic Man—but left out the part about the perv flashing me and Desi the winter before. I was afraid that a mob of irate PRs (like those angry villagers with torches in the old Frankenstein movies) would go after the magic dude if I told. Junior laughed at the story and at the thought that a whole neighborhood could be terrorized by some weirdo in a cape. "In Queens, we would just throw him a beating," he said.

When we got to the corner of Gelston, I noticed how dark it was underneath Mr. Santone's magnolia tree, which blotted out the streetlight. Junior and I were only a half block from my house. He stopped and held my hand. I worried that it felt sweaty, clammy, but if it did, he didn't seem to notice or care. Junior bent slightly and kissed me on the mouth. Sweet and firm. I was worried that my braces might hurt him. But he obviously wasn't concerned because he parted my lips with his tongue and put his tongue in my mouth. (It might sound gross but it wasn't.) Softly at first, then more insistent, like his tongue didn't want to be ignored. I wasn't exactly sure what my tongue was supposed to do, so I met his with mine. I think it was right because he kept on doing it then pulled me closer.

I was conscious of a lot of things all at once: how good it felt, how beautiful I felt, the sensation of the fallen magnolia petals underneath the soles of my white Confirmation Thom McAn shoes, the bite on the heel of my left foot from the new pleather, the brush of Junior's stubble on my cheek, the sweet ache in my neck from craning up to kiss him, the Tic Tac (orange) taste of his tongue…

All of a sudden, I heard cheers rise up from behind a parked car. Matty and a couple of cousins had followed me and Junior, the little rats. Mr. Santone flipped on his porch light and yelled, "What the hell is going on out there?" and the magic of the moment was broken.

It was 8:59 anyhow and I had to get inside before I got grounded again. I told Junior that I'd walk the rest of the way home myself since Tessie might be hanging out the window. Sure enough, I heard the worn aluminum of the screen's sides creak up and saw my mother's head bob out the window when I reached the front of the Olsen's house a few doors down. "Ma!" I complained.

"Don't 'Ma' me," she hissed. "It's nine o'clock." My mother threw down the keys so I didn't have to ring the bell. I caught them and let myself in. On the way up the stairs, I touched my mouth, which felt a little sore and rubbed away. But I liked the way it felt. I liked it a lot.

EXILE

Desi was pissed off at me!

Only it had nothing to do with kissing her cousin Junior. But it *did* have to do with her Uncle Ernesto. "How come your Uncle Ernie doesn't come by anymore?" I asked Desi one day, soon after her Confirmation party.

When Desi didn't answer, I looked over at her. It was hard to get used to Desi not wearing her mushroom hat, which was in her hand. She thought it was high time to retire MushroomHat for the summer. At that moment, she was on her knees, putting her beloved chapeau into the flower-power patterned cardboard storage box under her bed. "How come you never told me?" Desi challenged. Her face looked hard and cold. I never saw my friend look like that before. At least not at me.

"Told you what?" I wondered.

"That my uncle touched you weird," she snapped. "You tell me everything! Why didn't you tell me that?" It was true. I even told Desi about Junior. Desi was happy about me and her favorite cousin. But not about this.

"I don't know...I..." I stuttered. "I didn't think it was important."

"Not important! What if he did that to someone else? Athena? Me, even?"

"Athena would bite his face off," I laughed; Desi didn't. "Look, I was embarrassed," I told her. "I thought maybe I'd done something wrong. I thought maybe it was my fault. That you might not want to be my friend anymore because of what happened."

Desi shoved me. "Your fault? You're a kid. He's a grown-up. He should have known better."

I hung my head. "How did you find out?"

"Matty saw," Desi said. "He had a nightmare about it and finally told Raffi."

"I'm sorry I gave him nightmares," I told her.

"You shouldn't be sorry. About anything. Except about not telling me. I thought I was your best friend."

"You are!"

"Then how could you not trust me?"

I shrugged. "It's not that I didn't trust you. I just didn't want to make a big deal about it."

Desi was all red in the face. "But it *is* a big deal. It's a big deal that my uncle did it. And in my house, too. Raffi almost ripped off his balls through the phone. Thank God she didn't call him out on it in person. You should have heard her. 'If you ever touch any of my girls again...'"

"Wait, I'm her girl?"

"Sure, you are." Even though Desi was mad at me I still smiled. Especially when she said, "You're my girl, too. We're better than sisters. Remember?"

I did. "Still?" I asked.

"Still," she told me. I was happy but I couldn't think of anything to say. "And sometimes sisters fight," she reminded me. I guess they did.

It took a few days but things finally went back to normal between Desi and me. We were awkward at first, kind of tiptoeing around each other. Being extra polite, extra cheerful. Our friendship didn't seem the same after she called me out on Uncle Ernesto but it would soon be right, I thought. And it was.

'Were Desi and I growing apart?' I worried. I didn't think so. 'Would we ever grow apart?' I hoped not. But everything changes, I knew. And I figured we would, too. But just not yet.

In that awkward phase, I spent more time on my own without Desi by my side. Sometimes I went up to the rooftop of the municipal parking garage on 86th Street. Five-stories high, on the upper level, you got a good view of the neighborhood: Century 21 Department Store, Insight, Loft's, Hinsch's Luncheonette. They were all spread out below me like they were part of my kingdom. I always brought a pad and paper when I went up there because for some reason, I usually felt like writing. Mostly a poem or something short. Like this:

> I expected to fall in love
> The way they do in late-night movies,
> And when there were no violins,
> I wasn't quite sure
> What I had fallen into.
>
> There were no crashing waves
> Or flaming sunsets
> Or bouquets of red roses
> At my door.
> There was just you
> In your sneakers and faded jeans,
> And a space between your front teeth.

Was I in love with Junior? I wasn't sure. I liked him a lot. The way he looked at me made me feel weird and wonderful and almost pretty.

There were other poems, I wrote up on the garage roof. Like this one. I called it "Airborne:"

> Where do they bury dead balloons?
>
> They bury people
> Under great chiseled stones
> Or in marble houses.
> Ashes are thrown into the sea,
> Set out on the wind

Or on a mantelpiece in an urn.

But where do they bury dead
balloons?

I like to think that balloons
Sail into bright blue corners
Through tufts of white floss
To the end of the sky
And back,
Tangling their strings in play,
Still rising.

Desi made me send my poems out to *Seventeen Magazine*, which we both read religiously, breathlessly, every month, as though their articles about the proper way to apply mascara (which neither of us were allowed to wear yet) and "How to Get the Most Out of Your Active Sports Clothes" would somehow save our lives. Although we would never be perfectly freckled like Patti Hansen or Naomi Oreskes—yes, we were so pathetic that we even memorized the cover models' names—*Seventeen* still gave us a breath of hope.

I have to thank Desi for telling me to include an SASE with my poems when I sent them out. We didn't know what an SASE was at first. But with a little research, we learned that it stands for SELF-ADDRESSED, STAMPED ENVELOPE. You put one in when you submit work to a magazine so they can return it with a rejection slip if they don't want it. "But you're not going to need one," Desi said confidently as she put a 10 cent Peter Max Expo '74 stamp onto it, then put another stamp on the business-size envelope. We addressed it to 850 3rd Avenue in Manhattan.

I crossed my fingers as I slipped the poems and a cover letter (we had to look up what that was, too) into the envelope. Desi suggested we give the envelope a good-luck kiss but I thought that was going too far. Then we walked to the post office to mail it. We didn't want to risk it getting lost or someone throwing a match in the corner mailbox, which sometimes happened.

There was a lot going on in our lives. Even with our Confirmation behind us, Desi and I were working hard to keep our grades up and practicing for the graduation ceremony. Sister Paschal Marie was still wielding that freaking annoying cricket clicker to tell us when to sit, stand and walk.

In September, I would be going to the local public high school, Fort Adams. That's where my mom went and it was still a good school plus it was nearby. I'd had it with nuns, religion class, having to wear a farty uniform and going to class with boys who weren't allowed to wear their hair past their shirt collars. (Come on, it was the '70s, man!) I managed to keep my big mouth shut when Miss Coughley asked me, "What's the matter, Celestine? Can't your parents afford to send you to a Catholic high school?"

Meanwhile, Raffi was set on sending Desi to Fontaine Hall Academy, a posh, private, all-girls Catholic school about a mile away from Fort Adams High. Big Matty's mother offered to cough up the cash because she knew it was important to her son that his kids have a Catholic education.

At first, I worried that Desi and I wouldn't be so close anymore but then she reminded me that we were "better than sisters." And besides that, we had promised to be best friends forever.

The two of us had it all planned out—each morning we would walk down 92nd Street to Shore Road then go our separate ways to our separate schools. (Fontaine was on 99th Street and Shore Road, and Fort Hamilton was on 83rd Street and the Shore). Each afternoon we would meet up on the same corner of 92nd Street and walk back up the hill together. It was fool-proof, or so we thought. Now I know that nothing's fool-proof, except to fools.

Desi and I were so busy getting ready for our graduation that we'd forgotten all about the poems I sent to *Seventeen*. Then, one early June day, there in my building's tarnished brass mailbox was the SASE. I was glad Desi was by my side when I slowly started to open it. I didn't want to face my first rejection slip alone. The envelope felt thick, thicker than the one I'd sent. Shit, maybe they were sending me one of their famous do's and don't lists, this time, on how not to write poetry.

I held my breath and tore open the envelope. Desi held her breath, too. I was surprised to find a bunch of papers inside, but not my poems. "What's this?" I asked.

"It looks like contracts," Desi said, taking a closer look. "Cici, they want to buy your poems. Both of them!" We did a happy, joyful, jumping dance in the vestibule. "At $25 a pop!" she added. I didn't know what to say. "This means you're a professional writer. You're going to be published. At 13."

We ran upstairs to show Tessie, who was wearing a fashionable housedress, as usual. She couldn't be happier and swore it was because I had "a room of my own" to write in. I didn't have the heart to tell her that a corner in a damp basement didn't exactly qualify as a room. I did most of my writing other places: car garages, the double R train, on busses. But still, I didn't want to bust Tessie's balloon. She made me and Desi (and herself) ice cream sodas to celebrate, which was a nice touch.

But all wasn't perfect and sunshiny in Cici Land. I hadn't seen Junior since Desi's Confirmation party a few weeks earlier. Our relationship was geographically ugly (as my classmate Paul Siederman would say), a long-distance relationship. I lived in the ass-end of Brooklyn and he lived in the ass-end of Queens, somewhere near Flushing, out past Shea Stadium. We were too young to drive. And the subway would have taken at least two hours each way. Junior and I talked on the phone every few days but because we were both shy, there wasn't much talking going on. There were long, awkward silences because we were long, awkward teenagers.

Almost a month after the party, Junior and his folks finally came to visit. I missed him like crazy but tried not to show it, not in front of everyone at least. He was acting all cool and suave but I could tell by the way his eyes smiled that he was happy to see me, too. It was a warm day, so the grown-ups decided to go for a walk then pick up some groceries at Penner's to fix something for dinner. This meant they would leave us kids alone for at least an hour. They tried to convince us to go outside but we told them that we didn't feel like playing stickball in the schoolyard or playing basketball either. Finally, they just shrugged and left. "It's too nice of a day to argue," Raffi said before they went.

Matty wrangled Junior into playing Rock'em Sock'em Robots but lost patience when he kept getting his block knocked off. Desi, Jacinta, Athena and I were messing around with each other's hair. The younger girls' hair was so long we could experiment with French braids and French twists. I was trying to grow mine out for graduation and it wasn't going too well. My hair got bushy instead of long, and more stubborn and unruly the bushier it got. We tried taming it with some of Raffi's Dep, which made me look too much like Bowser from Sha Na Na. I rinsed it out the best I could. Desi's hair was still short, so the only thing we could do with it was put in barrettes. I let her try the ivory clips Umbe had bought me from Reminiscence. They looked really nice on her, especially when we twirled her hair away from her face. It was a pretty face, even though Desi didn't think so.

Suddenly, Junior was standing in the doorway of the girls' room, waiting to be invited in. He and Desi exchanged weighty looks. "Come on," she said to Jacinta (who now wanted to be called "Cindy") and Athena. Instead of belly-aching, they got up and left, their hair half braided and half curled.

My heart was beating real fast. I started to leave, too. "Not you," Desi told me. "You jerk," she whispered so no one else but me could hear.

Junior closed the door and propped a chair under the knob to lock it. "Hi," he said. We had already said "hello" when he got to the house earlier.

"Hi," I said. My hair was almost dry. I could feel it starting to curl into a Bozo the Clown-like 'do.

"Let's sit down," Junior suggested. There was nowhere to sit but on the bed. I pushed aside the bobby pins, combs, clips, dips and hair ties. We sat. Junior moved his knee against mine. Although I shifted slightly on Desi's bed, his knee followed mine. Without saying anything, Junior gently pushed me back so that my head rested on Desi's pillow.

"I can't..." I stammered. We were only going out a month—I couldn't go all the way yet. And in my best friend's bed! Besides, everyone was there, right outside the door. I didn't want to lose my virginity like this.

"I just want to hold you," Junior said. Maybe I shouldn't have believed him but I did. He never lied to me before so why should he start lying now?

Junior lay on top of me, not moving. At first, I thought he might crush me because he was so much taller, had so many muscles. But it didn't hurt. I liked the sweet weight of him. He didn't move around or anything, just held me. Didn't even try to kiss me. I don't know how long we laid there, holding still, just breathing. I wondered what he got out of it. I didn't even feel a boner between us, just his skin on my skin, his clothes on my clothes. It felt good.

Suddenly, there was a loud banging on the door. I knew it would come eventually. It was Matty, ready for Round 2 of Rock'em Sock'em Robots. "Later," Junior told him.

"How much later?" Matty wondered.

"When I tell you I'm ready."

"When will that be?" Matty pushed.

Junior sighed and climbed off me. We both sat up. The magic was broken. "When I say."

Satisfied for the moment, we heard Matty's footsteps skipping away from the bedroom door. "I need to talk to you about something," Junior said, his voice shaking slightly. I thought that maybe he was going to give me an early graduation present: a delicate pair of turquoise earrings or a silver friendship bracelet.

But instead, Junior broke up with me. I heard bits of sentences like:

"Not fair to you..." and
"...live so far away..." and
"working this summer..." and
"I really like you but..." and
"I'm sorry..."

My stomach hurt like I'd been punched from the inside out. I wondered if I was going to throw up. But it felt worse than that. After you puke, you usually feel better but I didn't think I'd ever feel better about this. Not for a long time, if at all. Maybe when I was an old lady in the Norwegian Christian Home on 67th Street. Or at least in college.

I didn't say anything afterwards. Junior looked terrible, all puffy in the face, like he was trying to hold back the tears. I might have muttered something like "Okay" before I got up and left the room. I don't remember. Matty burst in, carrying the yellow Rock'em Sock'em Robots box. Jacinta and Athena were playing Old Maid on the living room couch. Desi was in the kitchen loudly stirring a glass of Tang and seemed to be waiting. Did she already know? Did her cousin already tell her that he was going to dump me? I figure he did.

I walked into Desi's arms and cried. And cried. And cried. It might sound weird, but I felt Big Matty's presence in the narrow kitchen, too. I felt his sadness for his daughter's sadness for my sadness. It was one big sad. In one way, it was a comfort, being in a group hug where one person was invisible yet still very present. But it didn't make the waterworks any less. In another way, it was worse—feeling like my best friend's dead father was comforting me. Creepy and nice and extra doleful.

I cried as quiet as I could. Which wasn't easy. I didn't want the girls to hear and ask what was wrong. I didn't want to make Junior feel any worse than he probably already felt. I also didn't want the grown ups to see me like this when they got back, especially Raffi. So, I left.

But I couldn't stop crying. Even when I ran down the steps and hit the street. I walked. And walked. All the way up to 86th Street, still sobbing. People stared but I didn't give a shit. I didn't know them and they didn't know me. I wouldn't see any of them ever again.

Where did I go? I went to my tower, to the tall parking lot. I ran up the stairs to the very top level, barely able to breathe because I was still crying. Would I ever stop? Would I ever run out of tears? Nah. I figured the body could always make more tears. I might never pee again, that's how much liquid I was using up to manufacture all those tears. It was a big, messy, snotty boo-hoo. I blew my nose on the balled up Wetson's napkin in my pocket. Then I stood on my tippy-toes, looking down onto 5th Avenue below. It didn't look bad from a distance.

No one knew I was up there. People were so into their own heads, they just looked straight in front of them and moved like they were on tracks. Like trains. They didn't deviate. They didn't waver. They didn't look up or down. They just moved. It seemed mindless. Pointless. I didn't want to be like them. I always wanted to think, to feel, to be, even if it hurt.

What would happen if I jumped? Would I break the sidewalk from five stories up? Would I just be a splat? Would I feel anything upon impact? Would I scream? Would anyone care? Would anyone stop? Would anyone cry? Would I die?

I decided that I couldn't do anything like that to Desi. Or Tessie. Or me. Instead, I sat down on the parking lot's asphalt coating and curled my knees up into my chest, still crying. I took the banged-up notepad out of my jeans pocket and fished out the Bic pen from the other.

Instead of jumping, I wrote. That's what writers did: they wrote.

GRADITATION

No matter how many times we corrected him, Matty still called it "graditation" instead of graduation. I think he just did it to annoy me and Desi. But graditation was right around the corner and Tessie had her knickers in a knot making plans, buying paper goods, plastic tablecloths, chips, dips and 64-ounce Key Food sodas (she wouldn't spring for brand names like Coke or 7 Up). She would load it all into her fold-up silver shopping cart and lug it home a bunch of blocks from 86th Street.

Whenever I saw my mother on the Avenue, weighed down with her supermarket booty, I wouldn't offer to help her. Instead, I would cross to the other side of the street and pretend I didn't know her. I felt bad about doing this but Tessie was so freaking embarrassing. I hated the way she walked around the neighborhood, in her cotton house dresses, without pantyhose and her snaky varicose veins popping. Or else, in polyester pants and Payless sneakers, which was somehow just as bad.

Desi would give me crap whenever I avoided Tessie like this. "Can't you just see past the Polyester? Your mom is one of the nicest people on the planet," she would say.

"No" and "I doubt it," I would answer.

This was another one of the things Desi enjoyed about my mom: seeing how much of a fuss Tessie made over even the smallest things. A good checkup at the dentist. A good grade in science. A good bowel movement. They were all causes to celebrate. And by celebrate, I mean Tessie would cook your favorite meal, buy your favorite dessert at Your Baker, or even better, take the time to make Pillsbury Slice-and-Bake Sugar Cookies with you. Whereas Raffi was known to forget birthdays or even school plays even when one of her kids (Matty, always a drama queen) had a lead role.

"I think Tessie's cute," Desi would say. To which I would just roll my eyes.

My graduation cake would come all the way from the Golden Loaf on 13th Avenue. My Aunt Bernie's best friend's husband owned it and we got a break on the price, even though my father had to drive to pick it up. Mickey Grillo made a great cake, and he also topped his creations with those little wafers that looked like rose petals. They tasted just like Communion hosts without the guilt.

Our graditation ceremony went off without any screw ups. Despite Sister Vivian's screaming at us during rehearsals, insisting that we were an unholy mess. That our formation was an embarrassment to Catholics everywhere (both living and dead). And that God Himself was covering His eyes in disgust, with both hands, because we couldn't space ourselves evenly when we walked down the aisle of the auditorium. Even monkeys could master the art of spacing better than us, Sister Viv said.

In spite of "The Lip's" epitaphs and verbal browbeating, nothing terrible happened during the graditation ceremony. No one even tripped. No one's dangerously high heels snapped. No one forgot their cue—not with that terrible cricket clicker haunting our dreams. (It seems that all nuns had one or maybe Sister Vivian borrowed Sister Paschal Marie's.) No one messed up their speeches. Even Desi, who was so nervous that she puked in the girls' room (twice!) before we filed from the classroom into the auditorium.

Because Desi had the highest GPA in our homeroom, she was among the three (one from each class) chosen to give a short speech. She asked me to help her put her thoughts down on paper and I did. Even cold-hearted Sisters Viv and Paschal Marie were honking into their Kleenexes by the time Desi finished. Sweet Sister Joelle, too. Especially when Desi thanked her mother and her dead father for their love and support. I even cried a little myself.

St. Fi's didn't believe in titles like Valedictorian, Class Clown or Class Writer. (Anything that took attention away from God and His glories were no-no's in their sectarian book.) But they did mention "Space Children" came in first place in the diocese poetry contest. And they surprised all of us by announcing that Desiree Rebecca Matthew Ruiz had been awarded the school's first annual Father Mulvaney Memorial Scholarship, which was enough to pay for one year at Fontaine Hall Academy. I'm sure *Abuelita* Raquel would be glad to hear that she didn't have to shell out as much as she thought.

After the obligatory photos with our parents, siblings, teachers and Father Parsons in front of lamb-toting Jesus, we headed to the Tiffany Diner for a quick bite. (As the name implies, it's fancier than Venus II, if a diner can be considered fancy.) Desi's graduation party was later that night while mine was the following day. Raffi was in no rush to get back because Umbe, Stefan and Sylvie were at home setting up so she said "yes" when Phil invited her and the kids to come with us to Tiffany's. Unlike most of the casual, relaxed parties Raffi threw, this one wasn't a potluck. Stefan offered to do the cooking as a graduation present to Desi. Which we thought was really nice.

I couldn't believe how well Tessie and Raffi got along at Tiffany's. Even Phil, who could be very cranky, managed to be semi-charming. Maybe it had to do with Raffi being such a hottie. Was my father flirting with her? I almost fell over when he grabbed the check and insisted on paying the whole thing. Like Tessie, Phil wasn't very spur-of-the-moment. Doing things like footing the bill for four extra bodies was mildly shocking. (We didn't eat much, just appetizers, because of Desi's party in a few hours.)

"Thanks for being so good to my daughter," Phil told Raffi when he handed the waitress the money for the check. Raffi actually blushed. Again, she invited them to one of Desi's parties. Again, they politely refused. Again, I was secretly relieved.

It wasn't as awkward as I thought it would be, seeing Junior again after our big breakup. (Maybe it was only "big" in my eyes.) We talked a little bit, small talk, mostly, and he didn't give me moon eyes nearly as much as I'd hoped. Raffi and Stefan were all lovey-dovey, though. Maybe it was all the

Coronas (with a wedge of lime squeezed into the bottle then shoved down the neck) they guzzled.

When Junior offered to walk me home, I didn't say no. This time, we stopped under Mrs. DeCapa's maple tree. I let him kiss me and even feel me up. He rummaged around in my bra cup as though there were really something in the cups besides my "baby bottle nipples." (Thanks for giving me a complex, Laura!) Maybe I was a slut. Maybe not. But I didn't care because it felt good.

Would I tell Desi about swapping spit with Junior? Of course, I would. I told Desi everything. But in the end, I didn't tell her. She hadn't even French-kissed anyone yet, though lots of guys had crushes on the petite, curly-haired girl with glasses. Especially after she retired MushroomHat. Would Desi have understood me kissing her cousin just for the sake of kissing him? Probably. But I kept it a secret anyway. And maybe that's when it started: the beginning of the end.

My graduation party a day later turned out being better than I thought it would be. It was a minor miracle that everyone behaved themselves, even the grown ups. There was no poker game and therefore, no Phil ravings about wild cards. My cousin Gino even cooled it with the Puerto Rican jokes. I think he might have had a thing for Desi. For a quick second, when he offered to walk her home, I wondered if there would be tongue-kisses in store for Desi under one of the neighbor's trees. But when Gino asked if he could walk her home, she said "no thanks."

But first, there was cake.

Desi had never seen an overblown, Italian graduation cake before. Mickey Grillo really outdid himself this time. He pulled out all the stops. Besides the wafer-flowers, there were also those hard, edible pearls that cracked your fillings if you weren't careful. There were pink and white buttercream roses too, vanilla pudding filling and white cake. At least that's what Tessie said she ordered. I preferred chocolate cake and filling but my mother said a lot of people (like my father, who was paying for it) didn't like chocolate, so vanilla it was. "My father liked chocolate, too," Desi said, trying to console me because I couldn't even get the kind of cake I wanted at my own graduation party. "Big Matty used to say that if it wasn't chocolate, it wasn't worth it."

Our tiny four-room apartment was stuffed with people. Kids played games in me and Laura's room. Phil and Tessie's bed was reserved for purses and sports coats to be stowed. A big, folding table with a paper graduation tablecloth covering it was pushed up against the living room's wall-to-wall closet. The table was covered with platters of sweaty cheeses and cold cuts plus trays of potato and macaroni salad. Two cups were filled with mayo and mustard, already growing an appetizing crust on their surfaces. Fist-sized rolls, big as Spaldeens, were piled on top of each other at one end of the table. As promised, Aunt Jean and Uncle Fred didn't make the pilgrimage from Valley Stream to eat cold cuts (or to be with their family) but they sent me $10 in a Norcross (not even a Hallmark!) card.

The liquor was lined up on the kitchen table so the kids couldn't sneak any. But I think my cousin Gino somehow got into the Bacardi. Not only did his Coke smell funny but he was acting funny, too nice. The cake occupied a corner of the kitchen table, still hidden in its hard-sided cardboard box. Tessie was perking coffee in the big urn she borrowed from my Aunt Bernie whenever we had a party. She also boiled the water for tea. My Grandma Mae and my father's side of the family only drank tea. Tetley tea.

Desi and I sat at the top of the blue linoleum steps in the hallway, the only private place we could find to talk. I could tell she was worried about something. "Great party," she said. "Different than the ones Raffi throws, but still great."

"It's all right," I told her. "What's really on your mind, Desi?" I pressed.

She shrugged. Even with the big deal of Desi getting the Father Mulvaney scholarship, I could see that she was kind of bummed about going to a Catholic high school. Fontaine girls were known to be mean and stuck up, and Desi was neither. The both of us were shy but she more so than I was. Plus, lots of times, I jumped to her defense without thinking when she was too scared to speak up for herself. It was a knee-jerk reaction for me. I didn't think. I just stood up for her. "I'll always have your back," I assured Desi.

"Even when you're not there?" she asked.

"I can kick their butts when I meet you after school," I told her. That got a tiny smile out of her.

"Are you sure you can't…"

I knew what was coming next. Desi was forever trying to get me to go to Fontaine with her. "Desi, my parents can't afford that place," I explained as patiently as I could, for the millionth time. "And besides, I can't go to an all-girl school. I'm too boy crazy." Desi shook her head. "Don't worry, nothing will change," I assured her.

"Things change all the time," she said. "Whether you want them to or not."

Even though I knew Desi was right, I didn't say anything. Fathers don't come home from hunting trips. Best friends aren't best friends forever. Then Laura opened the apartment door and told us that they were ready to cut the cake.

After smearing my name for good luck and digging into the first slice, my mother's face dropped like I'd stabbed somebody. The cake was chocolate, all chocolate inside. Desi and I looked at each other. "Big Matty strikes again," she whispered.

Ice ran down my spine like a cube melting along its length. "Stop," I told her.

"It's true," she said, and didn't say anything else.

When my mother called The Golden Loaf the next day, Mickey Grillo swore he'd made an all-vanilla cake. He'd bet his life on it, he said.

Yep, Big Matty strikes again...

SUNSHINE STATE

Two days after my graduation party, Tessie, Phil, Laura and I, plus more luggage than four people could possibly need, stuffed ourselves into the Ford Falcon and headed toward I-95 in New Jersey, which would eventually bring us to Florida. My dad always took his vacation the last two weeks of June. He swore places weren't too crowded because Catholic school let out a couple of weeks before public school did. At least in New York City. And that's all that mattered to my folks—beating the crowds and getting a bargain because it wasn't the high season.

Tessie always insisted we go someplace, at least for part of the time. Even though Phil would have been more than happy sweating onto the plastic slipcovers, sipping Manhattans and watching old movies on WPIX. Some years it was the Catskill Game Farm or Lake George, where Laura got so many mosquito bites on her chest it was tough to tell which two bumps were her nipples. (Hint: the two that weren't covered in calamine lotion.) Other times, it was Pennsylvania Dutch Country, Niagara Falls or Colonial Williamsburg.

This time, Phil had gotten a big raise when he took a job with Rupp Southern Tier, where he would start in July as a rate analyst. The "relaxing" trip to Florida was supposed to be a celebration (for his new job and my graditation). It turned out to be anything but. I didn't complain about being away from my best friend because Desi was visiting her father's mother, *Abuelita* Raquel, upstate so there wasn't much happening in Brooklyn. Desi, Matty and Athena would be gone for almost a month.

I tried not to miss my best friend too bad but it was tough because the two of us were joined at the hip. I'd saved up a stack of quarters so I could call Desi on pay phones. I had *Abuelita* Raquel's phone number scribbled on an old assignment pad that I carried with me to the Sunshine State.

Phil drove practically the whole way there and back. My father was an easily-annoyed driver, especially when me and Laura fought in the back seat. "Ma, she's on my side!" and "Ma, she touched me!" was enough to send Phil into a litany of curses. And forget about when my sister and I rolled down the back window to send Laura's dolls flying around the Falcon in a mock hurricane! It was Tessie's job to calm Phil down. And to dispense the snacks that sat in the sacred Century 21 Department Store shopping bag at her feet. And to supply cheerful, titillating conversation so my dad wouldn't fall asleep at the wheel.

Tessie would also dole out iced tea made from Nestea powder packets, pouring it from a plaid, padded Thermos with a steady hand into waxed Dixie cups while Dad did 70 down I-95. She never spilled a drop. Tessie gave out the Nestea sparingly like sacred wine at mass. We were never allowed to buy snacks or soda at a rest stop, even if we were dying of hunger and thirst. Even if a roadside stand boasted boiled peanuts (North Carolina) or fresh peaches (Georgia).

A real treat was stopping for gas at Stuckey's. (This was the only time we were permitted to poop or pee, during gas stops, my mother holding us in suspended animation above the putrid bowl when we were too young to do "the dry squat" ourselves.) With a fill-up, you got a free bag of chocolate at Stuckey's. Only it was white chocolate, which tasted like wax. I mean, who liked white chocolate? Nobody except my dad, who wasn't nearly as food-savvy as Big Matty, who thought chocolate-chocolate was the only worthwhile kind. But where was Big Matty? Dead. I was stuck with my alive but ornery father, who was driving us down to Florida in the old Falcon, his t-shirt pasted to his back and sweat rolling down his face, cursing like a demon.

Sometimes Tessie took the wheel after lunch but she was such a nervous driver, none of us could relax. Especially not my father. My mom drove with her shoulders hunched up to her ears and her fingers white from clutching the steering wheel like a life preserver. Inevitably, it would start to hail or pour whenever Tessie took to the driver's seat and she'd start to panic. Then my father would start to yell, which made her panic even more. So, it was just easier for him to do all the driving.

By about five, we would start looking for a motel. But it had to have:

(A) a pool;
(B) a slide; and
(C) Magic Fingers.

A and B were all right if C was unavailable. In a pinch, just A was fine if Phil had already started ranting about how tired he was. Oh, and the motel had to be affordable. He always opted for Howard Johnson's over Holiday Inn, which was too ritzy and too expensive for the likes of the Piccolos.

That first day on the road, Phil refused to tough it out to reach South of the Border, just over the South Carolina State Line, because it was too pricey and too far. So, North Carolina it was for us Brooklyn Guidos.

Laura and I were happy because the HoJo's in beautiful Dunn, North Carolina had both a slide and a pool. Tessie was happy because they had a clam strips special. (Plus, it was June, HoJo's "Strawberry Month," and they had a strawberry sundae special—which Tessie loved. My mom never met a dessert she didn't like. Phil hated all things strawberry, too. He was a boring Vanilla Man all the way.) Tessie was nuts about seafood but Phil refused to let her cook it at home because it stunk up the apartment for days. And my dad was happy with HoJo's because the price was right.

I swore I wasn't going to do it but I did. That first night on the road. Maybe it was sliding down the slide for an hour, the warm water hitting my privates. Maybe it was the delicious smell of Coppertone, which always made me feel weird and mushy. Maybe it was all of the above. But Day # 1 in HoJo's sparkling clean bathroom, I found myself sprawled out on the bottom of the tub with my legs spread wide, arcing my hips up toward the shower's spray until I shuddered and spasmed.

I was definitely a slut. And a pig, too. What would Laura think if she knew what I'd done just minutes before I slid into the double bed next to her? Maybe she did the same thing. No. I was sure I was the only one on the globe who did this disgustingness that was so gross there wasn't even a name for it.

I also swore that my sister Laura sharpened her pinkie toenails when she knew we would be sharing a bed on vacation. Laura took great delight in cutting me with those lethal weapons before she began drooling onto the starched white pillowcase next to me. Little witch. When I complained to my mother, Laura turned sugary-sweet and gave that sickening "Who me?" smile. I slept as close to my edge of the bed as I could but still, Laura managed to snag me with her talons.

The drive south was mostly uneventful. We made it past the Florida border on the second night and stopped around Jacksonville. I wouldn't recommend it. An ugly town, except for that lonely phone booth on the beach. Armed with a pocketful of quarters, I tried to call Desi. I kept feeding coins into the slot like it was a hungry beast. We just managed to get in a "Hi" and "I miss you" before the recording cut us off and I ran out of quarters. It was going to be a long two weeks.

We got to meet my Uncle Nick (real name: Dominic) and my Aunt Millie who ran a Gulf station down in Delray Beach. Uncle Nick looked exactly like my Grandma Lou, his sister, but without the housecoat and pearl earrings. He and Aunt Millie were nice but the real treat was their three-legged German Shepard named Baron, who didn't seem to know he had three legs. Baron could run and jump and fetch like any other dog. He balanced his single front leg between the other two like a camera tripod and away he went. (Baron had jumped out the car window when he was just a puppy and was run over. My cousin Maria was too heartbroken to let them put Baron down, even after her pup lost his leg. Baron did what we all do—he adapted.)

Since it was the first time in Florida for the four of us, the Piccolos hit all the touristy spots, weaving from the East Coast to the West Coast to Disney World and back. We got a flat tire on Alligator Alley, just after Laura finished the last of the iced tea. I never saw a man sweat so much or curse so hard at a poor tire iron as Phil did.

Then there were the mermaids at Weeki Wachee and the two dogs getting married at the Ringling Circus Museum in Sarasota. There was a launch-pad visit to Cape Canaveral but no rockets were taking off. There was alligator wrestling in Margate and a loud airboat ride in the Everglades that rattled my fillings.

Phil splurged for a trip on the glass-bottom boat in Silver Springs. When the tour guide threw a quarter onto the glass at the end of the ride to encourage tourists to give him a tip, Laura snatched it up with a shriek of, "Look, Dad, I found a quarter!" And refused to return it to the guide. Thanks to Laura, we could never go back to Silver Springs again.

There was Monkey Jungle and Parrot Jungle in Miami. We even drove the Falcon on the hardened sand of Daytona Beach. Being on vacation was exhausting.

Since we were going to be in the Fort Lauderdale area for a few days, Phil sprung for an efficiency apartment across from A1A. Nothing fancy, just a simple Mom and Pop place but my folks would have their own room and Laura and I would have our own beds. No more toenail slashing, at least for a few days.

We loved everything about Nordick's—the homey Colonial furniture, the Formica and chrome kitchen table and chairs, and the big windows that let in the breeze from the beach, which was just on the other side of A1A. But the best thing about Nordick's was its name. It was a clever combo of the owners' first names—Nora and Dick.

Not only did Nordick's have a pool but a slide, too. Laura and I wore ourselves out going up and down the slide while my parents said they'd be "out in a minute." P.S. they never came out. And when my sister banged on the door because she forgot her nose clips, they wouldn't let her in. My dad's hairy arm just flung the nose clips out the door and luckily, Laura caught them. She had no clue what was going on in there but I did. And I was grossed out. I doubted I could look at my parents during dinner. Or ever.

I tried to focus on the delights of Nordick's pool instead of the delights in Room 36. Every time I climbed up the slide's ladder, a man sitting in a nearby lounge chair smiled at me. I didn't realize why he kept smiling until I got changed later on. I'd gone down the slide so many times, I wore a hole into the butt of my bathing suit. You'd think Laura would have said something to me. (Desi would have!) I was horrified. I hated that babyish ruffle-bottomed two-piece more than anything but hated baring my behind to a stranger even more. I could never go to Nordick's pool again.

Burgers at the Ranch House consoled me a little bit. I had burgers at almost every meal, except breakfast. Hamburgers were usually the cheapest thing on the menu and I was so afraid my father would run out of money on that trip that's what I ate. All the time. So much that Phil started calling me "Wimpy." You know, the character from those old *Popeye* cartoons who always said, "I'll gladly pay you Tuesday for a hamburger today."

The Ranch House also had $3.99 breakfasts which included two eggs, two pancakes, two strips of bacon plus toast, so we went there a lot. One thing we didn't cheap out on was dessert. (Tessie never forgot dessert, which was part of her problem.) In her defense, the key lime pie at the Ranch House was unforgettable and incredible. The perfect mixture of tart and sweet.

That trip, we were "regulars" at Ranch Houses across the Sunshine State. Glorified diners, they were all over Florida, and like HoJo's, they offered something for everyone, even my super-picky sister. The Ranch House in Pompano Beach even had a waitress who looked like Lou Costello. Although, she was very efficient in her white-on-white outfit and squeaky, sensible shoes, we had to hold back the giggles when she served us because that's how much she looked like Lou Costello. My father threatened that he was going to ask her "Who's on first?" but never did. I think he left a big tip because he felt sorry for her. I mean, what woman wants to look like Lou Costello?

Besides the Ranch House, the thing I remember most about our trip to the Sunshine State was hemorrhaging. Bleeding like a stuck pig. It's something you never forget. I woke up early one morning feeling wet and crampy. I had my period but usually a mini pad did the trick. When I looked under the sheet, I thought I was dreaming. I was soaked in red goo. I swear, it was like I was wearing a bikini bottom of blood.

When I got up, I felt a big blood clot slither out. I sat on the toilet and more clots plopped into the bowl. My knees were weak at the sight of so much carnage but I made my way to my mother's side of the bed. Naturally, Tessie was pissed at me waking her before the sun was up but when she saw the bloodbath, she changed her tune. She jumped out of bed, got one of Nordick's cheap towels with their name striped in blue across one side, laid it down and told me to get in bed next to my father. Reluctantly, I did. I tried not to touch him. And not just because of his yellow toenails. (My mother said it was because he didn't eat enough—read that as *any*—vegetables but I didn't believe her.) The reason I was so creeped out was because I was a still a little shaky on where babies came from.

You see, my mother's friend Margie Rolon had recently gotten pregnant and she supposedly "didn't know how." I was confused. I mean, how could you not know how you got pregnant or where babies came from? Didn't Margie ever hear Michael Pollock's limerick? Even I knew where babies came from…sort of.

Tessie sprung into "panther mode." She was back in a flash, a chunky feline protecting her young. In the space of five minutes, she'd ripped my soiled sheets off the bed (blood had soaked through to the mattress), apologized to Nora, found out where the nearest hospital was, got directions then woke up my father. All four of us piled into the car. Even on her best day, Tessie was a frantic driver so my sleepy, crabby father navigated the unfamiliar streets. Laura complained about not stopping for breakfast at the Ranch House and having to eat a dry box of Apple Jacks from a Kellogg's Fun Pak. Phil reached into the back seat and backhanded her. Laura was too stunned to cry and didn't even squawk when I needed to lay down because I felt faint.

Somehow, we made it to North Broward Medical Center. It looked like something out of *Marcus Welby, M.D.* It was tall, surrounded by greenery and had an actual parking lot with plenty of spaces. (The parking lots at Brooklyn hospitals like Maimonides were always full.) It looked more like a hotel than a hospital.

The second I got out of the car my legs went out from under me. Tessie held me up until Phil could get a wheelchair. What happened next was fuzzy. Blood pressure cuff, thermometer, my mother's voice wavering the way it did when she tried not to cry. A doctor examined me as best he could through the goop and Tessie's harsh whisper of, "Careful…she's a virgin…" (How did she know? Maybe I wasn't. But I was. Of course, I was.) I didn't even care that they gave me a shot. The doctor explained that it was the same injection they gave to women who were having miscarriages and that it would slow down the bleeding. Almost immediately, it did.

Then I had a terrible thought: did I start bleeding like that because of my intimate relationship with the showerhead? With the bathtub faucet? Did I hurt myself? I was too scared and embarrassed to ask anyone. Especially not my mother.

Although I didn't hemorrhage to death, I almost died of embarrassment when we got back to Nordick's only to see Dick and one of his hunky workers carrying a bloodstained mattress down the open staircase of the two-storied motel. My bloodstained mattress. For all to see. By the way he looked at me, I knew the dreamy handyman knew it was my menstrual blood. And so did everyone else who stayed at Nordick's. It was blazing hot and the pool was full. I swear everyone stared down the bedding like it was from a crime scene instead of from a hormonal imbalance.

But that wasn't the worst part of what I call "Bloody Monday." The worst part was that I couldn't go in the pool for the rest of the trip. And forget about the ocean across the street. I was afraid I'd draw sharks, even if I waded. Of course, Laura took great delight in annoying me and rubbing in that she could go in the pool, down the slide, off the diving board (looking fetching wearing her nose clips) and in the Atlantic. Which, she said was as warm as bathwater. She could and I couldn't.

Just for a second, I wished my mother had drowned Laura in the bathtub when she was a baby. For one second, maybe two.

The rest of the trip to Florida was pretty forgettable and getting back to Brooklyn was even more so. Because Desi would be at her grandmother's for another two weeks. (But who was counting? Me!) I didn't know how I'd survive it without her. But somehow, I did. We always do, don't we?

THE SUMMER OF RUDE AWAKENINGS

Whenever I looked back, I would think of the summer of 1974 as "The Summer of Rude Awakenings." A bunch of things I thought I knew, I didn't know at all. For example, I had no idea my Aunt Bernie was a racist.

Let me start by saying that Aunt Bernie was a pain in the ass. Nobody really liked her. Not even her husband. Especially not her husband, Uncle Guido, who was a saint. Not even her parents—and my grandparents liked everybody. Not even my mom, her only sister. Tessie just barely tolerated Aunt Bernie and was much closer to my dad's sister, my Aunt Cookie (real name: Carmella). Aunt Bernie tended to make much ado out of nothing. She not only tortured Uncle Guido, who was a nice, gentle guy, but she also tortured her son, my cousin Gino, who was an only child.

It was no secret that Aunt Bernie, who wouldn't let Uncle Guido touch her cystic breasts (and who would want to anyway?), had a big, fat, sloppy crush on Tom Jones. She had all of the Welsh singer's records and blasted them when Uncle Guido was at work. I got used to hearing "It's Not Unusual" played at maximum volume. (Maybe Aunt Bernie was confused because that's what David Bowie advised on the cover of "The Rise and Fall of Ziggy

Stardust and the Spiders from Mars"—TO BE PLAYED AT MAXIMUM VOLUME—not Tom Jones.) Anyhow…

Everyone on Gelston Avenue got used to hearing "What's New Pussycat?" so loud it would shake the street signs. I mean, she played Tom Jones louder than John Rubio across the street played Led Zeppelin. And that was loud!

Aunt Bernie even had a picture of Tom Jones Scotch-taped to the air conditioner next to her bed so she could look at him as she drifted off to sleep each night. She even sang "She's a Lady" to me the first time I got my period. Yes, her crush was that bad.

Aunt Bernie was equally as crazy about Al Green the first time she heard him. Soon, "Let's Stay Together" and "How Can You Mend a Broken Heart?" were sharing the bill with "Delilah" and "The Green, Green Grass of Home." Aunt Bernie couldn't get enough of Al's silky-smooth voice. For two whole years, she carried a torch for him.

So, when I saw a picture of Al Green in *TV Guide*, I cut it out and gave it to Aunt Bernie to tape to her air conditioner next to Tom Jones. "Who's this?" she asked.

"That's Al Green," I told her. Her face dropped like I told her it was a picture of Jack the Ripper.

"You mean, he's colored?"

I thought everyone knew Al Green was black. Everybody but Aunt Bernie apparently. Al Green's voice, I mean, it was so soulful, it sounded black. (Wait…am I a racist for saying that?)

My aunt stood there staring at the grainy picture in her hand then looked at me in shock. She didn't know what to do or say. Which was odd for Aunt Bernie because she always had something to say about everything, even when she knew nothing about it. "Thank you," she finally stuttered, almost as an afterthought.

But Aunt Bernie never did tape the *TV Guide* picture of Al Green next to Tom Jones on her AC and I knew why. She was a stone-cold racist.

Things like this, Desi and I would have giggled about. I would have run around the corner to tell her and she would have eaten up my every word like a Pyrex cup of My*T*Fine butterscotch pudding. But the story lost something in the translation when I told the *Reader's Digest* version to Desi over the crackly telephone line. Every couple of days, we were allowed to talk to each other for five minutes, Desi at her grandmother's place upstate in Cairo and me in Bay Ridge. This was a poor substitute for a best friend.

The summer crawled by slowly on its hands and knees. A bunch of us would take the train out to Manhattan Beach. It was a long walk from the D line to the beach but it was much nicer than Coney Island or even Brighton Beach. (Read that as cleaner, much fewer hypodermic needles and less used condoms washed up on the shore.) Not so many boom boxes either, no gangs and Manhattan Beach wasn't as crowded as the other beaches. There were lots of families. But oddly enough, there were the same guys hawking "Fudgie-Wudgies" in their gravely, Methadonian voices.

That summer, I went to the beach so much, my nipples got scabby. (I know it's gross but I'm telling all here.) I'm not sure if the irritation was from the sand or from the salt water but I was scaly under my bikini top. After a few days and lots of Vaseline, it cleared up, but not before Laura tortured me about it.

I was shocked that Tessie actually broke down and got me a proper bikini to replace the flouncy two-piece bathing suit that had worn out to expose my butt when we were on vacation in Florida. This new bikini was adorable and skimpy, yellow with a halter neck and ties on the sides and in the middle of the bra top. Even though I was flat-chested, I must admit I still looked pretty good in it. Instead of having boobs, I was okay in the Behind Department. My olive skin tanned easy so while most of my friends looked like freckled lobsters, I was golden brown.

A few days before Desi got back from upstate, a handful of us girls decided to go to Manhattan Beach together. I had all my stuff—two towels (one to lay on and one to dry myself off on) and some snacks—in a big canvas bag. We took the RR to Dekalb, then went up the stairs and switched platforms for the D going in the opposite direction, toward Coney Island instead of toward Manhattan. (Despite what Linda Berger said, this was quicker than taking the B1 bus from Bay Ridge, which took forever.) From the Sheepshead station, we crossed the Emmons Avenue footbridge to Manhattan Beach.

Me and my friends set up camp at the south end of the beach near the jetty. Away from it all, the stay-at-home moms and their annoying, noisy kids didn't seem to go there. It was also far from the guitar-playing stoners who couldn't play or sing...and it didn't stop them from doing either.

That day, it was hot as hell out, at least 90, without a breeze. I wasn't in the mood for the peanut butter and jelly (and sand) sandwich Tessie had made for me and wrapped in tinfoil. She refused to give me money for the concession stand when there was "good food" at home. And she wouldn't make me anything but PB&J because she was afraid cold cuts would get "funny" in the heat. It was so hot that nobody else wanted to eat either, even though they had money for fries. We popped into the water as soon as we set up our stuff.

The surf was rough and kept knocking us down. We kept laughing and getting back up. Kind of like in life. When Paola Manducci shook the water out of her curly 'fro and onto us like a wet dog might do, we laughed even more. "You Gelston Avenue Girls look better wet than dry," someone said. It was a voice we all recognized. Charlie Yeltsin, who lived down Shitty Gelston, across the street from Erik, Derek and Peanuts.

Charlie seemed to be alone. "That's more than I can say for Gelston Avenue Guys," Paola said. She was broad in the shoulders and bigger than most boys our age. Nothing scared Paola. Especially not a pretty boy like Charlie Yeltsin, with his Norse god good looks and blue-green eyes the color of March's birthstone. But good-looking as he was, Charlie wasn't the brightest bulb in the box. He went to public school and from what Candy Olsen told me, was in the dumbest class. Charlie was *exactly* the kind of boy who didn't like me. "You're too smart and not pretty enough," Paul Siederman would tell me whenever I got hung up, yet again, on another blonde Adonis. (Paul wasn't trying to make me feel bad; he was just being honest.)

Charlie ignored Paola's snippy comment. "Where's Desi?" he asked. Boys were always asking about Desi. She was cute, petite and curvy. All the things I wasn't.

"Upstate," I told him. "At her grandmother's."

"Too bad," Charlie said. "I would have liked to see her in a bikini." I didn't tell Charlie that Raffi wouldn't let Desi wear a two-piece. But even a maillot was sexy on Desi the way she was developing. It showed off all her nooks and crannies. Plus, it was white. Even my cousin Danny, who was only 10, knew that white bathing suits became see-through when they got wet.

Paola gave Charlie a shove. He went down like a rock but came up laughing and sputtering sea water. And just like that, Charlie started hanging around with us. We played tag, tossed around a Frisbee, ranked each other out. I guess we were kind of obnoxious. All the other beachgoers kept their distance from us, which was fine. The few moms there probably told their little brats to stay away from us. I bet they thought we were on drugs, which we weren't.

I don't know how it happened but somehow Charlie Yeltsin ended up on my back in the water with his legs wrapped around my middle. He wasn't heavy; the ocean held him up. I kind of liked the way he felt: his damp skin against my damp skin. I liked the way he smelled: Coppertone and salt and sweat. Smelling him, feeling him, lulled me into a mellow place. I could have stood there forever, waist-high in the water, with handsome Charlie Yeltsin pressing into my back.

When his hands strayed to the flat of my belly...well, that felt even better. Charlie traced invisible circles onto my moist skin. He talked to me about silly stuff, about what he'd done that summer, which was pretty much nothing. Just hanging around the schoolyard, playing stoop ball, playing stick ball. The same old, same old. His breath felt nice on my neck, in my ear. It smelled like Original Trident.

When Charlie's fingers slipped underneath the water, I started to protest. In fact, I almost let go of his legs and sent him flying. "Shush," Charlie told me. So, I shushed and I enjoyed it. I probably...no, not probably, I was *definitely* a slut. But then again, I didn't care. That's how nice it felt.

Would Desi understand? I guess. But I decided right then and there, with Charlie Yeltsin's fingers tracing an invisible path down my belly, that I wasn't going to tell her. I wasn't going to tell anyone. Until now.

The water at Brooklyn beaches is murky and a grayish-green even on the best of days. When you swim under the surface, it's hard to see even a foot in front of you. Maybe it's because thousands of pairs of feet stir up the sand on the bottom. Maybe it's because the water's so polluted. But whatever the reason, I knew no one could see what was going on with me and Charlie under the water.

But just to be sure, I turned my back to the beach itself, turned my back to my friends, who were starting to leave the water and get lunch. I turned my back to the mothers and kids and fathers taking a day off and *abuelas* soaking their swollen feet in the shallows. The waves were breaking way out in the surf now and by the time one got to us, the water was only a ripple. The tide rocked me and Charlie, who was moving almost imperceptibly against my back.

I felt something poking into my spine. His thing? Maybe. Probably. Yes, definitely. Charlie's fingers ventured underneath the elastic of my bikini bottom. This time, I didn't try to throw him off my back. This time, I let him. Charlie toyed with my pubic hair but didn't go any further. For some reason, he didn't try to poke inside. I'm not sure what I would have done if he had tried. Now I understood what Annette Ryan felt when Andy Mangano did that to her in the corner of St. Fi's schoolyard. Now I know why she let him. Because it felt good. Because at that moment, that's all there was in the world and that's all that mattered.

Charlie was pressing harder against my back now. I held his legs tighter. His breathing changed, got quicker, sharper. I felt his body shudder, his voice in my ear gasping, sighing. Big, strong, mean Charlie Yeltsin had just come against my back. And I let him. (And between you and me, I would probably let him do it again.)

Charlie climbed off my back. His splooge was nowhere to be seen. It probably drifted away, became part of the Atlantic, just like fish splooge did. Became part of the circle of life. Turtle food. Algae food. A snack for the jellyfish.

"Well, I've got to get going," Charlie said, not even looking me in the eye. And away he went. Just like that. But I didn't feel bad. I felt good. Pretty, even. I let Charlie do what he did because I wanted him to. Because it felt nice. And I knew that night, when I got in the tub, I would lock the bathroom door, then turn on the bathtub faucet full force, scooch down underneath it and think of Charlie Yeltsin.

When I went back to our blanket nobody said anything to me. Paola was chowing down on a cheeseburger and fries with a side order of sand. Like me, Betty had a PB&J, though not with chunky PB, but crunchy sand. Judy had sandy olive loaf on Golden Circles Bread. (Laura and I loved Golden Circles Bread but Tessie refused to buy it. She said it cost twice as much as Wonder Bread even when it was on sale.) Nope, there were no comments about Charlie Yeltsin and I was glad.

The girls went in the water a couple more times after applying more baby oil. By three, we were tired, briny, hungry and cranky. And none of us had any money left besides our train tokens. We headed back home, this time taking the B1, which was there when we were ready to cross Oriental Boulevard, so we decided to go for it.

The four of us sat in the back of the bus, dozing, quiet, happy for the air conditioning which made the bus feel like an ice box. When it pulled close to West End Avenue, I saw Charlie Yeltsin walking toward the train station by himself, backpack slung over one shoulder. I didn't call out to him or bang on the window. I just let him go. None of my friends saw him and it was better that way. It took close to 90 minutes to get home but we didn't care. We'd be back in more than enough time for dinner.

On the kitchen table waiting for me was a postcard postmarked Cairo, New York. There was an old-timey picture on the front of the card of Main Street about a million years ago when it was unpaved. For Desi's sake, I hoped it didn't look like that now. On the other side of the postcard was Desi's teeny-tiny squished Catholic school handwriting filling up the back with so many words, it was probably illegal. She got more than her eight cents worth in postage for a postcard.

Desi's note was all about how she missed Brooklyn and me and Vito's slices and White Castle and Kentucky Fried Chicken and me. And how boring Cairo was. How the people up there pronounced it "Kay-ro" like the corn syrup instead of the way it was spelled, like the capital of Egypt. Even Grandma Raquel, who was born in Ponce, Puerto Rico, said "Kay-ro." Desi liked being outdoors all day, she wrote, and was getting a dark suntan. It would have been a lot better if I could be up there with her, she wrote. Only one more week, she said, and she'd be back.

Funny how different someone sounds in writing. Even though Desi was a good writer, it wasn't the same as her voice-voice. Kind of formal, uncomfortable. You don't get nuance in a postcard. Or the way someone's eyes sparkle when they're making a joke. Or the smile in their voice when they talk to you. Writing is different.

Another weird thing is that when someone is away you expect everything to be the same as when they left. You expect *them* to be the same. And it makes no sense. Because you're not the same, why should they be?

You think everything's in a kind of suspended animation when the truth is that entire worlds can shift. Desi could have had her own "Charlie Yeltsin" experience at Colgate Lake where she said *Abuelita* Raquel took them swimming sometimes.

I thought I might run into Raffi while the kids were away. But I didn't, not even once. Maybe she was celebrating being childless for a month. Maybe she was missing them. As much as Raffi complained about them and screamed at them, I knew she loved them. Was she still running around with Stefan? Did she hang out with Sylvia and Umbe? Did she go up to visit the kids some weekends? And if she did, did she borrow a car or take the bus?

All I know is that I was counting the days, the hours, the minutes, till Desi came back at the end of July. That would leave us more than a month to hang out together before school started after Labor Day. Five weeks to be exact.

Would we be different people? Or would it be like slipping back into a favorite pair of sneakers? Cozy. Comfortable. Safe. Familiar. I would soon find out.

COMFY SNEAKERS

I shouldn't have worried. Things were exactly the same as they always were with me and Desi. Being apart for a month didn't make any difference. I shouldn't have been such an insecure jerk.

On our last phone call before Desi came home, we made up that we'd meet on the steps in the PS 104 schoolyard at 10 in the morning of the day she got back. Desi predicted that Grandma Raquel would wake them up at the crack of dawn and drive down the thruway real early, before rush hour. Either at her usual snail's pace, white-knuckling the steering wheel. Or else driving crazy like Mr. Magoo.

Desi told me later that on the drive down, her *abuela* wouldn't let anyone in the car talk, even in a whisper. And that Grandma Raquel never changed lanes—she stayed in the right lane all the way. They made it home by nine because they left before six, eating breakfast in the car (raw strawberry frosted Pop-Tarts), stopping only once to get gas near Exit 15 and to pee.

Desi was waiting for me at the schoolyard steps. Though it was a half-block away, I saw her the second I left my house. One of Casa Piccolo's walls bordered the schoolyard. (It made my grandparents nuts when someone bounced a softball off the wall we shared with PS 104.) As soon as I stepped out the front door, I could see Desi through the chain-link fence, waiting expectantly.

The boys were already playing basketball in the little schoolyard, which was shady early in the day. I could hear the rhythmic bounce-bounce-bounce even though I couldn't see them. A group of older guys were playing stickball in the big yard. There were two games going on side by side, with chalk squares drawn on the brick wall behind the batter to indicate the strike zone. (This stopped all kinds of arguments about strikes and balls because if the pink Spaldeen bounced back with blue chalk marks on it, well, that was a strike.) I could hear the regular whack-whack-whack of the broom-handle stickball bat versus Hi-Bounce Pinky.

Desi stood up when she saw me coming toward the gate and I started jogging to meet her. We were both smiling so wide I thought our faces might crack. My eyes actually filled with tears, that's how happy I was to see her. We hugged each other and spun around in a circle. We kissed each other. On the cheek, not on the mouth. That would have been too lezzie. Especially in public. As it was, Willie Peanuts yelled, "Get a room!" at us, laughing. But me and Desi, we didn't care.

It was too early to get sliders at White Castle. Desi didn't know what she wanted to do first. We decided to get bagels at Mike's on 86th off the corner of Gelston. "I miss Brooklyn bagels," she confessed. "*Abuela* Raquel's frozen Lender's bagels just didn't cut it." We both got everything's—"for people who can't make up their minds about anything," Stefan liked to say. The bagels were still warm so the butter melted into the dough, making them perfect. We walked a couple of blocks to the Golf Links, which is what everyone in Bay Ridge called the Dyker Beach Golf Course. We sat on a stone-and-wood bench outside Dkyer to eat.

Even though Desi and I hadn't seen each other for more than a month, it was like slipping into a pair of comfy sneakers. We picked up right where we left off, like it had been 30 minutes instead of 30 days.

We talked fast, excited, words spilling over each other like waterfalls. She was sick of rice and beans because *Abuela* Raquel served them with every meal, even breakfast when she didn't break out the Lender's. And always black beans and white rice, refusing to make red beans and yellow rice to mix it up, explaining, "*Chica*, what do you think, I'm *Dominicana*?" (Like most Latinas, even grannies, Old Raquel thought her particular *isla* was the best.)

Whereas Desi was sick of Puerto Rican soul food, I missed rice and beans, any type of *arroz con frijoles*, because all Tessie made was macaroni. Besides real bagels, Desi missed Your Baker's Napoleons plus the Green Tea Room's grilled cheese and tomato sandwiches. And like she said in her postcard, she missed me.

Turns out there was a Charlie Yeltsin upstate for Desi. But she didn't go as far as I had. I almost told her all the gritty details about Charlie but for some reason, the words wouldn't come. Desi's "Charlie" was named Josh and he only got to second base, not third. Josh said he would call and write, but Desi figured he wouldn't. She didn't seem too bothered by it even though she wasn't going to meet any guys at an all-girl Catholic high school and most of the boys in our neighborhood were pretty lame.

To wash down our bagels, Desi and I shared a Manhattan Special (or *colita*, as her family called it—pure coffee espresso soda). I let her take the last slug. "I felt his vibe, even up there," Desi told me, putting the empty bottle with the dancing couple on the yellow label onto the bench between us.

"Him who?" I asked. "Joshie? Up where?"

Desi gave me a playful shove. "Him. My father. Big Matty. *Abuela* Raquel lives near where it happened."

It being Desi's father's "accident." Or murder, depending on how you looked at it.

"He was shot in the woods nearby," she went on, without me asking.

"I remember," I said. "You told me once."

"Sometimes I felt like he was watching us. Watching over us kids. Even watching over his crazy mother. Once I even felt the bed move in the corner near my feet, like someone sat down on it..."

A chill shot through my spine but it had to be 95 degrees outside. "Did it creep you out?" I asked.

Desi shook her head. "No. It just made me sad. Sad he wasn't there."

A poodle peed near the bench we were sitting on, narrowly missing my buffalo shoes. The owner didn't notice. Or care. "I didn't know they could travel," I told Desi.

"Spirits can go anywhere they want, I guess," she said.

"Do you believe in that stuff?"

"Cici, I felt it. I thought I saw him once, behind a tree, as the sun was going down. It was almost dark so I couldn't be sure. It could have been a shadow."

"But you were sure."

"Yeah."

"You feel him a lot. Like he's right around the corner."

"Yeah."

"How about now?"

"You do too, right? Or am I crazy?"

"You're not crazy," I told her. We finished our bagels. I wiped a tiny smear of butter from Desi's cheek with my pinkie. I licked off the butter. She laughed. Then cried. Then put her head on my shoulder. I let her. Cry, I mean. Sometimes you just need to cry, you know?

"I can't tell anybody else this," Desi sniffled. "Especially not Raffi."

"Did you ever try?"

She nodded. "It just makes her mad. And when I told Athena, she punched me. Hard. On the arm. And forget about Matty. He'd just cry. Worse than I am now."

We didn't say anything for a while. I thought about it. About what to say. "Maybe you just have to let it," I said finally.

Desi wiped her nose on the back of her hand. I gave her a thin bagel store napkin. She used it on her eyes, then her boogers. "Let it what?"

"Let it be. Let him be. Let him come to you. Maybe he needs to."

"What about what I need?" she asked. "It scares the shit out of me sometimes."

"Maybe it shouldn't."

Desi rolled her eyes. "Easy for you to say. You're not the one getting spooked."

"What if he didn't want to scare you? What if he just wanted to make you feel better? Less sad."

"Who says I'm sad?" Desi challenged. I just gave her a look, raising one eyebrow. "Okay, maybe a little," she admitted. Desi balled up our napkins and took a two-point shot at the overflowing Department of Sanitation garbage can. It went in. "Well, if my father wants to make me feel better, he has a strange way of showing it," she sighed.

I walked our Manhattan Special bottle to the trash can. (I wasn't as good a shot as Desi.) "He doesn't have much choice, does he? I mean, he's dead. His communication options are pretty limited. He can't just call you on the phone. Right?"

I thought Desi was going to strangle me the way she looked at me. In shock. In disbelief. Like she was thinking, 'I can't believe I'm stuck with an asshole like you as my best friend.' Then she started laughing. We both did. Until tears leaked out the sides of our eyes. A woman pushing a stroller with a sleeping toddler inside steered it away from us, like she thought we were wacko. But we didn't care. Her kid was funny-looking and so was she.

"It's like Mami's Jamaican friend Ethelyn always says, 'The ghost knows who to scare,'" I told her.

"And it's me," Desi snorted through her tears. "It's me."

"It could have been Athena. Or Matty."

"My brother would bug out. So would Athena. And Raffi…Raffi would just get pissed off and yell at Big Matty for leaving her 'with three brats.'"

I nudged Desi's shoulder with mine. "You're not brats. Well, not all of you." No smile, no nothing. "But Desiree can deal with it."

Desi wiped her eyes with her fist. "Don't you ever get tired?" she asked. "Of being the strong one? Of being the one everyone thinks can deal with everything? All the freaking time?"

I got up from the bench. "Yeah. But you can. And you do."

We started to walk alongside the golf links toward Poly Prep, down to what I would always think of as the pond where Salvatore Angarri died. It was one long stretch of manicured "park" and we didn't have to cross any streets until we got to Poly. The Dyker Beach Golf Course cut the neighborhood in two, separated Bay Ridge from Dyker Heights, in a way. And snobby Bay Ridgers like us all knew we lived in the better neighborhood. Dyker Heights was full of *cugettes* with poofy hair, dumb guys who hung around on street corners and overblown McMansions, some with heated sidewalks so the owners didn't have to shovel snow.

Of course, Bay Ridgers weren't really than better Dyker Heights people any more than Puerto Ricans were better than Dominicans. But it made us feel superior. When all was said and done, no one was better than anyone else. Especially not because of the place they lived.

Desi and I talked about this and that. Nothing important. Just easy stuff, not emotional stuff. Safe stuff: school coming up in a few weeks, movies we wanted to see…like *The Longest Yard*. (I'd gotten a peek of Burt Reynolds' hairy nude centerfold pic in Aunt Cookie's copy of *Cosmo* and had a crush on him ever since.) Then there was and *The Gambler*, which was supposed to come out around our birthdays. (We both agreed that James Caan was a cutie. We loved him even more since we learned that his mom went to the same beautician as my Aunt Adrienne did in Sunnyside, Queens. Because he signed a bunch of 8 x 10's without complaint for Aunt A's nieces, Jimmy Caan would have our undying devotion.)

Soon, the hulking orange brick frame of Victory Memorial Hospital came into view. The only good thing that happened at Victory Memorial was that my cousin John Jr. was born there. Otherwise, it was like a roach motel for my family because once you went in, you never came out…alive. Even my poor, sweet Uncle Frank (half of my uncles were named Frank) who hallucinated about seeing golfers in the snow of the Dyker Beach GC hours before he passed. God rest his soul. It was Uncle Frank's favorite place to golf with his brother, my uncle Joe, who seemed to always have a Guinea stinker cigar permanently wedged in his face.

I told this to Desi as we passed the hospital and she laughed. She seemed to love all of my crazy family sagas. Or maybe she was just being polite. But I don't think so. Once more, Desi told me, "You should write all of these stories down. They're hilarious."

"Who else but you would think so?" I shot back.

"Just try it, you'll see," she smiled. And sure enough, years later, when I wrote a fiction piece called "Saturday Night" about a typical Saturday night at Casa Piccolo, a magazine called *Buffalo Spree* bought it.

About some things, Desi was always right, but not that we would be forever friends. Life changes and sometimes people change along with it.

Desi and I crossed at 7th Avenue and walked down 92nd Street, toward home. High school would start in less than a month, beginning a whole new chapter in our lives. I should have been excited about this new chapter but the problem was, I really liked the old one.

TOO COOL FOR SCHOOL

When you're in grade school, the summers seem to drag by. July is forever and forget about August. As the summer comes to a close, you start to get slightly bored, even with day camp, family vacations, the playground sprinklers, open fire hydrants and the beach. You almost...*almost* look forward to starting school after Labor Day.

But when you're older, things start to fast-forward. You go from flat to boobs, from climbing trees to having periods. And you don't remember how it happened. You barely remember being five when you're ten. And when you're 13, ten is like someone else's daydream.

It seemed like only seconds after Desi got home from upstate that we were starting high school. Our respective high schools. I didn't remember what school was like without Desi being in it, and she had only been at Saint Fi's for a year. She not only felt like my best friend—she felt like my only friend. The only one who mattered.

When Tessie took me to Dee & Dee Discounts to get school supplies (only the best for me!), she said something about broadening my horizons, finding other friends. New friends. "I don't want other friends," I told her, looking at a Bobby Sherman homework folder, then deciding against it. I wasn't sure if he was adorable, too girly or so last year. "I have one friend," I said to my mother. "The best friend."

Then Tessie mumbled something about not putting all my eggs into one basket. "What if Desiree moves away?" she asked. "Her mother has no ties here, nothing holding her here." I thought of Mami, who still lived upstairs from them, but wasn't going to live forever. I thought about Aunt Cassie and how Uncle Orlando was always bugging her to bring Jacinta back to PR. I thought of the fights Raffi had with Stefan. I thought about how Umbe had Sylvie and didn't seem to need us anymore.

Suddenly, I didn't want to go to the Green Tea Room, where they put cheese on both halves of the bun when they made you a cheeseburger. It was supposed to be me and Tessie's "girls' afternoon out" without the always-annoying Laura in tow. My mom even dressed semi-normal—not in a duster but in elastic waistband jeans and a half-decent top. Tessie forced me to think about how things might change between Desi and me, about how they were already changing. I was pissed off at my mother for making me consider the inconsiderable: my life without Desi in it.

Shit, who was I kidding? My life was already changing. In a week, I would be going to high school without Desi. I would be having all of these big and small experiences without her. And Desi would be going through the same huge and inconsequential changes without me.

Instead of my usual cheeseburger, I got the Green Tea Room's grilled cheese and tomato. (Which was Desi's favorite.) What can I say? Gooey cheese makes me feel better. Tessie tried her best to get me to talk. She even suggested we get a chocolate shake to share. But I wasn't having it. I was too sad for even chocolate. And mad at my mom for making me face the reality of what might happen to Desi's and my friendship in the next few months.

On Labor Day, we had a barbecue in the family's concrete backyard. As I chewed a dried-out hockey puck of a burger, I looked around: hurricane fence locking us in on two sides, the third bordering the schoolyard and the fourth J.R. Stock's parking lot. We had raised pebbled concrete flower beds, the obligatory weathered fig tree in our Italian-American garden, surrounded by flimsy tomato, zucchini and basil plants which were also a "given" for Brooklyn Guineas like us. I looked at everyone surrounding me:

brown-skinned even without suntans, shadows of mustaches (even on the women), round, loud. My people?

Although my London shag was blue-black in color like their hair (except for my grandmother's which was Miss Clairol's Old Lady Blue), I was skinny, angular and stringbeany. My skin was slightly darker than theirs from playing punch ball, riding my bike and walking in the sun. But were they really my people? I might look like them but I didn't feel like them. I had more in common with a girl whose family came from a vaguely football-shaped island in the Caribbean than this cast of characters who trace themselves back to the tip of the toe of Italy's boot. Did that make any sense? Yeah, it made perfect sense. At least to me. I felt like I was stuck between two worlds.

I kept looking down the alleyway to see if Desi was coming. She was at a barbecue at her Cousin Roberto's place in Queens. (I knew Desi would see Junior and that he'd ask about me.) But Raffi and the kids usually left early, before everyone got too drunk on *cervezas* and a fight broke out. And a neighbor called the cops. Desi said she'd come by my barbecue afterwards if she could, and I knew she would.

The folding table was covered with food but I didn't have much of an appetite. Even for Grandma Lou's potato salad, which had a touch of garlic like every dish she made—except desserts. Aunt Bernie was all "blood of Jesus" about anything anyone said—she was a born-again Christian, Pentecostal, much to the embarrassment of my super-Catholic grandparents. I wondered how long it would take for my father to get fed up with Aunt Bernie and storm off, an unfiltered Chesterfield dangling from his lips. We probably wouldn't see Phil until my grandma brought out the Sealtest, a Manhattan or two later. My dad having a Manhattan (or three) was as predictable as a fight breaking out at Mimi and Roberto's in Corona.

For some reason, the builder of our two-story, unattached, four-family brick house didn't see the need for a garage. Instead, there was a wide, shared alley big enough for a car and with a backyard for each homeowner on either side of the alleyway. Mr. Dietrich's backyard was grassy—with German precision, he mowed it twice a week with a push mower. Ours, as I said, was covered with concrete, except for the U-shaped raised beds crammed with sad fruits and vegetables that struggled to suck up the city sunlight. I have to admit that the tomatoes were pretty good but I didn't care much for the scrawny green peppers which gave me *agida*.

After peering down the alley for what seemed like the hundredth time, Desi finally appeared. Before I could talk to her, there was a machine gun-like barrage of questions from the Piccolo, Narducci and Del Vecchio women. The men couldn't care less because they were struggling to hear Phil Rizzuto and Bill White announce the Yankees game over the crackly AM transistor radio.

"How was your summer?"

"Are you really going to Fontaine?"

"How's your mother/brother/sister?"

These were a few of the queries they shot out at Desi. She answered them politely and slowly, each in turn, with a big smile. My family loved Desi because she was so well-mannered. I found them annoying and couldn't wait till the Spanish Inquisition was over.

"Your family's so nice," Desi grinned when we were in the alley, slapping a Spaldeen against Mr. Dietrich's wall, hitting it back and forth to each other with our open palms. (It was a game Desi and I invented, kind of like table tennis but without a table…or paddles. Not competitive like slap ball but kind of gentle, feeding the ball to each other instead of trying to make the other one miss.) Somehow, this made talking easier…it was something to keep our bodies occupied while we had a heart-to-heart. Normally, Mr. Dietrich would get pissed off and yell about the thumping against his wall but that afternoon, he was in the backyard with us, eating bad barbecue.

"My family? They're all right," I shrugged. "But they ask too many questions."

"It's just because they care," Desi pointed out.

"They're nosy," I said. "*Ficcanasi*. Busy bodies."

"*Ficcanasi*…I like that," Desi smiled.

"It literally means 'fig-nosed,'" I told her, then…"Are you ready for high school?"

She shook her head. "I mean, I have the uniform and all that stuff but I'm not ready. I won't know a soul at Fontaine."

"Isn't LoriAnn Mancuso going?"

"Loose LoriAnn?" Desi grimaced. "That's like knowing nobody." We laughed because it was. "I'm kind of scared," Desi admitted.

"Don't be," I told her. "You'll make friends."

"That's what I'm scared of."

My dad appeared, flicking his Zippo, sensing that dessert was coming out. The women brought platters out through my grandparents' bedroom where the house's back door was. Watermelon, a Sealtest ice cream carton (Neapolitan, of course, with stripes of vanilla, chocolate and strawberry, except nobody liked the strawberry, nobody but Aunt Bernie) and an Entenmann's blackout cake. (It was too hot to bake, the women apologized, too hot to even walk up to Ebinger's for their blackout cake, which was far superior.) And red Jello. For some reason, there was always red Jello.

Grandma Lou manned the ice cream scoop with the trigger lever, moving quickly before the Sealtest melted all over the plastic tablecloth. Desi said she was too stuffed to have anything but Grandma Lou insisted. No one ever left her table, even her outdoor table, without eating. "There's always room for Jello," Grandma Lou said, just like in the TV commercial. "Force yourself," she added gently. My grandmother said this so sincerely that it usually got the person to force themselves. Which is why most of the family was so grossly overweight.

So, Desi forced herself.

Uncle John had saved a few 4th of July fireworks for Labor Day. He even let us kids set them off with the light of a punk which glowed red in the darkening night. I hated the ashcans: too loud. Some people called them M-80s and they were supposedly made with a quarter stick of dynamite. But my cousin Gino loved ashcans. (It was no wonder he would grow up to be a cop. He loved guns and all things explosive, even as a kid.) Uncle John knew his nieces' preferences so he saved the pretty ones—the Roman Candles, the fountains—for me, Desi and Laura. I loved that my uncle refused to buy the screaming ones—which the street kids called "n*gger chasers." I hated them because of their racist name. But n*gger chasers pretty much chased anyone regardless of color or creed.

We set off the fireworks in PS 104's schoolyard next to my house because of the wide-open space. So, there was no danger of a bottle rocket going under Carmine Rubio's car and setting it on fire, which almost happened one year. (Desi loved hearing that story.) This way, the old folks could watch from the backyard, oohing and ahhing appropriately and still be safely out of striking range.

Uncle John kept the lone M-80 until last because Josephine, the Rubios' wacky upstairs tenant, invariably called the cops. The French lady said it reminded her too much of the German invasion of her little town during the Second World War…and the baby girl she lost…and being locked up in that convent. Besides, M-80s scared her shabby white poodle Sammy so much, it made him puke. And her drink. So, no ashcans till the very end.

After the fireworks, it was too dark to play stoop ball so Desi and I sat on two of the four big concrete slabs on either side of the front steps. Stoop ball was another way we could talk about things that weren't so easy to talk about face-to-face. But the shelter of the Brooklyn night would have to do. The streetlight in front of Dale's house across the street winked on and off. Out of the blue, Desi said, "Raffi's sending Matty to a psychiatrist."

"Why? He's not crazy."

"No," Desi admitted. "But he cries a lot. About my dad. Says he sees him, hears him. All the time."

"Well, we do, too," I reminded her.

"But I don't tell my mom. It bugs her out."

"So, being crazy or not being crazy has a lot to do with what you say and or don't say to other people, not what you believe," I said.

"Right." Desi grabbed a firefly in her fist. She opened her hand, watched it, then let it go.

"You and me, we know not to talk about Big Matty to anyone else." Desi smiled. "Now you're getting PR logic. It's okay just so long as you don't talk about it."

"Sounds more like Pretzel Logic."

"That's a good album," Desi said. "Steely Dan."

"Stop trying to change the subject," I told her.

"'Rikki Don't Lose that Number,' 'Any Major Dude…'"

"Steely Dan…I think the band was named after a dildo," I threw in. "The one from *Naked Lunch*. You know, William S. Burroughs."

"What's a dildo?"

"Never mind," I sighed. "Hey, why'd you bring up the psych if you didn't want to talk about it?"

"I thought it might help," she said, looking up at the faded stars.

"Did it?"

"Not really. Raffi wants us all to go, too. As a family."

"Oh, boy…"

"Right?"

"I hope he's ready for PRH. The psych."

"She. He's a she. And she sounds really nice. Her name is Jackie. A pretty blonde lady. Matty says that Miss Jackie does all sorts of cool things with him. Like she colors with him while they talk. Or sometimes they even go out for Baskin-Robbins."

"I can just see Matty crying into his Pink Bubblegum cone."

"That's just it. My brother says he hardly cries with her. That Jackie makes him feel better. The Baskin-Robbins makes it easier to talk."

"But you don't want to talk about it," I teased.

"Yeah."

"When are you going?"

"Tomorrow," Desi sighed. A mosquito buzzed in her face. She caught it as quick as Master Po in *Kung Fu*. "Snatch the pebble from my hand, Grasshopper…" I told her, mimicking Kwai Chang Caine's teacher on the show. Desi gave me a small smile, getting the reference. Then I got braver, "What are you afraid of?" I wondered.

Desi shook her head then spoke. "That I'll lose him. That I'll lose my father. The memories. That I'll forget the way he smelled: like cigars and Old Spice. That I'll forget the sound of his voice, all gravel and roses."

"Maybe you should be the poet," I smiled. "No one can take that stuff from you. Ever. Unless you want it gone."

"I don't," Desi said.

I could see Athena and Little Matty down near where Gelston Avenue met 92nd Street. They had just turned the corner. I bet Raffi had sent them to get Desi, who'd missed her curfew to go home when the streetlights came on. "Look," I told Desi quickly. "Just tell this Jackie person what you want her to know. Save something for you, keep some secret for yourself. Then you should be alright."

"So, that's the trick, to have a secret?" Desi wondered. "Do you have secrets from me?"

Luckily, Desi's brother and sister were already upon us. Athena was all sweaty from winning her race down the block against her little brother. Even if she gave Matty a big lead, he always lost. He ran with his arms and legs akimbo, his body flying out in all sorts of bizarre directions. Hadn't anyone taught him how to run? Was that the sort of thing a father taught a kid or was it something you just knew? How not to run like a girl when you're a guy?

Before they went home, I convinced the kids to come in the backyard for some dessert. Raffi would understand because it was the day before the day before school started. "There's always room for Jello," I told them.

And they laughed.

THE WALK

The first day of high school, Desi was waiting for me at the corner. She wore a gray skirt, white shirt, navy blue sweater with FHA above the left-hand pocket, sensible, flat black shoes and gray knee socks. It was a more grown-up uniform than St. Fiacre's but still baggy. Those Sisters of St. Joseph sure didn't want girls to look like girls, even in an all-girls school.

Meanwhile, I was wearing the new carpenter jeans Tessie let me get from Alvy's, a red shirt and my trusty Olaf Daughters clogs. I was letting my hair grow while Desi still kept hers short. When mine was in that awkward stage, it got all wiry, like an unkempt houseplant. I admit, it was in that yucky "in between" messiness, yet Desi didn't point it out to me. "I like it," she told me, taking a thick wisp in her hand.

I ran my fingers along the collar of her FHA sweater. "Fontaine Hall Academy...as though 'Fontaine Hall' isn't stuck up enough?" I said. "They had to add Academy?"

"Yeah, I know. Right?" Desi laughed. "I hate it. I look like a refugee from one of those *Madeline* books."

"'And Madeline cried...'" I began.

"…boo-hoo," we finished together. When Desi and I first met, we were surprised to learn that we'd both read—and loved—that silly *Madeline* series as little girls. Now we weren't little girls anymore…we were going to high school.

"Speaking of crying, how was therapy yesterday?" I guess I could have said it better. The words just sort of shot out of my mouth. Desi winced and didn't answer right away. Why was I being so snippy with her? Was I trying to hurt her? That was crazy because Desi was my best friend. But at that moment, I couldn't stand her. I hated her penny loafers without any pennies in them. (There's a reason they're called "penny loafers!") I hated her gray knee socks. I hated her ridiculous uniform. Why was I so mad at her? Maybe because I knew it was all going to change soon. Like, that morning.

But my displaced anger was probably because I was also scared. High school was a big deal. The next step in growing up. And here I was, going to the morning session at Fort Adams High School with 2,000 other kids. I didn't know any of them. Well, all except for Brenda Corbo, who ate her crusty boogers when she thought no one was looking. I mean, who could be friends with someone like that? Maybe someone like Joey Santino but not me.

Desi didn't pick up on my bitchiness. Or if she did pick up on it, she overlooked it. (Desi was such a good person and I didn't really deserve her as a friend.) I bet she was just as nervous as I was to start off at a new school. For Desi, it would be her second time doing this in as many years. "It was all right," she said, finally answering my last question. "Miss Jackie is cool. We'll probably be seeing her for a while. At least Matty will be."

"He's pretty messed up, isn't he?" I pressed. There it was again, me being a creep. Like a dog biting when she's scared.

"We all are," Desi said softly.

Her classes started earlier than mine so I had time to spare. I walked Desi the whole way to Fontaine that first day. We went along 5th Avenue, between White Castle and Kentucky Fried Chicken (where it was rumored that the employees spat in the batter), past the firehouse and Grand Union, past Charlie Yeltsin's apartment building, past St. Fi's, where 4th and 5th Avenues merged into one, and past Dr. Henry Amen's office. We made a right at the 101st Street softball fields where only boys could play on Little League teams. Then we turned down 3rd Avenue where it made a bee-line to Shore Road.

The houses were big and swanky down there with gates, electrified fences and views of the Narrows. They were houses our families couldn't afford, houses no one we knew could afford.

Desi and I paused at the corner and turned back to look at the Verrazano which yawned across the Narrows Strait to Staten Island. It was a grand bridge, elegant with its light blue paint, stretching like a seductive lady in a long, trailing gown. I knew this bridge always made Desi think of her dad, of the work he did on it, of her name scrawled into the once-wet cement on the day she was born, which was five days before the day I was born. "We're going to be all right," Desi said.

"Yes," I told her. Even though I wasn't sure who "we" was. Her family? She and I? But we were all okay. Everything usually worked out, didn't it? Except when it didn't.

The sight of Fontaine Hall Academy holding court on Shore Road almost took our breath away. I think Desi even gasped out loud but then tried to cover it up with a cough. It was a white stucco-ish network of buildings with red terra cotta roof tiles enclosed by a black wrought iron fence, FHA looked completely out of place in Brooklyn. It might have looked more at home in Florida or California but not here.

Desi stood still, like she was paralyzed. "I can't go in there," she said.

Girls were already filing in the wide double doors. Every one of them was taller than Desi. They all had lighter hair, fairer-skin, even the ones we knew were Italian-American princesses and *cugettes*. "Sure, you can," I told her. But deep down, I didn't know how she could either.

"Cici, I don't belong here," Desi said.

"Who does?" I joked. But I could tell Desi was going to cry, not laugh. "You're gonna do great," I told her. "I can't wait to hear all about it afterwards." Desi bit her lower lip. Her nostrils quivered. "Besides, your scholarship already paid the tuition. Raffi'll freak if you don't go." When Desi looked at me this time, nothing was quivering. She was smiling, at least a little bit. "All that PRH. It won't be pretty."

"Yeah," Desi sighed. "I guess you're right."

"I'm always right," I told her.

"I'll meet you here after school," Desi said.

"Okay," I told her.

Desi turned and left. I watched her go. She smiled at an older girl and they started talking. I couldn't hear what they were saying but they were both grinning. I don't know why but my eyes filled with tears. Desi and the girl disappeared inside the blue set of double doors which were almost the same color as the Bridge.

I turned and headed to the Fort.

THE FORT

Fort Adams High School really *did* look like a fort. I was the second generation from my family who went there. The Del Vecchios: my mom, her sister Bernie and brother John went to FAHS, too. I remember Tessie telling me that when they built the Fort back in 1941, they had to choose between putting in a swimming pool or putting up a clock tower. The jerks went for the clock tower. Wrong choice. But at least you know what time it is when you zip by the school on the Belt Parkway, right? Big whoop.

Nobody went in through the school's front entrance, which was pretty much just for show. It had a zillion steps and a bunch of columns. I must admit, it looked pretty impressive. Foreboding even. (But not as menacing as Fontaine.) I was glad they made us use the back doors near the ball fields because they were less imposing.

My first day at the Fort, kids streamed past me like they knew exactly where they were going. I just stood there, gawking. I felt lost. I probably looked lost, too, like one of those yokel tourists who stare up at the skyscrapers in the City, their mouths wide open like they're catching flies.

"It's not so bad," a sweet voice with a slight lisp said to me. I turned around to see a short, solid girl with a curly crown of chestnut hair. My Guinea radar went off and I guessed that she was Italian American like me. The girl introduced herself as Amy (Anna Maria but everyone called her "Amy.") "Come on, let's go inside," Amy said. We did, moving past kids who towered over us and looked mean, older. But I wasn't so scared anymore with Amy by my side.

Turns out Amy and I were in the same homeroom, 1E18. That's what our yellow slips of paper said. There were at least 18 homerooms (hence the number of mine) with 30 plus kids in each of them. And that was just the morning session! But it sure seemed like more than 500 students were dodging past us, rushing to get to homeroom before the bell. It was a big change from St. Fi's which had only three classes in each grade. I had a feeling there would be a lot of changes for me at the Fort—and there were.

Like me, Amy came from a Catholic school. St. John's down in South Brooklyn. It was a few doors away from the row house she lived in so Amy didn't even have to cross the street to get to her grammar school. Though she and her friends were zoned for John Jay, which was a rough high school in their neighborhood, they got into the Fort on what was called a "Latin Variance." Amy's father wrote a letter to the principal, Herman Sherman (his real name!) explaining that Amy and her pals wanted to be doctors so they just *had* to take Latin. It was even funnier when I met Debbie and Donna later. The three of them were so *not* doctor material. Whatever doctor material was.

I soon learned that half of the Fort's basketball team was there on "Latin Variances." Guys like Tony Fickley, who I could tell was a real ladies' man with his crooked million-dollar smile, his short 'fro and perfect, honey-colored skin. Then there was a guy named Albert who was at least a foot taller than me and real shy. Albert reminded me of a giraffe in an elevator—he tried to make himself smaller, tried to make himself disappear but that was impossible because he was so noticeable. Amy told me that he was a fantastic basketball player. Al was a small forward, shooting guard (whatever that was) and had an older brother named Bernard who the Nets were supposedly interested in.

Then there were the girls who all seemed prettier and smarter than me. I wanted to crawl into a desk drawer and disappear. These girls *waxed* their eyebrows instead of just tweezing them. They were allowed to wear makeup and actually knew how to apply it correctly. Some even dyed their hair a shade of blonde that doesn't exist in nature when they were Italians named Ninfa. I bet "the curtains didn't match the rug," as Michael Pollock might say.

There was one girl who wasn't like any of the others. Her name was Jean and word was that she was a pool shark and even at 14, was better than grown men in the sport. Even better than pocket billiards champ Willie Mosconi. Jean had been on the TV show *I've Got a Secret* when she was six. When Tony Fickley asked Jean if it was true, she smiled, blushed and said, "Yeah, I guess."

My first impulse, sitting in that chipped, uncomfortable wooden desk, was to put down my head and cry like a kindergartener. Which, in high school-speak, I was. But unlike a kindergarten kid, I didn't want my mommy. I wanted my best friend. I wanted my Desi. But she wasn't there.

When I looked to my right, there was Amy. To my left was Crystal. Behind me was Rene and behind her was Ginny. They would have to do. For now. For the next four years.

Amy smiled at me. I smiled back. It was going to be all right. Maybe.

The chatter stopped when our homeroom teacher walked in. He seemed like an okay guy. Not old and crusty like a lot of the other teachers I passed in the hallway. Maybe a little younger than my dad. He even looked kind of like my dad. Maybe that was a good sign. Maybe it wasn't.

The teacher had a beard and mustache, longish, brown hair (which curled past his open collar) and kind, blue eyes. He had an easy smile yet somehow you knew he wasn't a pushover. The teacher introduced himself to us as Clifford Helm. He said that he taught Sociology and Psychology besides being 1E18's homeroom teacher.

Mr. Helm wrote his name on the blackboard then passed out these buff-colored attendance cards. We had to write our names at the top in a space that was barely big enough to write your initials in. Right off the bat, I wrote in Cici, not Celeste or Celestine. I didn't care whether or not it was my legal name. I wanted to start off in a different school as a different person. Or the same, old person, only better.

When Mr. Helm checked our cards against his Mimeographed attendance list, he nodded knowingly, "Cici it is," he told me and smiled. Maybe, just maybe it was going to be all right after all.

Fort Adams was so crowded that we didn't even get a lunch break. There wasn't enough space for all of us in the cafeteria even if they split us up into different periods. Supposedly, more than 1,800, and that was just the freshmen and sophomores. The juniors and seniors went to class during what they called the late session. Tessie packed me a bag of Funyuns but I was too nervous to eat. Or maybe I was more excited and not nervous. But whatever I was, I wasn't hungry.

The first day was a run through of a regular day at the Fort. We went to our classes, bolting to the next one at the sound of the bell, trying to figure out what was where. The school was only three stories high (not counting the basement where the gym was) but it was huge and shaped like an H. The short part of the H was a long hallway which connected the other two hallways together. If you were at the wrong leg of the long end, you had to run like hell down the connector, past the terrible reproduction of Picasso's "Three Musicians," to get there. (Yep, I knew what the painting was thanks to Umbe and Sylvia taking me and Desi to MoMA in late August.)

Amy was in a couple of my classes—English and Algebra—so we stumbled around together the first two periods. I also met this really cool girl named Sue, who was a twin and a PK (Pastor's Kid), though she hated being referred to as either. Sue just wanted people to get to know her and hopefully like her for who she was, not make judgements before they did either.

In Social Studies, I got to meet Sarah, Sue's identical twin sister. Most people couldn't tell them apart but I could. Sarah was bigger boned, while Sue's face was slimmer, her voice slightly deeper. I liked them both for different reasons. I thought Desi would too. And this got me to thinking—who was Desi meeting that I might like? Or hate? Or be jealous of?

Along with Psych and Socio Mr. Helm was teaching freshman Social Studies that year. Word on the street was the old Social Studies teacher had thrown a chair through the window at the end of last semester and he still hadn't recovered from his nervous breakdown. I had a feeling Mr. Helm wouldn't do something like that. Throw a chair, I mean. He seemed like a good teacher. And a good person. I couldn't picture him throwing a chair or even throwing a fit. He remembered my name from homeroom and didn't even try to call me "Celeste" once.

After last period, everyone drifted into clumps outside the Fort near the running track. There were the Cool Kids, the Bookworms, the Jocks, the Sluts, the Stoners and everything else between. I didn't think I fit into any of those categories except maybe...

Then Amy called my name and called me over to where she was hanging out. She introduced me to Debbie and Donna, the other Latin Variance girls she knew. Most people went to the busses but the four of us walked up the hill toward 4th Avenue. Everyone except the Stoners. The Stoners went across the street. To smoke a joint on one of the stone benches that lined Shore Road.

It was too nice a day not to walk, even though I'd gotten my student bus pass in homeroom. Donna said that the B16 was always crowded, so crowded you didn't even have to hold onto the poles to stay standing when it moved. Besides, the girls said there was always some creep trying to feel you up on the bus and everyone was so crushed together you couldn't tell who the pervert was.

As we walked up 86th, I shared my Funyuns with my new friends. We had a smorgasbord of crap: Hostess Donettes, Fritos and Chocolate Babies, a symphony of sweet and salty that somehow worked. Kind of like all of us. The RR station at the corner of 4th Avenue came into view. I was feeling pretty happy. It had been a good day, despite all the dread. Then my stomach filled with ice. I had forgotten to meet Desi!

I handed Amy what was left of my Funyuns and ran toward Fontaine. It was three avenues down and more than a dozen streets over. I was a wet rag when I saw Desi standing near the fence, alone. "You forgot all about me!" she said.

"No," I told her. "I didn't. How could I forget you? We got out a little late." In all honesty, I really *had* forgotten Desi. It was the first time I had ever forgotten her. Or lied to her. But not the last.

THE GREAT DIVIDE

Looking back even a few years, the dates and the faces during my high school days jumble together. What year was the United Federation of Teachers strike? When was Mr. Stevens thrown out of Fort Adams for smoking pot with his students? When did the best art teacher ever, Eugene Greenman, die? (He just didn't come back to school one Monday, had a heart attack over the weekend. Mr. G was the coolest…the winter the Board of Ed was trying to cut back on heating costs and kept the classrooms frigid, Mr. Greenman brought in a hot plate, set it up in an unused coat closet and made us hot chocolate while we drew and painted.) When did I become best friends with Sue and Sarah? When did Mr. Fonti take us to see *The Threepenny Opera* with Raul Julia starring in it? (Raul was so dreamy, all the girls swore he was staring straight into our souls when he sang "Mack the Knife." It didn't matter that Mack was a serial killer.)

And when did Desi and I start drifting apart? When did we stop walking to and from school together?

Oh, we still saw each other and hung out occasionally. But it got less and less the more time passed. How could it not? We didn't get the same homework assignments. We didn't read the same books. We didn't go on the same field trips. We didn't have the same life experiences or go to the same dances. Yes, we were growing up but we were also growing away from each other.

Sure, it bothered me, but in a way, I just stood by and let it happen, watched it happen. I guess I was so caught up in the moment, in living my life, that sometimes I felt like a spectator, like I had no say in it. Some days, it was like I was just watching the days pass in wonder.

It got better when Desi and I were off long stretches for holidays. Though public school and private school vacations weren't in perfect sync, they always had an overlap. Whenever Desi and I reconnected, there was an awkward phase the first few minutes or so—there was so much to say that we didn't know where to start. There were uncomfortable silences. Uneasy glances. But then we fell back into step.

Some things never changed but other things changed drastically. Raffi was no longer working part-time at Mary's Dress Shop. "She makes more money tending bar at the Cordial," Desi told me when I ran into her one day. Also on the plus side: Rocky, the owner, let Raffi pick her shifts and Hygiene, the other bartender, wasn't a creep.

The Cordial was a nice, neighborhood place. So nice that Larry, our mailman, brought his tinfoil-wrapped sandwich from home every day and ate it right there at the bar. Hygiene slid a ginger ale in front of Larry every afternoon, free of charge. The whole neighborhood knew Larry was eating there because he left his mail cart parked outside. That is, until someone complained that Larry was getting wasted in the middle of the afternoon, on the government's dime no less. (We figured it was cranky Mrs. Penner because Larry didn't buy his lunch from her.) From then on, Larry took his mail cart inside the Cordial when he ate his brown-bagged midday meal.

This was one of the many fun bar stories Raffi told us after her shift. "You should write a book," I told Raffi laughing.

"I'll leave that to you," she said with a wink.

"Maybe I will," I challenged.

"You better not write anything about me," Athena snapped.

"There's nothing to write," I told her. To which Athena huffed through her nose like the stubborn bull she was.

Since the Cordial was right on the corner, Raffi felt it was okay to leave the kids alone. She thought Desi was old enough to look after them. (She was.) Even though Athena could be a real witch with her "You're not my mother!" comments and pinching Matty so hard he bruised. And cried. Though it wasn't tough to make Matty cry, even at 12 or 13.

"Sounds like your sister keeps getting meaner," I said, spooning up the last of my chocolate ice cream from the glass boat. Desi and I were talking over banana splits at Woolworth's, just like the old days. We were celebrating our October birthdays in November. That year, we were so busy it was the first chance we'd had to get together.

"I didn't think that was possible, but yeah," Desi admitted. "Just before her period comes Athena is the worst."

"I remember when we used to get our periods together," I told Desi wistfully. This menstrual synchronization stopped when we started going to different high schools.

"Those were the days," Desi said, scratching away at the mound of maple walnut ice cream in her dish. It had surpassed chocolate as her favorite flavor and she saved it for last when she had a three-scoop banana split. While I always gobbled up the best one—chocolate—first. "I can never see that happening with Athena," Desi added. "Getting our 'friends' together. Even though we share the same room." Then after a thoughtful beat, she added, "I can't see it happening with anyone else either."

"Me neither," I said quick, without even thinking. Did Desi mean it? I wasn't sure it was true anymore.

Weeks, months, passed. I'm a little foggy about it now. Desi and I went from talking on the phone a few times a day to a few times a week. Then less than that. At some point, our school schedules changed and it no longer worked to go to and from school together.

A lot of "Desi-less" things happened that I couldn't believe. Like having my first drink without her. Doing my first drag on a Marlboro Light without her. Taking my first toke of pot without her—though Desi was such a good girl, I doubt she would have done this, even *with* me. (Besides, where would we have gotten the joint?) Was I turning into a bad girl? Turning? I think I already was one.

At my Uncle Frank's retirement party, the band's drummer kept checking me out as he played. He was cute in a rugged, broken, rough kind of way. Oliver Reed vs. Mark Lester. Jack Wild vs. Donny Osmond.

Normally, I would have told Desi about meeting Zach, the drummer, the second I got home from my uncle's party. No matter how late it was, I would have snuck the phone into the pantry and called Desi after my parents went to sleep. I knew Raffi usually worked at the Cordial on Friday nights so Desi wouldn't have gotten in trouble.

But for some reason, I didn't tell her about Zach. Just like I didn't tell her about Charlie Yeltsin during the summer.

As much as it hurt to admit it, Desi and I were going our separate ways. How could we not? Our life experiences were different. I couldn't imagine her reading "Hills Like White Elephants" at Fontaine. (Spoiler Alert: It's about an abortion!) But that story changed my life. It made me think that maybe I could write great short stories too, not just poetry. (Not that there's anything wrong with just writing poetry.) And maybe even more than short stories someday. Maybe even a novel.

I couldn't share my discovery of Hemingway with Desi. Well, I could, but she probably wouldn't get what I was talking about.

But I could—and did—talk about stuff like this with Amy and with Sarah. Because they were in Mr. Fonti's American Lit class with me. Desi wasn't. She was more than 10 blocks away behind the thick adobe walls of a strict all-girls Catholic school.

And that time in English Lit, when Ms. Folwell had us do a scene from *Julius Caesar* and filmed it in an empty science lab... Even though I tried to explain it to Desi, she couldn't understand how funny it was when Sarah played Caesar's dead, stabbed corpse and kept laughing under the bedsheet we used as a shroud. The story lost something in translation. Or maybe it was the way I told it. Maybe I had no business wanting to be a writer after all. Or maybe I did.

I think it was sophomore year when we had to do an oral report with a classmate in Ms. Ruckert's Home Ec class. Sarah picked me, and together, we picked embroidery, something we were always doing to our jeans and jackets, anything we could get our hands on. (I don't think Desi even knew how to sew. As for me, it was in my blood.)

Since Sarah loved all things Elton John (just like I did!), it was a no-brainer to use Elton's album "Madman Across the Water" in our presentation. Why? Because it had an embroidered front and back cover. Which would demonstrate just how cutting-edge embroidery could be. Sarah and I even brought in some of the stuff we'd embroidered ourselves: jeans, shirts, handkerchiefs. Ms. Ruckert gave both of us an A.

At some point, I realized that I was spending more and more time with Sarah and less and less time with Desi. The first time I admitted this to myself, I felt a cold chill in my chest. Then I just shrugged it off. It was what it was, I tried to convince myself. But what exactly was it?

Sarah and Sue's folks were so hassle-free. Even though her dad was a pastor, he didn't act like one, all stuffy and religious. But they did say Grace at dinner, which I kind of liked. Saying Grace with the Gilberts always involved thanking me for being there, which made me feel happy and embarrassed at the same time.

Supper at the Gilbert House was always so relaxed. Not nearly as dramatic as the Ruiz House with all of that PRH going on. Mrs. G, who insisted I call her "Barb," was so laid back. (Sometimes she calls/called me "Third Daughter," which I love to this very day.) To make extra money for the family, Barb temped at law offices in the City. When she came home at six, she could whip up a hearty chicken soup and orange muffins from scratch in less than an hour. At the Piccolo House, that would just be the appetizer. Plus, it would take all day and lots of fuss to make.

I was also close with Sarah's sister Sue, who I'd met first. For two people who looked almost exactly alike, the Gilbert Twins were very different personality-wise. I learned to like them for who they were, not who they weren't. I could always tell which one was which. (And for the record, twins hate when you ask them, "Which one are you?") Together, we'd have flea markets to raise money to support Cesar Chavez, the United Farm Workers and Proposition 14. If that wasn't enough, the three of us sometimes made unleavened bread for Zion Lutheran Church's communion. Tessie worried that I was turning Protestant on her but I wasn't. I just liked the Gilbert Girls.

The family lived in the old brownstone parsonage right next door to the church. I'd sleep over most Friday nights, Sarah giving me her bed while she slept in a bedroll on the wooden floor. Those nights, I would try not to touch myself, still convinced that I was the only one in the world who did something so disgusting. I wasn't comfortable with asking my new friends if they did it, too.

Some nights, I just couldn't relax and was all twitchy down there. Those times, I couldn't sleep without doing it. But when I did, I tried to be quiet about it, laying on my hands on my belly, flat as a board, struggling not to gasp or shake the bed when my body spasmed. I swore Sarah knew but was too polite or embarrassed (or both) to say anything about it.

There were Ice Cream Socials at Zion Lutheran and once, they even invited me to go see *Godspell* on Broadway with them. There were more school projects and more subway trips to the City alone. I hardly got lost on the trains anymore.

Junior year, Sarah and I had to go to an art gallery for Mr. Greenman's class (before he died, obviously). We took the IRT to the East Side and wandered around, finally getting enough nerve to go into a camera club's photography show. The pictures were big, silvery and slightly blurry but I liked them. There were lots of huge flowers and nude torsos. But one in particular stood out for me. Literally. I was fascinated by it. The photo showed a woman's hand at the root of a man's erection. The hand wore pink, iridescent nail polish and was the only splash of color in the whole piece. I couldn't take my eyes off it.

When Sarah saw the photo, her pale skin blushed purple. I turned my head to get one last look as she pulled me out of the gallery by the wrist. Horndog that I was, I wanted to see that dirty picture one last time. I wanted to remember it. And to this day, I still do. Sarah's reaction reminded me of Umbe the day he yanked me and Desi out of that poetry reading in the Village.

Umbe... Where was he now? Was he still with Sylvia? Did he come by Raffi's anymore? It had been years since I'd seen him or Stefan. Months since I'd seen Desi. We had different lives now. All of us did.

Bay Ridge reminded me of an old, Italian lady leaning out a tenement window, her rough, chapped elbows on a pillow, watching the world go by. In other words, Bay Ridge was one big, fat busybody. Meaning, I heard all sorts of gossipy things about the Ruiz Family:

- That Raffi was a hooker...
- That Matty'd had a nervous breakdown and was in Creedmoor...

- That Desi was pregnant…
- That Athena had been pregnant but got an abortion…
- That Raffi'd had a nervous breakdown and was in Bellevue…
- That Desi was going to become a nun…

I didn't think any of it was true but still, the rumors flew.

More and more, I spent my time below 86th Street, with the Gilberts. When I wasn't at school, I was most likely at their place on 63rd and 4th Avenue. When the movie *Tommy* came out, Sue and Sarah's older brother Peter took us to see it at the Waverly Theater in the Village. (Their younger brother Karl pouted because he had to stay home—Karl was too young to even sneak into an "PG" movie. I knew Karl really wanted to go because he had a crush on me. And I could tell he had a crush on me because he kept punching me in the arm.)

We got to the Waverly super-early so Peter took us to a loud, crowded Irish bar nearby named the Blarney Rock. It smelled like stale pee and beer and puke rolled all into one. Peter ordered a pitcher of beer and asked for four small glasses. (The bartender didn't even proof us.) I didn't like the way beer tasted but I drank it anyway. Us girls were too young to drink but that didn't stop us. Besides, I didn't want Peter to think I was a baby or a prude.

Peter may or may not have been flirting with me when he told me that I reminded him of a woman he knew when he was a kid in Alaska—that's where the Gilberts' last church was before Brooklyn. It was on the Kenai Peninsula, in a little town not far from the Homer Spit called Soldotna. At Grace Lutheran Church.

"Her name was Connie," Peter said. "She was really something. She hunted and skinned moose. You remind me of her."

"I don't know if that's a good thing or a bad thing," I told Peter, taking a slug of the warm Bud and wincing. It really did taste like piss.

"It's a good thing," he assured me. "She was petite, just like you. And she was pretty, too."

Nobody had ever called me "pretty" before, so I didn't know what to say. Instead of saying something dumb, I said nothing. I remembered what Mrs. Rizzi at St. Fi's had once told us, quoting Abraham Lincoln: "Better to remain silent and be thought a fool than to speak and remove all doubt." So, I kept my lip zipped.

At *Tommy,* there were no seats together, so we all decided to stand, clustered behind the back row. I felt Peter's beer breath on the back of my neck all night, which wasn't entirely unpleasant. But I couldn't concentrate on *Tommy,* not even when Jack Nicholson, who I had the hots for, came onscreen and pretended to sing. All in all, it was a good night. Peter didn't try to kiss me like Junior had but it was still a good night.

Not long afterward, I ran into Desi outside of Ann and Harry's Candy Store. I was coming out with some Jujubes and she was going in. It was good to see her. Desi's hair was longer, straighter but she didn't seem any different besides that. Except that she was slightly nervous. "You got your braces off!" Desi smiled at me.

"Yeah," I admitted. "But I still have to wear a retainer at night."

"Your teeth look good," she told me.

"Thanks," I said. "You're lucky you have such straight, perfect teeth."

"Horse teeth, my dad always used to say," she shrugged.

It was quiet for a few seconds. I shifted the box of Jujubes and they made a scraping sound. "I guess you heard about the Magic Man," I said. "That he was arrested?" she chirped. I nodded. "Is it true?" I shrugged. "In this neighborhood, you hear all sorts of crazy things about people," Desi added knowingly. "Half of them I don't believe."

"More than half," I said. "But it makes sense that someone's dad finally beat the crap out of him because he showed the kid his wiener. Remember when we..."

Desi grabbed my arm, squeezed it. "I still have nightmares about that. I was so scared I peed a little."

"Me, too," I admitted.

Desi and I walked back toward the corner, toward the Cordial. I could see Raffi working behind the bar. She saw us too and waved. Larry the mailman was there, nursing what looked like a tall Coke.

Soon, we were in front of Desi's building, which was only a few feet from the Cordial. She said that she had a paper to write on the fall of Saigon. "The war was a lot more than those silver POW bracelets everyone liked to wear," Desi said. (Neither of us had one. It was embarrassing to realize how little the war had affected us. More than 50,000 had died but no one we knew, and the Vietnam War had been going on for most of our sheltered childhoods.

But maybe the soldiers wanted it that way. Maybe they wanted us to live good lives and be free while they got shot and trudged through the muddy jungles. Maybe not.)

"I have to finish reading *Othello*," I told Desi.

"That's it?"

"And then write an essay from one character's point of view."

"Who are you going to pick?" she wondered.

"Maybe Desdemona. I kind of like her." In Mrs. Beauregard's English class earlier that afternoon, she'd asked Debbie Mendoza why Othello was so upset and Debbie said it was because Othello thought his wife was a "who-a," pronouncing "whore" the way we did on the street. Mrs. Beauregard kept asking Debbie to repeat what she said and Debbie kept saying "who-a," slower and slower, enunciating the two syllables more and more with each repetition. Finally, Mrs. Beauregard turned to me, exasperated, and asked me to translate. I did, in my best Larchmont lockjaw. Mrs. Beauregard understood because that's the way she talked. It was pretty funny. I thought about telling Desi but wasn't sure if it would be as hilarious in the retelling. Probably not. Nothing ever is.

"I like Desdemona, too," Desi agreed. "But I would probably pick Emilia."

"Why?" I wondered.

"Because she always thinks the best of people. Even of Iago. Emilia reminds me of you in that way," Desi blushed.

"I'm not nearly as nice," I told her. "Deep down, I have a lot of ugly stuff."

"Same as anybody," she said.

I shrugged. "Not like I do."

"Try me," Desi pushed.

I shook my head. "How's Matty?" I wondered, changing the subject.

"The same," she said. "Maybe a little worse."

"That sucks," I told her. And I meant it. I really liked Matty, who wouldn't hurt a mosquito even if it was biting him.

"It does," Desi nodded. "His therapist wants to put him on meds but Raffi won't have it. She thinks he's just being stubborn."

I asked her, "And what do you think?"

"I think he's just being Matty. He can't help it. That's just the way he's built."

The nuns at St. Fiacre chewed Matty Ruiz up and spit him out. The lay teachers like Miss Coughley weren't as bad. The mean kids were worse. Matty had a couple of friends, mostly girls, and that was it. "I'm scared for him," I said quietly.

"Yeah, I am, too," Desi said, looking at the pebbles in the concrete under our feet. "I am, too."

That should have been my cue to go but I just had to ask, "And how's Big Matty?"

This got a smile out of Desi. A big one. "Still there," she admitted. "He's still driving Raffi crazy, more than when he was alive." Before I could ask how, Desi told me. "He keeps leaving doors wide open. The front door. Even the refrigerator door."

"How do you know it's him?"

"Believe me, those superstitious PRs...they know. Mami always makes the sign of the cross when it happens and mutters something in Spanish."

"What?"

"I don't know if it's a blessing or a curse...And Raffi, she sure thinks it's a curse. And then she curses my dad. For leaving her to go hunting. For leaving her alone with three kids. You name it, she curses him. But especially when he leaves her little presents."

"What kind of presents?"

"Cigar bands, mostly. They're everywhere." I remembered how Desi's parents had gotten engaged with an *El Producto* cigar band. I smiled. "They're on the floor mat outside the apartment. They're on the bar when she goes to work. They're on the seat of the B64 bus when she's about to sit. 'Fuckin Matty,' Raffi says under her breath."

"Remember the tape?" I asked Desi.

"I should have kept it."

"How could you? Little Matty was bugging out. You did the right thing by destroying it."

"I guess," she said.

There was so much more to say but no time to say it. "I have to get to Vietnam," Desi sighed.

"And I have to get to Willie Shakespeare, the shit. I hate reading that crap. I mean, why doesn't he just stay stuff straight out? In English?"

Desi rolled her eyes at me. "It *was* English, Cici. Way back when."

I turned to go, then stopped. "We should hang out more." I said.

"We should," Desi said. "But we can't. School…and life. It was different when we went to the same school. When we walked to and from St. Fi's together and were in the same class. But now…"

"…there doesn't seem to be enough time, does there?"

"No," Desi agreed. "There doesn't." Desi was the one who turned away, then turned back. "But you'll always be my best friend. My first best friend."

"You, too," I told her.

Desi pushed hard to open the steel and glass door to her apartment building. It closed with a metallic thump. I started to walk toward Gelston but stopped dead in my tracks. Under one of my Olaf Daughters clogs was a cigar band. An *El Producto*.

"Fuckin Matty," I said out loud, then just kept walking.

DEAR MS. D'ANGELO

ENGL 313 — Workshop in Fiction 2
Hunter College of the City University of New York
Semester: Spring 1982

April 19, 1982

Dear Ms. D'Angelo,

First, let me begin by saying how impressed I am with your writing. Your attention to detail is to be commended. You possess the skill (though raw it may be at times) to make minutia meaningful. The pace is brisk and the story moves along well. The characters are believable and engaging. I can even overlook your use of run-on sentences, mild racism, your abuse of semicolons, your fondness for incomplete sentences, the spelling of "MushroomHat", phrases like "way handsomer," excessive (and often unnecessary) parentheticals and ellipses, your clunky device of directly addressing the reader and your grammatical errors. (e.g. It's "Desi and I" not "me and Desi"—but I know you know this, Carla.) And would a 13-year-old use a word like "specter?" Some characters are fully drawn while others seem wooden. But all of this can be amended in the rewrite.

That being said, you can't leave us hanging like this! I want to know, need to know, what happens to Desi, Matty, Umbe and all of the others. I realize the assignment states that the final project needs to be at least 50 pages and you're well beyond that, but I urge you to continue.

Looking forward to hearing your thoughts,

Professor Daniel Winner

•

April 20, 1982

Dear Professor Winner,

First, I wanted to thank you for letting me add your Workshop in Fiction 2 late in the semester. I know registration had already closed when you let me sign on in January and I know how crowded the class is. But I wouldn't have been able to graduate on time because I would have been three credits short. How the hell was I supposed to know that Remedial Math wouldn't count toward my 120 credits? (Total disclosure—I rushed through the placement test at freshman registration—and flunked!—because I wanted to go hang out with my boyfriend.)

But anyway, I know I thanked you about a million times already but I just wanted to thank you again. So, thank you.

I get the feeling I'm trying to stall and change the subject. That I want to avoid going back to the story. In my mind, it's done. Over. *Finito*. Things end. Friendships finish. That's the way it was for Desi and Cici. They taught each other stuff, helped each other grow. And now it's over.

I would appreciate it if you'd use my final paper in its current form as my end-of-term project. Of course, I have no problem with edits and fixing the grammar errors, incomplete sentences, excessive parentheticals, clunkiness (!), etc. (By the way, I spell it "MushroomHat" to convey that it's like a person, like a name. That's staying.) But writing more is out of the question. I have a very demanding schedule: four other classes, I work part-time and have said boyfriend besides. But I appreciate how much you like this thing. (There I go with incomplete sentences again.)

Also, are we still on for our face-to-face meeting on the 26th?

Carla D'Angelo

•

April 21, 1982

Dear Carla,

I can only imagine how busy you are. (This coming from a professor with dozens of students.) But I think you owe it to yourself and you owe it to the story to continue. I think you might even have a novel here. (Though the explicit details of adolescent sexuality might not make it very marketable.)

That being said, I feel very strongly that people—women, some men and especially teenage girls—will relate to this story of true, pure, intense friendship; about the ones who teach us how to be good friends, how to love, how to *be*, and then slowly trickle from our lives.

No promises, but I know an editor at Knopf. But that's far off in the future. First, you've got to finish this book!

And yes, we're still on for April 26th.

Looking forward to our MAC during 4th period on Monday,

Daniel Winner

TRANSCRIPT
4/26/82 MAC MEETING

Student: Carla D'Angelo
Instructor: Professor Daniel Winner
Course: ENGL 313 — Workshop in Fiction 2
Institution: Hunter College, City University of New York
Semester: Spring 1982

Mandatory Advisory Conference (MAC): April 26, 1982 between Professor Daniel Winner and Carla D'Angelo, a student in my Workshop in Fiction 2 course. The purpose of this meeting is to satisfy the requirement of having one conference with the student to confirm the parameters of the final project, which is to be the beginnings of a novel at least 50 pages in length.

WINNER: I hope you don't mind being recorded, Carla. It's just to have documentation of our meeting and to make sure you know what's expected of you in this class.

D'ANGELO: Whatever. I already know what's expected of me.

WINNER: I know you do. But this is to avoid the dreaded "I didn't know" when final grades roll around. Trust me, it happens. A lot.

D'ANGELO: What do they do with the recording?

WINNER: Believe it or not, Hunter pays for someone to transcribe it. Legal says it's easier to pay for a transcription service than to go back and forth with a student who claims they weren't aware of their final project and shows up on May 12 empty handed.

D'ANGELO: How is that even possible? It says it right there on the syllabus.

WINNER: Believe me, it's possible. This is just a CYA move for CUNY.

D'ANGELO: CYA?

WINNER: Cover your ass.

D'ANGELO: Got it. Are you allowed to say 'ass' on a transcript?

WINNER: I just did. Anyhow, as usual, you're doing what you do best. Avoiding the subject. We only have 45 minutes so I'd prefer not to waste any time.

D'ANGELO: Okay.

WINNER: I'd like to pursue why you're so reluctant to continue the story.

D'ANGELO: Because it's over.

WINNER: That's it?

D'ANGELO: Yeah. It's over. Done. No *mas*. I have nothing more to say about it.

WINNER: Oh, but I think you do. I think you need to tie up loose ends.

D'ANGELO: Let the reader draw their own conclusions.

WINNER: That's a cop-out, Carla. You're the writer. It's your story. Though it could be any of our stories.

D'ANGELO: What do you mean?

WINNER: I mean that everyone has that one friend, that one good, close friend who you were like glue with growing up. Who was there with you through all of the important things and all of the bullshit. And suddenly, they're not there anymore. Everyone can relate to this.

D'ANGELO: Then they know the drill. They can fill in the blanks.

WINNER: But as a writer, it's *your job* to fill in the blanks. Filling in the blanks is what writers do!

D'ANGELO: I don't have time. Look, you've got your 50 pages. Way more than 50 pages. Why isn't that enough?

WINNER: Because I think you need to finish this. You need resolution. Even though you know how it ends, you need to end it on paper.

D'ANGELO: Well, maybe I don't want to finish it. Maybe it's too painful... Hey, I don't know if you got this from the story but it really happened. Most of it, anyway. It's true.

WINNER: Most great fiction comes from fact. Camus said, 'Fiction is the lie through which we tell the truth.'

D'ANGELO: Whoa, that's deep.

WINNER: 'Fiction reveals the truth that reality obscures.'

D'ANGELO: Maybe *you* should be the writer.

WINNER: Well, it just so happens that I *am* working on a novel. I have been for about five years. But I didn't say that. Emerson did.

D'ANGELO: Look, maybe I don't want to go back there. Maybe I don't want to look at what happened next anymore. Maybe it hurts to go back there.

WINNER: It's okay for it to hurt. Hell, it's *supposed* to hurt. Your hurt…that's what makes others feel.

D'ANGELO: Wow. Who said that?

WINNER: Me. I just made it up.

D'ANGELO: You really should finish your novel, Professor Winner.

WINNER: Deal. And you need to finish yours. If not for the reader, then for yourself. Bring some closure to what happened. Look back on it. Try to make some sense of it. I think you'll find it cathartic.

(SILENCE OF SEVERAL SECONDS, then…)

D'ANGELO: I'll see. I'll try.

WINNER: It doesn't have to be long. Maybe just a few pages. But I think this story needs to be laid to rest. Kind of like Big Matty.

D'ANGELO: Like a dead thing?

WINNER: Not like a dead thing. But like something that deserves to be felt, heard. Have a voice. You at least owe your story that.

D'ANGELO: I think I know what you mean.

WINNER: Okay, so for the record, we're clear. You've satisfied the requirement of 50 pages for this class's final project but you agree to continue writing and conclude the story. Plus make the edits I suggest. I should have those to you by the end of the week.

D'ANGELO: Yes. Right. That sounds good. No promises, though. I'll just see what comes out.

WINNER: Carla, writing isn't a bowel movement. You don't just 'See what comes out.' You make it come out.

D'ANGELO: Like Dulcolax?

WINNER: No, but yes. So, we're good?

D'ANGELO: Sure. We're good. Thanks, Professor Winner.

DULCOLAX

Some things are better left alone. Some things are just too painful. You don't want to look at them closer. But those are probably the best things to write about. Because when you write about those things, you get to look at them. Examine them. Pick them apart. Like a science experiment or a scab, I'm not sure which. And then you get to make them neat and pretty. Tie them up with a purple ribbon, then give them away. Like a present, a gift. You know that kids' song "Magic Penny?" The one about how love is something if you give it away? Hokey as it sounds, kind of like that.

Some things served a purpose then suddenly don't anymore. Like Desi's mushroom hat. She wore it every day practically the whole year we met. Then one day it was gone. Kind of like me. Kind of like our friendship. Gone but not. Tucked away in a box for when you need it. If and when you need it.

I didn't see Desi for a long time after I ran into her on the sidewalk in front of Ann and Harry's. Months. Maybe a year. The Ruizes still lived around the corner but our paths rarely crossed. My sister Laura sometimes brought home Athena to work on a school project. At that point, they were in their last year at St. Fi's and getting ready to graduate soon. Laura told me that Athena refused to go to Fontaine Academy. She was going to the Fort, just like Laura was. Athena rarely said anything to me about her family but then she was never the talkative type. The screaming type, sure, but not one for small talk. Maybe there was a nod or a "hi" or a grunt between us but that was it.

More time passed. Senior year of high school, I started seeing that drummer, Zach. Though I was too young to date him the first time he called, apparently he had put a star next to my name in his little black book. (To signify that I was special, I guess). Zach called me back a couple of years later. This time, I wasn't playing in the schoolyard with my friends. I was home and we talked on the phone. Then we started going out.

I wasn't sure where it would lead—or if I wanted it to lead anywhere because shit, I was only 17. But I guess I was in love. Or at least I thought I was in love. Which was pretty much like almost being in love. I knew I didn't want to go to sleepaway college like Sue and Sarah were even though Mrs. Yaminsky, the guidance counselor I did Service for at Fort Adams, pushed me to apply to Antioch in Yellow Springs, Ohio. (Where the hell was Yellow Springs anyway?!) And I got in. With a partial scholarship.

But jerk that I was, I didn't want to leave my boyfriend. No, I was going to be a writer. Just like Hemingway. He didn't go to college; he went to war instead. He didn't go to school to learn how to write; he just wrote. And look at him. Ended up blowing his brains out, but before that, it worked out pretty good for Old Hem.

"You're too smart *not* to go to college," a friend of Sue and Sarah's parents told me at their Christmas party the year before we were going to graduate from Fort Adams. I thanked Pat for being so nice (she always said such positive things about my writing which I really appreciated) and told her that it was too late to apply to colleges plus I didn't want to go away. "It's not too late for CUNY schools," Pat said. "I went to Hunter College and it served me well."

Pat worked for United Cerebral Palsy (and not just but because she had CP herself, but because she was good at what she did). Plus, Pat was a teacher, so maybe she knew what she was talking about in reference to me.

Sure enough, CUNY's deadline wasn't until May, so I applied after I took a look at Hunter. It was uptown on East 68th Street with no campus to speak of, just a bunch of buildings scattered around the East Side. I was accepted, even though I screwed up the Math Assessment Test. (I admit, math isn't my strong point but like I told Professor Winner, I rushed through the test because I wanted to get registration over with and get to my boyfriend's apartment. And screw Zach. But I ended up getting screwed because I had to take Remedial Math. I mean, who takes 15 credits their first semester—including "Art of Early Renaissance" and "The Foundations of America"—gets all A's and B's and has to take Remedial Math? Me, that's who.)

I'm getting off topic. Trying to avoid talking about Desi, maybe.

Desi and I yapped on the phone maybe once or twice our last semester of high school, then not even that. From Athena, I managed to wrangle that Desi was going to Marist, a private college upstate in Poughkeepsie which used to be run by these Roman Catholic brothers. (Man, Desi couldn't get away from those damned Catholics, could she? But at least Marist was co-ed, though.) Desi had always been a smarty-pants and got herself a full scholarship, Athena said. Athena was looking forward to getting the room she and her sister shared all to herself when Desi bunked up at Marist. Raffi didn't like the idea of Desi living in a dorm but Brooklyn was too far of a commute from Poughkeepsie for Desi to live at home. Plus, Desi would be close enough, a Metro-North and subway ride away. I guess Raffi figured it was time to cut the cord. Sort of.

I'd lost my virginity that winter but didn't tell Desi about it. There wasn't much to tell. Lots of fumbling. Lots of pain. A tinch of blood, then pop. I wasn't sure if I liked sex or not but I was willing to try it again. It seemed silly, all that in and out. Yet somewhere under the hurt, it felt pretty nice.

And while we're on the subject, I hate the phrase "lost my virginity." I mean, "*lost it*?" Where the hell did it go? Did I misplace it? You know, like a set of keys: "It was right here a minute ago…" No, I didn't lose my virginity. I gave it away. Willingly. Good riddance.

I hated being new at this sex stuff. I wanted to know everything all at once but I knew next to nothing. Not even how to move. I was struggling to move with my lover, to slither like a snake, but I soon learned that this was the exact opposite thing I should be doing. Luckily, the guy (it was Zach, the drummer) was very nice about it and didn't laugh in my face. "We're getting nowhere," Zach said, then explained the ins and the outs. Then we did it. But I felt like such an ass to be doing it the wrong way at first.

Desi and I would have snort-laughed about this until Sprite came out of our noses if we had been tight like we once were. But we weren't so we didn't.

When I lost mine, I wondered if Desi had lost hers, too. (I admit, there's no way to avoid saying "losing it," so I guess I have to.) Maybe she met some cute Xaverian guy at one of Fontaine's high school mixers. You know, horny seniors from two same-sex Catholic high schools who spontaneously combusted on the dance floor when the DJ played "Don't Leave Me This Way."

But then again, maybe Desi was still chaste. Underneath it all, she was pretty withdrawn and quiet. Not a shower-head defiler like me. Only you just can't tell something like that about a person just by looking at them, can you? They might seem all normal and button-down on the surface but you never know what's going on deep inside their dark recesses. Hey, they could be cutting themselves with an X-Acto knife on their inner thigh when nobody's looking. (Athena told my sister Laura that she sometimes did this just to feel, to feel something, anything, even pain.) They could be going into those token booths at Show World Center on 42nd Street to see "live sex acts." (Once I saw my old algebra teacher doing this when I was at Tad's Steaks with some friends across the street. I don't know which was worse, the thought of Mr. Stein wanking to strangers or me eating a $2.99 steak. Probably the steak.)

My point is that we all have dirty, little secrets. We all have our shame. But in reality, sometimes our secrets are not very dirty but we think they're huge and gross and that makes us shameful.

Maybe my shame, my not feeling good enough to be Desi friend anymore, pushed me away from her. Maybe she and I just grew apart. Maybe we served a purpose for a while then suddenly didn't anymore. Just like Dulcolax serves its purpose. Then you don't need to take it. I'm still trying to figure that one out.

THE LAST TIME I SAW DESI

The last time I saw Desi was during winter break 1979. We were both college sophomores at different colleges. She was home from Marist and I had just gotten back on the RR train from my last final that semester at Hunter. It was "Introduction to Music," where we basically sat in class, listened to music and talked about it. Classical. Jazz. Everything. It was fun and easy and I was thinking of taking "Gershwin & Porter" the next semester with Professor Schwartz, who'd written a book about each songwriter.

I was in my room, lying on my belly with my feet up, working on a poem about a carved wooden box (which was a metaphor for me) in my wire-ring notebook. Laura was out, miraculously leaving me some alone time to write and think in the two-by-four room we shared. I had a couple of hours before I had to get ready for my date with Zach. We were going to see the Christmas tree at Rockefeller Center then maybe go ice-skating.

The doorbell rang, which I ignored because I knew Tessie would get it, even though she was elbow-deep in meat loaf. I pictured my mother wiping her hands on her apron, then opening our beige, painted door to shout "Who is it?" into the semi-dark recesses of the hallway. (We never, ever buzzed anyone in without knowing who it was, just in case it was an ax murderer.) I heard, "It's Desi," and then a buzz.

My heart jumped. Or did it sink? Maybe both. It wasn't like Desi to come to my house unannounced. Or at all. Before that, I hadn't seen her for... could it have been a couple of years? More?

When I looked up, Desi stood at my bedroom door, like she was waiting to be asked in. Her hair was much longer now, way past her shoulders. She didn't wear any makeup but then again, she didn't have to. Desi had perfectly-arched eyebrows and Latina lashes as thick as paintbrushes. "Come in," I told her and stood up.

We didn't hug although that was my first impulse. (Maybe it was hers too because her hands sort of moved an inch or two, then dropped back down to her sides.) Desi looked good but agitated. Worried about something. Someone. "Hey," she said.

"Hey," I said back. Then nothing. "Is everything all right?" Desi shook her head 'no.' "Is it Matty?"

"Matty is fine," she assured me. "Finishing up his second year at the High School of Performing Arts."

"The one from that big movie coming out next year?" I asked.

"Yeah," she said. "*Fame*. Matty was in a couple of scenes, dancing in the background."

"That's nice," I told her.

"It is," Desi agreed. "My brother finally found a place where he fits in."

There was that silence again, creeping in like a cold, gray fog. I remembered a time when Desi and I tripped over each other's words. So much to say, so little time to say it. But not now. Not anymore.

"Look," Desi said with a deep sigh. "There's no easy way to say this. So, I'll just come out and say it: Junior died."

Junior! It had been how long? At least five years, right? I can't say that I thought of him often. Or at all. And yet...and yet. Those French kisses, sweet as an éclair in my memories. That time he laid on top of me, just holding me. Those lovely experiences had shaped me in a big way. And now Junior was gone? Just like that?

I was floored. Flattened. Someone I had swapped spit with, someone who had touched my boobs, was dead. Gone. And he was only...how old? I remembered he was a few months younger than me.

"Junior's dead? But how?" I finally managed to get out.

Desi sunk her head. "A heart attack."

"But he was only 19."

"Eighteen," she corrected me. "It turns out he had an undiagnosed heart condition." Desi explained that it had happened at work—he was training to be a welder. Junior was an apprentice; it was a good job. She swallowed hard then spoke. "The first time he went out onto the hot workroom floor, he passed out." Desi stopped, took a deep breath. "They say Junior died before he even hit the ground." She wasn't crying but her eyes were wet. Mine were, too.

"Did he...did he..."

"No, I don't think he suffered much." It had been years since Desi and I had what you'd call a deep conversation, but here she was still reading my thoughts, just like old times. "Junior probably didn't know what hit him," she added.

I was stunned. Didn't know what to say. But I had to say something. "I am so, so sorry," I croaked out. "He was such a good guy, so sweet."

Desi nodded. "Junior was the best."

"How is Mimi taking it?"

Desi shrugged. "How do you think? I mean, he was her only child, her son...*Mijo! Mijo!* She keeps crying out. They had to give her a sedative. My cousin Roberto has been great, so strong. He loved Junior like his own flesh and blood but..."

My mind tried to picture it: Mimi's grief so raw and ugly, filled with tears and mucus and aching. Roberto trying to console her and failing. The whole family, not knowing what to say or do. Helpless. This was much more than PRH. This was real.

But I didn't know if I could deal with real. Maybe I *could* deal with it but I didn't want to. I was a coward, a shit, I know. But that was the truth.

Desi was still talking. I tried to catch up. "We couldn't talk her out of it," Desi said. "Mimi is having Junior's wake in the house. In the living room. In Corona."

"That's almost Medieval," I told her.

"Real Old School Puerto Rican," Desi agreed. "Look, I know you don't have wheels. And it's kind of far. Almost two hours on the RR, the N and the 7 train. But if you wanted to…"

But that was the thing, I didn't want to. Going to Junior's wake was the last thing I wanted to do. Look, I hadn't seen the guy in years. I didn't want to dredge up the past. I had a boyfriend. We'd fucked, for God's sake. We were fucking. I didn't want to go see some dead ex laid out in his mother's living room! "When is it?" I asked. But only because I felt I had to.

"Tomorrow. Just tomorrow day and night. We convinced Mimi to have the wake for only one day, not two. It's too draining. As it is now, Mimi is…"

I drifted off again. No way in hell was I going to Junior's wake. I didn't owe it to him. I didn't owe it to anyone. I had my own life. I had a path. Jesus, I was on a path! Two more years at Hunter and I'd have my BA. I had Zach and we were talking about moving in together after I graduated. I had my own shit! I didn't need a dead ex-boyfriend. Who did?

Except when I thought about it, about not going, I felt guilty. Well, screw it! People feel guilty about a lot of things. People feel guilty about crap their whole lives and do fine. Or not. Sometimes they're okay and sometimes the guilt eats away at them like gangrene and the next thing you know, your index finger is falling off, then your right arm, then your… And what the hell was that smell?

Besides, did I want to be one of those people? I'd spent almost 20 years trying *not* to be one of *those* people, yet here I was…

The car ride from Corona was uncomfortable. And not just physically—because there were eight of us stuffed into the Town & Country station wagon Stefan managed to borrow from his friend Frank. Athena and Matty grumbled about having to sit in the jump seat near the tailgate and ride backwards. Matty moaned that it made him carsick. Raffi snapped that he should stop being such a little girl and threw him an empty Key Food shopping bag to use as a barf bag.

Maybe Matty was a girl, I thought, but didn't say anything. Was he wearing eyeliner? Foundation? Was he even old enough to wear makeup? How old did a boy have to be to wear makeup? I remembered when Desi and I would sneak home compacts of Maybelline from Woolworth's and pray our mothers wouldn't notice. But they always did and the makeup kits ended up in the garbage until we saved enough allowance to buy another one.

Why am I writing about makeup when I should be writing about my emotions? Because it's easier, that's why.

Stefan insisted we wait until after the morning rush but there was still traffic. Even with tie-ups, it took less than an hour to drive from Bay Ridge to Corona, first taking the QEB (that's the way *Tia* Cassie would mangle the abbreviation for the Brooklyn-Queens Expressway) then the Grand Central. Sylvia argued that the Belt was shorter but then again, Sylvia argued about everything now that she was preggers, Umbe said. She even got pissed off that Umbe called it "preggers" and snapped that he'd be peeved too (yes, she actually said "peeved") if he had to pee every 15 seconds.

I loved the back and forth, the banter, the jibes. I missed the tennis match of words that was life in the Ruiz household; it even made long car rides sizzle.

Desi and I talked about our classes, which were as different we were. From the back seat, Athena shouted something about accounting and creative writing being like apples and oranges. To which Raffi added, "Yeah, but they're still fruits…and together, they make a good salad."

I was smushed between Desi and her mom in the back seat. Raffi leaned over (was that Michelob on her breath?) and whispered in my ear, "I missed you, *mija*." I still remembered the Spanish shorthand for "my daughter." I felt myself blush even though I missed Raffi, too.

"*Yo también, mamita*," I whispered back. "Me, too, Mom." Or at least that's what I meant to say. My Spanish was a little rusty. On my left, I felt Raffi smile. On my right, I felt Desi stiffen slightly. Or I could have been imagining it.

I had never been to this part of Queens before. Corona reminded me a lot of Brooklyn, but a sad, run-down, wanna-be Brooklyn. 55-12 102nd Street (why did the house numbers in Queens have dashes in them?) was an unremarkable brick box of a building. Ugly really. A concrete front yard. Starburst wrought-iron fence painted black, in serious need of a paint job. A narrow space not even a foot wide separated it from the unremarkable brick box of a house next door. It was like the builder ran out of imagination when he got to this block in Corona.

Mid December, it had barely snowed, and not for a while. What little snow on the ground was topped with black lace from the car fumes and other junk we breathed. There were Christmas decorations on the potted tree in the areaway (faded tinsel and a few silver balls).

Stefan managed to find a spot to park his friend Frank's "boat" a few houses away from Mimi and Roberto's place. The eight of us silently got out of the Town & Country and walked to the front door in a clump; no one wanted to be first. It was Raffi who put her hand on the doorknob and turned it, not even knocking. She just went in, knowing it was open. I took a deep breath and followed.

As much as you try to prepare yourself, nothing quite prepares you for the grief of a mother with a dead teenager. At first, I didn't recognize Mimi—I thought she was her mother, even her grandmother. That's how bad she looked. Her hair was in curly clusters and didn't look like she'd taken a pick to it for days. Her eyes were all puffy, just slits. Mimi sat by one of the three front windows in a folding chair with Roberto beside her. It was as far away as she could get from her son's coffin yet still be in the same room. The second she saw Raffi, she stood and fell into the smaller woman's arms, crying, "*Mijo... mijo.*" My son, my son.

Junior's coffin... After Mimi, it was the second thing you noticed when you walked into the house. I assume it was the living room but all of the furniture had been moved out to make space for the rows of folding chairs and the pine box. And that's all it was, a simple pine box. All of the Italian wakes I'd been to had fancy, polished wooden caskets that probably cost at least $1,000. But Junior's looked like something you'd see in a John Wayne Western. Something Junior, who liked woodworking, might have made himself. Except he didn't. Instead, he was in it.

Surrounded by the sound of wailing, I was afraid to look around to see who the terrible noise was coming from. But just like when I saw *The Amityville Horror* at the Fortway a few months ago, against my better judgement, I had to look.

Mimi, who outweighed Raffi by at least 50 pounds, was still collapsed against her petite cousin's body. Stefan and Umbe were helping them both to a chair. Conjoined, they looked like a horrible, sobbing creature with two heads, four arms and four legs. Roberto scooted over one seat to make space for them. They sat, Mimi melting onto Raffi's slight body.

Matty was snort-crying, black circles growing under his eyes. (Not only was he wearing eyeliner but mascara too!) Even Athena, who we used to swear had no heart, was sobbing. Sylvia held onto her soccer-ball stomach and lowered herself into a metal folding chair. Desi was coming back from the kitchen with Dixie cups of water for her mom and cousin-in-law.

Luckily, Tessie had taught me how to behave properly at a wake. She said that you go up to the person who'd lost the loved one and you tell them how sorry you were. I figured the rules were the same when the wake was held in someone's living room instead of in a velvety funeral parlor so that's exactly what I did. Or tried to.

When Mimi saw me, she started crying even harder. She stood and surrounded me with her fleshy body. "*Él te amaba...Él te amaba*," she said like a mantra.

"He loved you," Raffi managed to choke out, translating for me. "He loved you."

"*Fuiste su primer amor*," Mimi gasped.

Raffi shook her head at that one, unable to translate. "She says that you were Junior's first love," Umbe told me in a quiet voice, peeling Mimi off my body and depositing her back into the chair next to Raffi.

"I'm sorry" was all I could say. "*Lo siento*."

A bleached-blonde girl was glaring at me. I assumed she was Junior's current love. I hoped her light hair, eyes and skin meant that she didn't understand Spanish. But I hoped wrong because *La Rubia* was charging toward me like a pissed-off goat. That's when I knew I had to get out of there. Fast.

It wasn't even an Irish good-bye—sneaking out without saying a word to anyone—because there was no sneaking out when everyone was staring at you. I just left. Bolted. Not even closing the door behind me. Desi chased me to the areaway, calling my name, but I ignored her.

I zipped up my jacket and just kept going. To where I didn't know.

QUEEN OF CORONA

The only thing I knew about Corona was from that song "Me and Julio Down by the Schoolyard." Something about Rosie being the Queen of Corona. For some reason, that song kept spinning through my head as I ran, then walked through Corona after I ran out of breath. What did Mama Pajama see? And why did they call her Mama Pajama? And what did Mama saw that was against the law?

Yeah, my first impression of Queens had been correct. The borough *was* a low-rent Brooklyn. Everything seemed smaller, duller, shabbier than Kings County. I didn't feel unsafe in Corona but I didn't like it. It didn't feel comfortable. It didn't feel like home, and of course, it wasn't.

I walked up one street and down the next. They all looked the same to me. Brick houses, apartment houses, three-story concrete blocks, wood-frame houses that seemed tilted. Down Martense Avenue, down Waldron to Otis, which put me onto 108th Street. I took Corona Avenue to see where it led. It led to National Street. This took me to Roosevelt Avenue, which was a big shopping area. I remember hearing about a mall somewhere, Roosevelt Field, but I wasn't sure if it was nearby. And it didn't matter, anyway. I wasn't there to shop.

No, I was there to escape. To get away from the stifling, overheated room. To get away from Junior's coffin, which I didn't even have the balls to look inside. To get away from the sobbing, the hurt, the messy emotions. To get away from the blonde *chica's* icy blue eyes that looked like they wanted to kill me. I was wandering the unfamiliar streets to hide. To hide from what I was feeling, which was not good. I guess I'd never lost anyone close to me before. My all four of grandparents were still alive and so was my great grandmother. No one I'd ever kissed, *tongue kissed*, had ever died before. This was all so weird and new.

I was starting to panic, both from the crazy emotions and from not knowing where the hell I was. Then I heard it. Like the voice of an old friend: the rumble of the El, of the elevated train, in the distance. I followed the sound until it stopped. Then I followed where the sound had come from. Minutes later, there was the clatter of another train to guide me, coming from the opposite direction. Then another. Then I saw it, the familiar green, peeling girders and the steel steps. From the street looking up to the top of the concrete platform, I could read the white and black sign that said, "103 Street – Corona Plaza." Mami always said that if you knew where you were, you knew where you were going. (But in Spanish.) That's when I knew I would be all right.

Mr. Rogers from the kids' TV show also said to look for the helpers when you felt lost or confused. Even though I was in Queens, unchartered territory for a Brooklynite, I looked for the familiar. There was a fruit and vegetable stand that resembled Pucci's place on 3rd Avenue in Bay Ridge. There was a candy store as crummy as Ann and Harry's, a corner grocery that reminded me of Penner's. I was home but not.

My skull was pounding from a hunger headache. (I hadn't eaten since the Thomas' English Muffin I'd had at breakfast.) I looked around and decided on Corona Queen Pizzeria. The guy making pies behind the counter was big and surly, just like Gio back at Luigi's down in South Brooklyn, Amy's neighborhood. The Gio clone snapped at his workers as they carried in a delivery of huge tomato sauce cans and 10-pound bags of shredded mozzarella.

Although Pizza Man just got finished barking at someone on the phone, he was nice as anything to me. "Regular slice and a small Coke," he repeated when I ordered. His smile was shockingly sweet for a guy who could be as snappish as a pit bull.

After I paid the guy the dollar he asked for, he pushed my order toward me on the chipped orange counter. "Thanks," I told him.

"Enjoy," he nodded. "You from around here?"

"Nah," I said, my mouth full of thin crust and molten cheese. It burned the roof of my mouth. I could feel a blister already forming.

"Whereabouts?" Gio's twin asked, twirling a circle of dough into the air, then catching it.

"Brooklyn," I said, after I swallowed. "Bay Ridge."

"You're far from home," Pizza Man told me.

"She's too young for you," a deep voice behind me said. "Stop flirting, Vinnie."

"I wasn't flirting," Vinnie, the pizza man, protested, circling sauce onto the dough with a ladle. "I was just being friendly." Vinnie spread mozzarella across the sauce. "Okay, maybe I was flirting."

I laughed. The baritone voice belonged to a man in the shadows of the pizzeria, where the chrome chairs and black wooden tables sat. When the man stepped out of the shadows, I gasped. He was a dead ringer for Desi's father, Big Matty. I had seen enough faded pictures of him to know those broad shoulders, that chipped front tooth, his curly black hair and big, brown eyes. The guy even carried a hardhat. And his voice...that deep, dark, creamy voice...it was the same one I had heard on that sealed cassette tape when Desi and I were kids.

"You look like you saw a ghost," Vinnie smirked.

"Maybe she just doesn't like your pizza," Big Matty's Ghost suggested.

"No, the pizza's great, almost as good at Brooklyn pizza," I said.

"Almost?" Vinnie snapped.

"You know, that old Brooklyn/Queens rivalry," Big Matty's Ghost remarked. Vinnie made a face while he sprinkled Parmesan on top of the pizza. "How everything in Brooklyn is better than everything in Queens."

Vinnie slid the wooden paddle underneath the dough and eased the round pie onto it. "That's total bull," he said, careful not to curse in front of a young lady, just like his mama had raised him to do. "You obviously haven't been to The Lemon Ice King."

"And you obviously haven't been to Spumoni Gardens," I told him.

"Fair enough," Vinnie agreed, displaying a gold-rimmed front tooth. He slid the pie into the oven and slammed the door behind it. "I bet this is your first time in our fair borough," he added.

I thought for a second. "I've been to Belmont."

"Close, but no cigar," Big Matty's Ghost said. "That's in Elmont which is technically in Nassau County."

Vinnie wiped his sweaty forehead with a handkerchief from his back pocket. It was as big as a small tablecloth. "What brings you to the Little Italy of Queens?"

"A funeral," I told him, chewing on the crust which was nicely crunchy and blackened in spots, just the way I liked it. "A wake, really."

"Over at Guida's?" Vinnie asked.

I shook my head. "It was actually at their house," I said.

"That's so old school PR," Big Matty's Specter commented. "I can say that because I'm Puerto Rican," he added quickly.

"Not the Quiles kid," Vinnie said. I nodded sadly. "Oh, Jeez. Damn it. Damn it to hell. He was a good egg, that Luis."

"He was. But nobody called him 'Luis,' though, did they? Nobody but his mom."

"Right, they call him 'Junior.' I mean, called," Vinnie corrected. "Because now he's…"

"…gone," Big Matty's Ghost finished. "Yeah, that happens to the best of us." His eyes flickered up to mine. He knew that I knew. Then his glance flittered away like a dark butterfly.

After I ordered another slice, I said, "He was laid out in the living room. It was kind of creepy."

"Lots of PRH, I bet," the GhostMan added.

"What the hell's PRH?" Vinnie asked, slipping my warm slice onto a sheet of waxed paper.

In unison, Big Matty's twin and I said, "Puerto Rican Hysteria."

"Except this was real. Real grief," I added.

"Full of *ai's* and *mijos*, I bet," Big Matty's double added. I looked at him, shocked that he'd know. "Been there," he explained.

Vinnie nodded. "Yeah, they're all the same, funerals. Whether they're Italian, Latino or freaking Chinese. There's nothing as bad as losing your kid."

Vinnie talked like he knew this firsthand but I didn't want to ask. It wasn't my business. "Your boyfriend?" Vinnie wondered.

"No. My friend Desi's cousin," I said.

"Desi," the other guy said dreamily. Then again, "Desi. Desiree." I stared at him in disbelief.

"Eat your slice, it's getting cold," Vinnie said. He was pretty bossy.

The guys were quiet for a few minutes. The pizza man busied himself making another pie, a square this time. (The corners were my favorite.) The other one fiddled with the liner of his hard hat, then watched me eat, which I did as fast as I could without choking. It was time to leave.

I tried to pay Vinnie for the second slice. "It's on me," he said. "Sorry about your friend. I liked him." I thanked Vinnie and left. Big Matty's Ghost didn't say anything but his sad eyes followed me out the door.

At first, the purple rectangle that announced the 7 train at the 103 Street – Corona Plaza station threw me. But then I remembered taking the 7 with my cousin Gino all the way out to Shea Stadium to see the Mets once, many years earlier. (Even though Gino was a die-hard Yankees fan, a Mayor's Trophy Game when both teams played each other, was the only reason Gino would ever set foot in Shea.) I knew to take the 7 toward Manhattan, to Times Square, where I could then switch for the RR which would take me home.

It was cold on the outdoor platform. The wind whipped around me hard and mean but I didn't have to wait long. The train's light bobbled in the distance as soon as I got to the top of the grooved stairs. I saw it before I heard it, swaying on the elevated track, coming toward me. It was an old, beat-up train, probably worn out from being on a line that was mostly outdoors. The metal cars' outsides were covered with graffiti, which I loved. This far out on the 7 line, the train wasn't crowded, even though it was rush hour. I had an empty row of speckled turquoise seats to myself. A bum was holed up with his blanket and shopping cart in the two-seater nearby but I was far enough away so I didn't smell his stink. Or his bum-juice, as me and Desi used to call it.

I had nothing to read, so I passed the time staring at the rooftops that blurred past the windows. "The Magic Hour," artists and photographers called it, those golden moments right before sunset. The windows of the tenements and row houses were painted electric orange and there was a lavender tint to the sky. It was nice. "Pretty," a now-familiar baritone nearby said.

I looked up. The Ghost of Big Matty was lowering his tall, thick body into the row of seats next to me, a few inches away. I could feel the heat of his body as his heavy, quilted jacket brushed my mittened hand. I could see his pores, his five o'clock shadow coming out of them, that's how close he was. "You following me?" I asked, trying to hide the shake in my voice.

"I'm from Brooklyn, too," he said.

"What part?"

"Here, there and everywhere," he told me. "Teo," he added, holding out his gloved hand for me to shake.

I took it. His grip was strong, not ghostlike but real. Sure. Safe. "Celeste," I said.

"But your friends call you 'Cici,'" he finished.

"How did you know?"

Teo shrugged. "Lucky guess."

Even I knew that Teo was short for Mateo. And that Mateo was Spanish for Matthew. Same name as Desi's father.

This guy just didn't look like Big Matty Ruiz; he *was* Big Matty Ruiz.

He took off his hardhat, his helmet liner and gloves, sat them in his lap like you might balance a small child. As he looked out the window, I studied the side of his face. His profile, his snub nose, his jutting chin, looked so much like Desi's, I almost cried.

But actually, it felt okay sitting next to this stranger. He was silent. Brooding. Weighing the situation. It felt oddly comfortable and good. Not creepy or scary.

Suddenly, I remembered what Grandma Lou had once told me about what superstitious Italians believe when you dream of dead people. It was this: if the departed one kisses you, it means that you would die soon, maybe even as soon as that night. Also, my grandmother said that it was impossible for ghosts to lie—they could stretch the truth, they could twist it, they could be vague but they couldn't tell a falsehood.

Was I dreaming this? Was Teo real? Was he dead? Was he Desi's father come back to life? Or was he just some charming creep who followed me from a pizza place onto the 7 train? I tried to figure out how to ask a potential ghost these things without really asking him. And came up blank.

The sun was almost down. The light show was over. Teo turned toward me, smiling. "You'll be fine," he told me.

I stiffened. "Who said I wasn't?"

"You did. You said you ran away. You should never run away."

"No, I didn't," I insisted. Teo shrugged. "Another lucky guess?" I pushed.

"I'm full of lucky guesses, I guess," he said to me.

This guy had a quiet sense of humor just like Desi's. Teo's whole face lit up when he grinned. Then he got thoughtful again and it was like a gray cloud darkening the sun. "But I'm serious about not running away," Teo continued. "Staying and dealing with stuff is part of growing up," he told me.

I was shocked. Now was my chance to challenge Teo, to find out for sure who he was. But I couldn't ask him outright. And he couldn't lie. "What about you?" I challenged. "You ran away."

Teo shook his head sadly. "I didn't run. I had no choice in the matter."

"We always have a choice," I said. "Don't we?"

"What do you mean, a choice not to go? How could I have known what was going to happen on that hunting trip? Besides, it was my time."

"And you're not mad? About getting murdered?"

Teo shrugged. "It was an accident. Things happen."

"Things happen?! But they need you," I pushed. My voice cracked with emotion.

"They're doing fine without me," he barked back.

"Fine? You call that fine? Raffi is still hurting. Athena is mad at the world. Little Matty...he doesn't even know what he is. And Desi..."

"Desi has you."

"Had," I told him. "We're not that close anymore."

Already at the Queens Plaza stop, the sky was fully dark now. The streetlights had come on without me realizing it. Windows glowed as we chugged past, illuminating late afternoon activities: kids doing homework at kitchen tables, moms getting supper ready for the family, dads reading a good book in an easy chair, lost souls watching the 7 train click by on the elevated tracks...

"It doesn't matter," Teo said. "What matters is that you had each other when you needed each other most. You helped each other grow up. You taught each other how to be a good friend. You showed each other how to love someone you weren't related to. You prepared each other for life."

"Yeah, but..."

"Yeah, but...everything changes. Everything evolves. It's important to know when it's time to move on. That's something else you taught each other." Teo looked at me. His eyes crinkled at the corners but his mouth didn't smile. "I know it sounds like a crock of crap but you've got to trust me on this one."

The big man buttoned his quilted jacket and pulled on his work gloves. "Besides, you're never really gone. Part of you is always there."

"Where?" I asked.

"Everywhere," he explained. "You just have to know where to look."

A homeless man in rags pushed his way through the subway car, jingling change in a paper coffee cup, mumbling some sob story about losing his job, his wife, his kids, his home. The combo platter of bum juice and cheap alcohol followed him. I held my breath till he passed. Teo dropped a few coins in the man's cup. Then he switched gears again. "You and Desiree, you've got something special."

"How do you know?"

"I think you know how I know," Teo told me. "What is it you two always used to say? That you're better than sisters?"

How could he have possibly known this? I wanted to ask him all sorts of things. About the tape. About the cigar wrappers. But I said nothing. He probably wouldn't have answered anyway.

The train car plunged into darkness as it went into the tunnel under the East River, the tunnel which separated Queens from Manhattan. When the lights flickered on, I thought Teo would be gone like the ghost he was. But he was still there, staring me down, looking amused at my shocked expression.

The motorman's fuzzy voice announced, "Next stop, Grand Central Station."

"That's me," Teo said.

"I'm Times Square," I told him. "The last stop."

The crowded subway platform came into view. Teo stood and plunked on his hardhat. Then he took it off again, leaned forward and kissed me on the forehead. "And it doesn't mean you're gonna die. Your grandmother was wrong about that," he told me, channeling Grandma Lou's old Guinea superstitions. "Just the opposite."

The doors opened and Teo made his way through the crush of bodies. Only two more stops to go but people still had to stand and hang onto those swinging pull things shaped like silver teardrops. The 7 was the only way to connect to the IND, the Sea Beach, the Brighton line and the IRT. I tried to follow Teo/Big Matty as he pushed through the crowd but lost track of him. He disappeared in the sea of souls forever.

As the train rolled into Times Square/42nd Street, I noticed something small and colorful at my feet. I leaned down to pick it up, careful not to wedge my head into the crotch of the man standing in front of me. Paper crackled in my fingers. I lifted it up and saw that it was a cigar band. An *El Producto* cigar band. Just like the one Big Matty had asked Raffi to marry him with. Red and gold and white.

Fucking Matty.

OLD FRIENDS, BOOKENDS

Before you say anything about it, Professor W, I realize that there are references to two Paul Simon songs in the titles of the last two chapters. But I swear, there are no hidden meanings. No secret messages. The names just fit.

Traditionally, angels and the dead always teach people stuff in books and films. *Death Takes a Holiday*. (My dad has a thing for old movies and that one's almost as old as Phil is, made way back in 1934.) *It's a Wonderful Life*. *Bridge to Terabithia*. It's a common device in the arts, even if the characters don't always come back to visit like Big Matty did.

Think about it. It's the same in real life. People coming back to teach lessons, I mean. There are signs all over the place. They talk to us in dreams. They leave doors open. They move things around your apartment. They want to make sure we don't forget them. They want to make sure we don't make the same mistakes they did.

So, what did Big Matty teach me? Not to talk to strangers in pizzerias? Not to run off into the crazy quilt of Queens? Not to run away from anything? Ever? No. Big Matty taught me that it's never really over. That love endures, no matter what. Although it might take a different form, love's still there.

Big Matty helped me realize that Desi and I will have an unbreakable bond which will be there for always. When we need each other most. In good times, like when we get married (hell, maybe Desi will even be my maid of honor). And when we have kids and when we write books. In bad times, like when someone breaks our heart, when we're feeling useless, unloved, unworthy of anything.

Like your favorite book that you can pick up anytime you need a lift. Like your favorite scene from your favorite movie that you can watch over and over again when it's on the *Million Dollar Movie*. Like your favorite pair of pants, your favorite pair of shoes that you can slip into at any time because they fit you perfectly. And not only do they fit but they make you feel good. They make you feel right. They make you feel like you. They make you feel. They make you *you*.

The first thing I did when I got home from Junior's wake was take out the box he'd made for me. (I'd hidden it in my bedroom closet.) Wait, did I mention that Junior had made me a box? (I even wrote a poem about it.) Not only did he carve the top with all sorts of intricate squiggles and deep triangles but he actually made the box itself. He cut the wood to size, sanded the sides, dove-tailed them perfectly together without using a smidge of glue. The top nested nicely into the bottom, no hinges. He said the curves and sharp edges reminded him of me. Said he tried to make it beautiful, like me.

Of course, I didn't believe him at the time. That I was beautiful, I mean. I thought Junior was just trying to get into my pants. Now I know better. Maybe he did love me. Like 13-year-olds can love each other. All deep and serious and dramatic and quietly stupendous. Like it's never going to happen again. But it does. It does, only different.

When Junior and I broke up, I put the wooden box away. High up in a neglected corner of my closet that I could only reach by standing on a step stool. Sometimes I forgot the box was there until I was looking for a purse I couldn't find or an old journal I wanted to check something in. Then my fingers would stumble upon Junior's box, rediscover its curves and all its edges, all its perfect imperfections. I would rescue it from its corner and look inside (it was empty) and sometimes cry, then put it back where I found it. Until I forgot it again.

Maybe me and Desi were like that wooden box. Something that was put away until it was needed. Except our box wasn't empty inside: it was overflowing.

If Desi came to me after five years, ten years, I would be there for her. We would pick up just where we left off and it wouldn't be uncomfortable or awkward. It would be just like we paused in the middle of a sentence. And we could continue that sentence dozens of months later, like nothing had ever happened.

Don't you have a friend like that? A forever friend, no matter what? I believe that everyone has at least one. A once-in-a-lifetime friend. Well, Desi was mine.

At first, I didn't know how to end this story—because relationships like this don't have endings, even after one of the people dies—but this kind of ending feels right. Finishing the book sort of up in the air. But not. Because, after all is said and done, Desi and I are better than sisters.

And that's not really an ending; it's just the beginning.

DEAR CARLA

ENGL 313 — Workshop in Fiction 2
Hunter College of the City University of New York
Semester: Spring 1982

May 6, 1982

Dear Carla,

First, I don't think the Paul Simon reference in the last chapter is
necessary. In my opinion, you should start the book's final chapter with
something stronger, something more impactful. Left hook, so to speak. Think
Muhammad Ali: "Float like a butterfly, sting like a bee." But with words.

And don't respond to me with your customary: "That's just the way the
words came out." You and I both know it's a lame excuse. I know you can do
it. And will.

I'm not sure about closing with the poem. I took the liberty of showing
it to Ms. Lorde, who I believe you had last semester. Audre said some great
things about your writing and your ability—and your laziness. She stressed
your tendency to take the easy way out when something hits too close to home.
Audre said she would give "First Kiss" five exclamation points and a set of

goofy eyes. (She also said you'd know what this meant.) I am including the poem here with Ms. Lorde's comments noted in green.

As it is now, I'd say your final paper, though much longer than the required length, is a solid B. Do the additional revisions I suggest by the 14th and you're looking at an A.

As Big Matty might say, close but no cigar!

Daniel Winner

•

May 7, 1982

Dear Daniel,

Thank you for your comments and for showing "First Kiss" to Ms. Lorde. I had no idea what a famous poet she was when I took "Workshop in Poetry 2" with her last semester. Maybe I wouldn't have given her such a hard time if I had. Who am I kidding? I would have busted her shoes just as much. Maybe even more. I guess that's just the way I am.

A week to do all of those revisions?! Is there any way I can get more time? I have four other classes, finals and work part-time besides.

Carla

•

May 10, 1982

Carla,

I can give you until Monday the 17th so you have another weekend to work on the revisions but that's it. I have dozens of other papers to grade but I'll give you a special dispensation because I believe you really have something here.

Now, stop wasting time writing me notes and start the rewrite!

Don't let me down!

Dan

•

May 11, 1982

Dan,

Okay. Thanks. I won't.

Carla

WRAP UP: WARTS AND ALL

After the edits, I ended up getting an A in Professor Winner's class. It brought my GPA way up to 3.71. Tessie was pleased as shit, even though she was never gung-ho about a girl going to college in the first place. Maybe, just maybe, there's more to life than being a secretary, Ma. Not that there's anything wrong with being a secretary. It just wasn't for me.

Phil seemed pretty happy and proud, too, though he didn't say much. I heard my big-mouthed Brooklyn crowd of three (Tessie, Phil and Laura) cheer like crazy when Donna Shalala announced my name and I crossed the stage at the Felt Forum. Yep, I graduated in Madison Square Garden, that's how big Hunter College's Class of '82 was.

Afterwards, my parents took the four of us out to a nice dinner at The Lamps of China back in Bay Ridge to celebrate. Although it's been closed for a lot of years now, The Lamps of China was *the* place to go for special occasions. It was huge with multiple levels and had fancy paper lanterns hanging all over the restaurant. They even had special drinking glasses with their name etched onto them in black Chinese-looking writing next to a picture of a lamp. (My Uncle Richard stole one when we were there for my cousin Ricky's communion.) The menu was complicated, all of this one from Column A and two from Column B nonsense but the waiters were happy to help you figure it out.

Who else happened to be at the Lamps of China that day? Desi and her family. Just the four of them. Marist's graduation was the same day as Hunter's and like Philly, Raffi didn't want to waste her hard-earned cash on a place she didn't know from Adam. The Ruiz clan was leaving the Lamps just as the Piccolos were coming in. There were smiles, hugs and congratulations all around.

Desi and I made plans to meet at The Mustard Seed that night to have a drink celebrating our graduations. We did and it was great.

Not counting seeing each other on the train or at Penner's, Desi and I hadn't really seen each other since I'd run out of Junior's wake a couple of years earlier. She never even called afterwards and neither of us ever brought it up when we ran into each other. What was there to say? It was water under the bridge, I guess.

When we met at the Mustard Seed, Desi said she'd gotten a job in the Accounting Department at Brink's on 47th Street in the City which she was supposed to start the following Monday. I didn't have anything lined up but I did have an interview with Dell Puzzle Publications as a Word Search Editor. I ended up getting the job. Turns out Desi and I worked a few blocks from each other. We met for lunch every once in a while. It was nice.

Over the years, Desi and I have drifted in and out of each other's lives. Mostly in. Which is also nice. She's like a life preserver to me, a buoy. Something I swim to when I get tired of treading water, something that sustains me, makes me stronger. Makes me strong enough to get back into the pool and swim some more.

All that time, even when I was a Word Search Editor, I sent out poems and short stories to magazines. But it was weird, after writing that assignment for Professor Winner's class, I never wrote anything longer than 10 pages or so. I kept the manuscript in a bright pink, three-ring binder in a box in Tessie's basement. Like Desi, I knew it was there when and if I needed it.

After a few years, I left Dell to do freelance writing full-time. My husband Billy (Yeah, I ditched the drummer a while ago. He was an asshole. I mean, who marries a drummer?) had a good job with the City and health insurance. I had a lot of pieces published and wrote just about anything they'd pay me to write: resumes, articles, interviews, personal experience essays for magazines nobody ever heard of like *The American Gardener* and *Disapora*, articles for the *Courier Life* newspapers. I even wrote an essay about Audre Lorde for *Essence*.

Desi and I were maids of honor at each other's weddings. (She married a wonderful guy named Sam who's a financial whiz at Deutsche Bank.) We were the godmothers to each other's first child: hers a boy named Matthew (what else? And yes, Frances Paladino's Ouija-board prediction about her having two girls was wrong) and mine a girl named Siena. They were born only eight weeks apart and though not best friends like Desi and me, they always had a great rapport, even as toddlers. Desi and I like to think they will be friends their whole lives. Not like us but different. But still good.

I was there when Little Matty graduated from SUNY Purchase. He majored in Performing Arts (no surprise there) and even had bit parts in *Fort Apache, The Bronx* and *Beat Street*. But mostly, he's a waiter. (No surprise there either.)

Desi was there for me when Tessie died of sepsis when a hernia she'd neglected for decades suddenly burst. She said I was a good daughter even though I doubted it. I regretted being so mean to my mom as a teenager; she did the best she could and nobody could be expected to do more than that. Desi consoled me saying that being mean to their parents is a teenager's job.

I was there when Mami had her stroke, when Raffi married a nice electrician named Kevin and Athena had twins. Amazingly enough, Athena finally met a guy who was brave enough to go out with her, let alone marry her. Motherhood and the years mellowed Athena's fiery temper somewhat but her dark eyes still burned like angry coals, even in her 30s.

Desi was there with me on 9/11. She called me from Long Island as soon as it happened. Not two hours after I told her that my firefighter husband was working that day, she showed up on my doorstep. And Desi didn't leave my side until she knew Billy was safe. We cried in each other's arms when he called from Methodist Hospital. From all the dust, the doctor said he had scratched corneas, which would heal. They did, but it took longer for our spirits, our souls to heal. But eventually, they did, too. But we never forgot what had happened that day, what and who we lost.

Although Desi and her family lived almost 60 miles away in Port Jefferson (she now taught Financial Accounting and Business Communications at Stony Brook University), she was with me every step of the way when I was diagnosed with ovarian cancer in 2013. Billy too, but there's nothing like having a good girlfriend at your side, someone with ladyparts who understands what it's like to lose them. Hers was the first face I saw in the recovery room after my hysterectomy. When her teaching schedule allowed, Desi was even there with me for a few chemotherapy infusions.

And even when she couldn't be there physically, Desi was always with me—knitting me warm skullcaps in crazy colors, taking my daughter Siena (who was terrified I was going to die) for sleepovers in Port Jeff, calling me after every doctor's appointment, sending me a deliciously fleecy blanket from Bath and Body Works, coming with me to buy a wig and laughing at how ridiculous they all looked.

Yes, my sister Laura was still in the picture but for some reason, me having ovarian cancer scared the crap out of Laura. Maybe she thought she was next. I didn't worry too much about it—I was too busy worrying about myself. I'd long discovered that expecting something that people couldn't give was a losing battle. Whatever Laura could give, I was glad for it. We all do the best we can for each other.

Now Desi and I are officially old bags. We're in our 50s. I dye my hair (which came back a curly afro after chemo) and Desi doesn't. She keeps it layered, to her shoulders, and it's almost all gray. "Chrome," Billy tells her, "Chrome like a motorcycle fender." Which she likes better than calling it gray. Would you believe that each of us still have the barrettes Umbe bought us at Reminiscence in the Village? We don't wear them anymore but we've both kept them in a safe place all these years.

Oh, and Desi confessed that she still had MushroomHat stashed away in a Ziploc bag under her bed. Like Junior's box, she told me that she takes it out every once in a while to look, feel, remember. It still fits. And it still smells like Tide from when we hand-washed it in my basement, she said.

I don't know what made me do it…maybe it was being diagnosed with cancer…but I finally showed Desi my "Junior poem." After close to 40 years. I could have emailed it to her but I wanted to watch her read it. I wanted to study her face when she read it. Desi's expression changed from happy to amused to sad to pensive like the phases of the moon in time-lapse photography. One lone tear rolled down her cheek. "I think Junior would have liked this," she said in a quiet voice afterwards.

Desi and I debated whether or not she should send it to her cousin Mimi, who was still with Roberto and late in life, had another child, a daughter this time. But we decided against sending the poem to Mimi. No sense in opening up an old hurt.

Desi's reaction to the Junior Poem gave me the courage to show her the manuscript I'd written for Professor Winner's class way back in 1982. When Billy and I bought his parents' place in Windsor Terrace, I'd rescued the pink binder from Tessie and Phil's basement. Now it sat on a bookshelf in my home office, untouched for years.

When Desi read it would she be mad? Would she be pissed off that I told family secrets? Or would she be glad these secrets were finally out in the open? Would she ever talk to me again? I felt like this was a big weight pressing down upon our friendship. The 800-pound gorilla in our room. For some reason, I wanted Desi to know. I wanted her to see. I wanted her to read.

Slowly, deliberately, I scanned the pages into my laptop, carefully placing them back into the binder one by one. When I was done scanning the manuscript, I printed it out, punched holes in it and made a new binder, also electric pink. Then I mailed the binder to Desi Priority Mail. Calvin at the Post Office said it would get to Port Jeff in two days.

On the third day, the phone rang. "This has to be a novel," Desi said, not even saying hello.

"I guess it already is," I told her.

"I mean it needs to be published," she pushed. "Other people need to see this. Just the way it is, warts and all."

Then we talked about Underoos, Umbe, Uncle Ernesto, getting lost on the double R, *Soul Train*, bathtub faucets (for Desi, it had been her electric Snoopy toothbrush…well, knock me over with a feather), *pernil*, Sylvie, Fontaine and Fort Adams, the Napoleons at Your Baker, Junior, me seeing Big Matty in Corona, and all the rest. We talked until our throats were dry and we were exhausted from smiling and crying and laughing. We could have stayed on the phone reminiscing forever but there were deadlines to make, papers to grade and dinners to prepare.

So, that's what I'm doing. Exposing my warts and all, in a manner of speaking. I'm entering this into my computer pretty much as is, just cleaning up some misspellings (or not…I kind of like the imperfections), making clarifications, etc. I'm trying not to do too much, though, because I'd like to preserve what my 21 year-old-self was writing about my 13 year-old-self. Some four decades later, it's like a time capsule of words, a piece of personal history. A part of me that I'm trying to preserve. Although I only got a 70 in Mrs. Fishberg's typing class at Fort Adams, it's going pretty fast.

Is this a Young Adult novel? Is it a women's book? Is it neither? Or both? We'll see what happens. We'll see what the publishing industry thinks. And as Desi says, if no one wants to take it on, then screw them. Lots of people are self-publishing these days. I'm sure Siena could help me. If I could tear her away from *The Legend of Zelda*.

Oh, and Big Matty, he still visits me and Desi from time to time. As he said to me on the 7 train, the signs and symbols are all around us. You just have to know where to look. Sometimes it's a cigar band. Others it's an old photograph that falls out of a long-forgotten paperback. Or else it's a man on the street who looks alarmingly like Desi's dead father, enough to be his twin.

If Desi and I are together when we see one of her father's signs, we'll just look at each other and smile. We don't need to say anything about it because we know. Silently, we know. Because after all, we're better than… But you already know that.

Oh, and here's the Junior Poem:

THE JUNIOR POEM (AKA FIRST KISS)
by Carla D'Angelo-Smith

My first French kiss
was beneath the boughs
of Mr. Santone's magnolia tree
which was in full bloom.
It was mid-May
and the waxy blossoms
lay on the sidewalk
beneath my fancy Thom McAn shoes.
I had just been confirmed
at St. Fiacre's Church,
had an unfortunate shag haircut,
no chest to speak of
and braces on my teeth
but Junior kissed me anyway.
Little did I know
that my friend Desi's baby brother
and a couple of her cousins
had followed us

and were watching
from the corner.
They broke into spontaneous applause
when Junior finally did the deed.

Our romance didn't last—
it was a long-distance relationship;
I lived in Brooklyn,
he lived in Queens,
and neither of us drove—
we were only 13.
We lost touch, moved on.

Years later,
I heard that Junior died
when he was only eighteen,
an undiagnosed heart condition.
He'd trained to be a welder
and passed out, collapsed
the moment he hit the hot workroom floor.
I couldn't help but wonder
if our sweet moment
beneath Mr. Santone's magnolia tree
was one of his last thoughts.
I hope it was.

PUBLISHER'S NOTE

While this book is inspired by real people, places and some actual events, *Better than Sisters* is a work of fiction and in no way meant to be a historical accounting. Any resemblance to persons, either living or dead, is purely coincidental. This book is intended solely for entertainment purposes.

ABOUT THE AUTHOR

Catherine Gigante-Brown is a writer of fiction, nonfiction and poetry. She was born in Brooklyn, where she still lives with her husband and son. Her articles have appeared in publications like *Time Out, New York, Ravishly, Essence* and *Industry*. Her poetry and fiction appear in several anthologies. A handful of her film and theatrical works have been produced.

Her first novel, *The El*, was published by Volossal in 2012, and her second, *Different Drummer*, was released in 2015. Her third, *The Bells of Brooklyn*, is a sequel to *The El* and was published in 2017. She is currently writing the last and final book in *The El Trilogy* and is also working with a creative team (which includes Volossal's Vinnie Corbo) to bring a musical version of *Different Drummer* to the stage.

ACKNOWLEDGEMENTS

Ever since I learned how to read, I inhaled books, all kinds of books, but the pickings were slim in pre-teen and teen novels when I was growing up. The genre "YA" wasn't even a thing in the 1970s. Since my son David turned me onto John Green, I've wanted to write a Young Adult novel of my own— but one with crossover appeal.

This is my fourth book-birth with Volossal. I can't thank Vinnie Corbo enough for always believing in me, for his creative vision and his dedication. He encouraged me to "go for it" when I told him I wanted to try a YA project— and also strongly suggested that I write the third (and final) installment in *The El* trilogy when I was done.

I'd like to thank the Young Adult authors who inspired me, including John Green, fellow Brooklynite Jacqueline Woodson, plus Judy Blume and Beverly Cleary before them.

Thanks also to my husband Peter who deals with my craziness and insecurity on a daily basis yet still loves me, cheers me on and supports all of my endeavors. Thank you for being my partner in crime, through sickness and health, and crippling self-doubt.

I'm also grateful to my son David, not just for introducing me to John Green's writing many years ago, but for being his awesome self. I don't know what I/we did right but David is a beautiful human being and I am proud he picked me to be his mom.

Thanks to my cousin Bobbi Wicks for being the book's first reader and proofreader extraordinaire. Bobbi hadn't read a YA book since the Nancy Drew mysteries and she weathered BTS's explicit passages well. And love to Jackie, as always, for being an early reader and cheerleader.

Gratitude to my teachers, who put up with my many questions, including Professor David Winn, Sister Lucide Maytrott and those who have moved on to that big blackboard in the sky like Audre Lorde, Eugene Greenburg, Mildred McVay, Sister Helena and Mary Coughlin.

I'd like to thank my childhood friends. Through their kindness and acceptance, they unknowingly taught a nerdy, insecure girl how to be a good friend. They are here between the lines and some even inspired characters, including: my sister Liz Dell'Alba (who was my first friend), Anne Marie Ischia-Paladino, Betty Duffy-Golembeski, Cindy Olsen Strommen, Judy Iannacone Lynch, Debbie Mendola Touhey, Pat Karlsen, Sue Gilbertson, Sarah Gilbertson Lampman, Crystal Angela Sada, Rene Myatt, Ginny Mayer-Reyer and many others. Apologies if I left anyone out but you know who you are.

Finally, to my friends today, too numerous to mention, thank you for being you. Paul Siederman, I will always miss you—and quote you.

CGB

CPSIA information can be obtained
at www.ICGtesting.com
Printed in the USA
LVHW041147180319
611004LV00004B/324/P

9 780999 691656